D1507998

LYON'S BRIDE

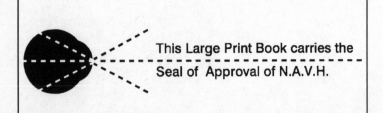

This Large Print Book carries the
Seal of Approval of N.A.V.H.

LYON'S BRIDE

THE CHATTAN CURSE

CATHY MAXWELL

THORNDIKE PRESS
A part of Gale, Cengage Learning

GALE
CENGAGE Learning·

Detroit • New York • San Francisco • New Haven, Conn • Waterville, Maine • London

GALE
CENGAGE Learning·

Thorndike Press® Large Print Romance.
The text of this Large Print edition is unabridged.
Other aspects of the book may vary from the original edition.
Set in 16 pt. Plantin.

LIBRARY OF CONGRESS CATALOGING-IN-PUBLICATION DATA

Maxwell, Cathy.
 [Chatten curse.]
 Lyon's bride : the Chattan curse / by Cathy Maxwell. — Large print ed.
  p. cm. — (Thorndike Press large print romance)
 Previously published as The Chattan curse
 ISBN-13: 978-1-4104-4946-7 (hardcover)
 ISBN-10: 1-4104-4946-7 (hardcover)
 1. Large type books. I. Title.
PS3563.A8996L96 2012
813'.54—dc23   2012012803

Published in 2012 by arrangement with Avon, an imprint of HarperCollins Publishers.

Printed in the United States of America
1 2 3 4 5 6 7 16 15 14 13 12

To my travel buddy —
Judy Gomes Rogers
I am wealthy in my friends.

THE CURSE

Macnachtan Keep
Scotland, 1632

A mother *knows*. 'Tis the curse of giving birth.

She feels life enter this world, a knife-sharp pain and one gladly borne for the outcome. She nurtures, protects and prays for her child's safekeeping with every breath she draws . . . and so is it any wonder she would also sense, *know,* the moment that precious life is cut short?

Fenella, the wife of the late Laird Macnachtan, was in the south gallery where the sun was best, plying her needle when terror seized her heart. She looked to her kinswomen, all gathered around for an afternoon chat as was their custom. These were her husband's cousins, his sisters, and her daughters Ilona and Aislin —

"Where's Rose?"

A mother should not have a favorite, but

Fenella did.

Her other daughters were merry and bright, but Rose was special. She shared her mother's gift of healing. Fenella had delighted in the realization that the powers of her mother and her *nain* — her grandmother — now flowed through her to her youngest. Rose would be "the one" to receive the Book That Contained All Knowledge.

Of course, Rose's golden beauty was the stuff of legend, and that set her apart as well. The suitors for her hand had formed a line across the land, but there had only been one man for Rose — Charles Chattan of Glenfinnan.

Rose's love for Charles reminded Fenella so much of her younger self, that self who had challenged and won the heart of the handsome Macnachtan. That self who was willful and bold.

But Chattan had proved a faithless lover. He'd handfasted himself to Rose and then accepted marriage to another — an Englishwoman from a family with power. *Sassenach* power.

With a jolt, Fenella realized today was Charles and the Englishwoman's wedding day. She should not have forgotten the fact. No wonder Rose had been so quiet this morning and was not here amongst the chatter of women this afternoon. Fenella's worry eased a bit.

Rose had loved Charles hard and well. Her heart hurt, but Fenella would see that Rose *would* recover. Thank the Lord, Macnachtan was not alive to witness the Chattans' dishonoring of his daughter. It had been all Fenella could do to keep her sons from calling Charles out. She refused to spill her family's blood over the traitor.

She could not see Rose's future — her gift failed her when she attempted to discern Fate — but there would be another love for Rose. There must be. The powerful gifts handed through accident of birth from one ancestress to another needed to take seed in Rose's womb. . . .

Suddenly a scream rose from the courtyard, an alarm of shock and grief.

In that instant, Fenella's foreboding gained life.

The other women scrambled to their feet and ran to the window overlooking the stone courtyard. Fenella didn't move. Her whole being centered on one whispered word. *"Rose."*

There were more shouts now. Fenella heard her son Michael call his sister's name, heard weeping, wails of distress and mourning. Her kinswomen at the window threw themselves into shocked grief. They turned, looked at Fenella. Ilona, her face contorted, stumbled toward her mother. Aislin knelt, bowled over in pain.

Fenella set aside her needlework.

She did not want to go to that window.

Tears burned her eyes. She held them back. She didn't weep. Not ever. She'd not shed one tear for Macnachtan's death. Death was part of life . . . that's what *Nain* had said. One didn't grieve for life.

Fenella stood.

It was hard to breathe.

She walked to the window. Ilona held out her arms and then dropped them, as if knowing she could not stop her mother.

Leaning forward, Fenella looked out upon the courtyard below.

Rose's body was sprawled there, her golden hair mingled with a stream of blood flowing from her head.

Her dear daughter. Her darling, darling daughter.

She'd thrown herself from the tower wall.

She'd taken her own life.

Michael looked up and saw his mother. Tears flowed freely down his face.

He was so like his father —

In that moment, Fenella's legs gave out beneath her. She fell to the cold stone floor.

Nain was wrong. Grief could not be contained. It started as a small flame that grew larger and stronger until it consumed her.

There was no doubt Rose of Loch Awe had taken her life because of Charles Chattan's perfidy, no saving her memory from the disgrace of suicide.

Fenella longed for the magic to reverse time and bring her daughter back to life.

For the next three days she poured over her *nain*'s book. Certainly in all these receipts and spells for healing, for fortune, for doubts and fears, there must be one to cast off Death.

The handwriting on those yellowed pages was cramped and in many places faded. Fenella had signed the front of the book but not referred to it often, at least not once she'd memorized the cures for fevers and agues that plagued children and concerned mothers.

She'd been surprised to discover Rose had also been reading the book. She'd found where Rose had written the name *Charles* beside a spell to find true love. It called for a rose thorn to be embedded in the wax of a candle and burned on the night of a full moon.

They found a piece of the burned candle,

11

the thorn still intact, its tip charred, beneath Rose's pillow.

Fenella held the wax in the palm of her hand. Slowly, she closed her fingers around it into a fist and set aside mourning.

In its place rose anger.

'Twas said the Chattan kin had run for England. The rest had scattered to other clans. They feared Fenella of the Macnachtan, and well they should. Grief made her mad.

They thought themselves safe. They were not.

There was no sacred ground for a suicide, but Fenella had no need of the church. She ordered a funeral pyre to be built for her daughter along the green banks of Loch Awe directly beneath a stony crag that looked down upon the shore.

On the day of Rose's burial, Fenella stood upon that crag, waiting for the sun to set. She wore the Macnachtan tartan around her shoulders. The evening wind toyed with her gray hair held in place by a circlet of gold, gray hair that had once been as fair as Rose's.

At Fenella's signal, her sons set ablaze a ring of bonfires she'd ordered constructed around Rose's pyre. The flames leaped to life.

"Rose." Her name was sweet upon her mother's lips.

Did Chattan think he could hide in London? Did his father believe his son could jilt Rose without penalty? That her life had no meaning?

That Macnachtan honor was a small thing?

"I want him to feel my pain," Fenella whispered.

Ilona and Aislin stood by her side. They nodded.

"He will not escape me," Fenella vowed.

"But he is gone," Ilona said. "He has become a fine lord while we are left to weep."

Feeling the heat of the bonfires. She knew better.

At last the moon was high in the sky. The time was right. *Nain* had said a witch knows when the hour is nigh. Tonight would be a night no one would forget. Ever.

Especially Charles Chattan.

The fires had drawn the curious from all over the kirk. They stood on the shore watching her. Fenella raised her hand. Her clansmen and her kin on the shore below fell silent. Michael picked up the torch and held it ready.

She brought her hand down and her oldest lit his sister's funeral pyre as instructed.

'Twas the ancient ways. There was no priest here, no clergy to call her out — and even if there was, Fenella's power in this moment was too strong to be swayed. It coursed through her. It was the beating of her heart, the pulsing in the blood in her veins, the very fiber of her being.

She stepped to the edge of the rock and stared down over the burning pyre. The flames licked the skirt of Rose's white burial gown.

"My Rose died of love," she said. She whispered the words but then repeated them with a commanding strength. They carried on the wind and seemed to linger over Loch Awe's moonlit waters. "A woman's lot is hard," she said. " 'Tis love that gives us courage, gives us strength. My Rose gave the precious gift of her love to a man unworthy of it."

Heads nodded agreement. There was not a soul around who had not been touched by Rose. They all knew her gift of laughter, her kindness, her willingness to offer what help she could to others.

Fenella reached a hand back. Ilona placed the staff that Fenella had ordered hewn from a yew tree and banded with copper. *"I curse Charles Chattan."*

Raising the staff, Fenella said, "I curse not just Chattan but his line. He betrayed her for a title. He tossed aside handfasted promises for greed. Now let him learn what his duplicity has wrought."

The moon seemed to brighten. The flames on the fires danced higher, and Fenella knew she was being summoned. Danse macabre. All were equal in death.

She spoke, her voice ringing in the night.

"Watchers of the threshold, Watchers of
    the gate,
open hell and seal Chattan's Fate.
When a Chattan male falls in love,
strike his heart with fire from Above.
Crush his heart, destroy his line;
Only then will justice be mine."

Fenella threw her staff down upon her daughter's funeral pyre. The flames now consumed Rose. Fenella could feel their heat, smell her daughter's scent — and she threw herself off the rock, following her staff to where it lay upon Rose's breast. She grabbed her daughter's burning body and clung fast.

Together they left this world.

Six months to the date after his wedding,

Charles Chattan died. His heart stopped. He was sitting at his table, accepting congratulations from his dinner guests over the news his wife was breeding, when he fell facedown onto his plate.

The news of his death shocked many. He was so young. A vital, handsome man with so much to live for. Had he not recently declared to many of his friends that he'd fallen in love with his new wife? How could God cut short his life, especially when he was so happy?

But his marriage was not in vain. Seven months after his death, his wife bore a son to carry on the Chattan name . . . a son who also bore the curse.

CHAPTER ONE

London
April 1814

Thea Martin's first thought upon receiving a letter from Sir James Smiley, Esq., renowned solicitor for Persons of Great Importance, was that her brother had hatched a new scheme to chase her out of London.

Her hands shook as she broke the sealing wax. So far, her brother Horace had attempted to bar all doors to her, an effort that had not succeeded, since London loved nothing more than a scandal — and the feud between the mighty duke of Duruset and his disinherited sister was great fodder for gossip.

Horace's next action had been to block all reasonable landlords from letting to her. His machinations came to naught, because Thea was determined. London offered opportunities for her to make a living, something difficult for a penniless widow with children to do on her own elsewhere. This had been her home before she'd run away to marry Boyd Martin, and it offered the only hope for her small family's future.

Thea had found a tiny set of rooms for let in a shabby building in a less-than-respectable neighborhood. It meant she would keep her boys in all day instead of giving them a garden for play, but it was a start, and that had been what Thea had needed — a new beginning.

Using the connections she'd made during her debutante years, she'd set about using the only skill she knew, matchmaking. She knew the ways of the *ton,* she knew marriage, and she understood the desperation of parents. She also knew how to be discreet.

And if her brother was not pleased? Well, she was already disowned. What more could he do?

Thea feared she'd discover the answer to that last question in Sir James's letter.

"What is it, Mother?" Jonathan asked. He was a bright, towheaded seven-year-old who wanted to be her protector. His brother, five-year-old Christopher, stood by his side, his little forehead wrinkled in concern. Their small family didn't receive letters often.

"I will tell you in a moment," Thea murmured. "Are you waiting for my reply?" she asked the messenger, who still lingered in the hall with a distasteful sniff at his surroundings.

"Yes, ma'am. I've been ordered to return with your reply."

Thea forced herself to focus on Sir James's slanting handwriting. He wanted to see her on "a matter of Some Importance." He mentioned he was the uncle of Peter Goodfellow, for whom she had "performed a service that was nothing short of a Miracle" and that he hoped she'd be willing to "assist Someone again facing the same Situation."

Peter Goodfellow had been one of Thea's matchmaking challenges. He was as tall as he was wide, had a squint, liked to pick at his face, and had a distressing tendency to burp. She'd found a wife for him, but it had not been an easy task. His family's handsome commission had compensated for the difficulty. Thea wondered if this request could mean another large commission.

Oh, were it to be so. She'd hidden most of the Goodfellow commission in her "Future Box," the small, wooden money chest kept under the floorboard beneath her bed. Her goal was to see that both her sons received a gentleman's education. Jonathan had an interview in a month's time with the head-master of Westminster School, a prestigious day school that would offer him the opportunity to meet boys from the right sort of families, families far different from those living in their present neighborhood.

"Sir James wished to know if you could meet with him today at half past two," the messenger said politely.

"Half past two?" Thea consulted the clock on the mantel over the hearth. It had been Boyd's mother's and was the nicest thing she owned. It was already one. "Yes, of course I can." She reached for her reticule and pulled out a coin to tip the man.

The messenger smiled as he saw her open her purse, a smile that turned brittle at the small amount she placed in his palm. She knew what he was thinking, but she didn't care. She must watch every penny.

"I shall return to him with your acceptance." The messenger bowed and was on his way.

Thea shut the door. For a second, she allowed herself a moment's relief over the letter not being from her brother — and then she danced a little jig. Christopher started dancing with her, his worry giving way to a huge smile.

"What was in the letter, Mother?" Jonathan asked, too dignified to join in their little party.

She knelt down to the level of her two handsome sons. "A chance to earn the money we need for your school fees." She wrapped her arms around them and gave them both a big hug. "I was so worried, but God does provide." Yes, yes, yes. She'd been living on what God provided ever since Boyd had abandoned them in Manchester right after Christopher was born.

"Do I still have the interview with the school next month?" Jonathan asked.

"Yes," Thea said, "and you shall do very well. Westminster will be happy to have you. But first, I must see Sir James." She was on her feet in a blink, her mind a flurry of activity.

She needed someone to watch her sons while she was out. She ran up the hallway stairs to Mrs. Hadley's door. Mrs. Gray, Mrs. Hadley's sister by marriage, answered. She'd only arrived last week, and Thea didn't know very much about her except that her late husband had been a country vicar. She was a petite woman with a comfortable bosom and sad brown eyes.

"I am looking for Mrs. Hadley," Thea said.

"Oh, she is off to care for my brother at

the hospital," Mrs. Gray replied. "You know how it is in those places. If your family doesn't see to your care, you can rot." Mr. Hadley suffered from consumption. Thea had been relieved when he'd been taken to the London Hospital, away from her boys, with his coughing and hacking.

"This is sad news," Thea said. "I wanted to ask her to watch my sons while I ran an errand. Mrs. Hadley is usually home by now."

"I don't know what has been keeping her, but if it is help you need, I'll watch your boys for you," Mrs. Gray volunteered.

Thea's first instinct was to refuse the kind offer. She hated leaving her sons alone at any time and was very particular about whom she asked for help.

However, this was a special circumstance.

"Are you certain it wouldn't be a bother?" Thea asked. "I dislike imposing."

"No trouble at all. I've seen your lads walking with you. They seem to be good boys."

She had such a soft, melodic voice and grandmotherly way — and Thea really didn't have another choice. Not on such short notice.

"Thank you," Thea said, meaning the words. "I must change my dress, but if you could come down in ten minutes?"

"Of course I will."

Thea didn't waste another moment. She flew down the stairs, changed into her best dress, a cambric gown in a brown with a reddish tint, then donned a very plain poke bonnet and dark green pelisse. Within ten minutes, convinced she looked every inch the part of a sensible matchmaker, Thea set off for Sir James's offices on Beatty Street.

Thea actually arrived a few minutes early for the interview.

The law offices of Sir James Smiley, Esq., consisted of two rooms. Sir James's clerk sat at a desk in the first room. At her entrance, he jumped to his feet. He was all of seventeen, with a slender frame and straight blonde hair parted to one side. He pushed his spectacles up his nose. "Mrs. Martin? Sir James is waiting for you."

Thea always used her married name. She never even thought of herself as Lady Thea, which had really been nothing more than a courtesy title, since she was the daughter of a duke. In truth, a true lady would never style herself above her husband, and at this point in her life, Thea was concerned about what was honest and real over "courtesy."

After all, her ducal father had disowned her, and, as Mrs. Martin, she was determined to stand on her own two feet . . . no matter how wobbly she felt doing so at times.

"I hope I'm not too late?" Thea said, nerves making her sound a bit breathless.

"You are right on time," the clerk assured her. "One moment, please." He crossed to the room's other door, gave a knock and opened it. "Sir James, Mrs. Martin has arrived."

"Send her in, send her in," a hearty male voice ordered.

The secretary held open the door. "Mrs. Martin," he announced, ushering her forward with a small sweep of his hand.

Her heart pounding in her ears, Thea crossed into the other room.

Sir James's book-lined office was the typical sort one would expect from a solicitor. The desk was huge and covered with neatly stacked papers, the ink-and-quill stand was solid silver, and there was a side table for the wig stand that held the curled peruke of his profession. Two comfortable wooden chairs were arranged in front of the desk.

"Come in, come in," Sir James said in greeting as he walked around the desk to welcome her.

He was a robust man with flinty blue eyes,

a hawkish nose and an air that proclaimed him no one's fool. "I've heard much about you, Mrs. Martin, and it is a pleasure to make your acquaintance. Please, have a chair."

Thea sat on the edge of the offered chair, holding her reticule in her lap with both gloved hands. Sir James took his seat behind his desk.

He smiled at her.

She smiled back, very nervous.

"I suppose you are wondering why I requested this interview?" he asked.

"You mentioned my assistance to Mr. Goodfellow," she murmured.

"I'm his uncle, and only one as familiar as I was with the situation can truly appreciate the miracle you wrought. All of us in the family adore his wife, Emma. How you managed to convince her to marry him is beyond our understanding, but we are thankful you did. In fact, his mother, my sister, has suggested I should think about seeking your services. She claims I'm too old to continue bachelor ways, but I am not ready to hand over my freedom yet. By the way, did you hear that Peter and his wife are expecting their first child?" Sir James asked. "One can hope the child looks more like Emma than Peter." He paused before adding thoughtfully, "You know, Emma seems to love him. She sees the better qualities in him."

And finding a suitable husband without the aid of even a modest dowry meant Emma had little choice in husbands Thea could have added, but didn't. "How wonderful for them."

"Yes, and when one of my clients mentioned he wished to find a wife to meet his most unusual specifications, I thought of you."

"Thank you," Thea said. She prayed this wasn't going to be a task as difficult as Peter Goodfellow had been. "But exactly what is the gentleman looking for in a wife?"

Instead of answering, the lawyer straightened in his chair, listening.

Male voices came from the other room, one the clerk's and the other a deep, well-modulated tone. Sir James smiled. "I'll let him tell you himself. I believe you will be pleased. He won't be as challenging a case as my nephew." He rose and crossed the room, throwing open the door. "My lord," he said in greeting. "Good of you to join us."

"She's here?" his lordship said.

Thea came to her feet. She caught a glimpse of the gentleman but could not see

26

his face from this angle. She had the impression he was taller than Sir James, and that was good. Women liked tall men.

"Yes, she is, and very interested in meeting you," Sir James said.

"I don't know," the gentleman said, doubt filling his voice.

"Speak to her. See what you think," Sir James said. He stepped aside to let the gentleman enter the room first.

Thea caught her breath in anticipation, silently praying this man was not an unfortunate-looking soul like Peter Goodfellow. After all, there was *usually* something wrong with all of her charges, else they wouldn't need her guidance —

Her breath left her with a small exclamation of surprise.

He wasn't her *usual* charge.

This man was everything a young lord should be. He was tall, taller than most, with square shoulders and no sign of belly bulge or flabby calves. Strong legs were encased in buff-colored breeches and shining, tall black boots. He was handsome. Slashing black brows, a resolute jaw, blue eyes that seemed to look right into a person. The material of his bottle green jacket was of the finest wool and molded to his shoulders in such a way that she knew he did not need padding.

Indeed, there was so much masculine energy about him that most women would find it hard to breathe, let alone think, in his presence. Thea was no exception. Her mind had come to an abrupt halt. She couldn't think, couldn't speak, couldn't do anything but stare, and not out of admiration . . . but from the shock of recognition.

Before her stood the wealthy, reclusive Neal Chattan, Lord Lyon — the most eligible bachelor in society, and a man who had once been her closest confidant until he'd rudely rejected her friendship.

"Mrs. Martin," Sir James said with the eagerness of someone very pleased with himself, "this is Lord Lyon." He shut the door behind him and came into the room. "My lord, may I present to you Mrs. Martin, the matchmaker I've suggested you enlist."

Neal appeared to be having his own bout of mind-numbing recollection. He didn't react to Sir James's introduction but stared at Thea with an unnerving intensity.

Or, perhaps, age had made his expression intense. She wouldn't know. Their paths hadn't crossed in close to fourteen years.

But he was here before her now.

She straightened her back and lifted her

chin, keeping both hands on her reticule for balance, for support. "My lord." She almost choked on the words. She'd heard his father had died several years ago, knew that he'd ascended to the title.

"*Mrs.* Martin?" He moved a step away, as if uncertain.

His movement allowed her to take two paces opposite his. "I married," she said.

"Apparently."

Sir James looked at Thea, looked at Lord Lyon, and then back at her. The welcoming smile left his face, replaced by uncertainty. "Do you two know each other?"

"Barely," Thea replied crisply even as Lord Lyon barked, "Hardly."

The twin words lingered in the air, followed by a beat of heavy silence, and Thea couldn't help but remember their childhood days together, back when her father had always banished his children to the countryside, where the favored sons had been encouraged to hunt and fish, and the girls had been left to sew samplers. Thea had escaped the house back then and come across Neal, who'd been just as lonely as herself.

Lord Lyon must have been thinking along the same lines. "I knew her when she was Lady Thea," he told Sir James. There was an accusatory tone to his voice that Thea did not like.

Sir James dismissed this bit of information with a wave of his hand. "Yes, yes, we all know she is the duke of Duruset's daughter. You needn't worry about the current Duruset's opinion, my lord. His father disowned her when she married. The current duke has stated publicly he won't have anything to do with her."

Lord Lyon frowned. "Is that true?" he demanded of Thea.

She was not pleased to have her business bandied about, yet she was also proudly defiant. "It must be," she said. "Sir James wrote the letter from my father cutting me off."

"Bad bit of business it was," Sir James said, moving around his desk to his chair. "Never enjoy those sorts of things, and I admit I've been doing what I can to help her out. She's widowed now. The marriage is done, but she is developing a very respectable reputation at putting the right sort of people together. She helped immeasurably with Peter, and you know we fretted of ever marrying him off. Considering your unusual desires for a wife, you'd be wise to listen to her."

"Perhaps his lordship would not care to

work with me," Thea suggested stiffly.

"Perhaps," Sir James echoed. He stood behind his desk now, his fingers resting on its polished surface. "Will you sit down and discuss the matter with her, Lyon? Or shall I toss her out?" He said this last with the familiarity of one who knew his customer.

Lord Lyon shifted his weight as if in indecision, and then he shrugged. "Very well, she may try. I suppose it doesn't matter who I use as long as she is effective."

"I believe you will be pleased," Sir James said. He smiled. "Perhaps someday I shall use her myself. Like you, I must marry sooner or later. Will you sit, Mrs. Martin?"

Thea had the urge to run from the room, but then she thought of her sons, of her looming plans for Jonathan's education. Lyon was rich. "I shall stay, but it will cost you a pretty penny, my lord," she said, wanting to give him a bit of his own arrogance back. "My services are not inexpensive."

"I can't imagine they would be," Lord Lyon replied. "In fact, if you find the wife I am looking for, I'll triple whatever your commission is."

Thea sat.

Lord Lyon took his seat.

"Now isn't this better?" Sir James said brightly, taking his own chair.

Thea forced a smile. Neal remained stony-faced.

She decided to really tweak Lyon's nose and take charge. "Sir James said you have particular qualities you are looking for in a wife. Please tell me what they are?"

He shifted in his chair, crossed his arms and his legs, not looking at her.

"Do you wish her to have blonde hair?" Thea queried in a pert, businesslike voice — one that she knew would needle him. "Or a brunette? Do you like voluptuous women? Or perhaps a more slender version?"

Lord Lyon looked to Sir James. "This is uncomfortable."

"They are reasonable questions, Lyon," Sir James said. "If she is to search for a wife for you, then she must know."

"Or," Thea said, "you could head out on the Marriage Mart and look for yourself." The "Marriage Mart" was the name given to the round of social parties and engagements during the season when Parliament was in session. Many a match had been made at these events.

"I don't want to do that," he said, still not making eye contact with her.

A memory came to her of the two of them sitting on the same rock beside a running stream, their secret place. She'd been what? Fourteen? He must have been sixteen. She saw them, their heads together, laughing, drawing courage from each other. Their friendship had helped make her world sane, and then the next day, she'd escaped to meet him again as they had done every morning for the past month or more, and he hadn't been there. She'd visited the site every day for the rest of her summer, and he'd never showed again.

No warning, no explanation . . . and then, in the fall, she'd heard that he'd left for school and she'd stopped searching for him. She'd not seen him again until this moment.

"Then I shall need to know what you are looking for if I am to sift through the large number of women who would be very pleased to marry a wealthy, well-respected nobleman." She heard herself sounding like a society matron planning a party. She liked the tone. It was distant and didn't convey the turbulence of her own emotions.

His jaw hardened.

When he didn't speak, Sir James prompted him once again. "Lyon, what are you looking for in a wife?"

His lordship stirred himself then to sit up. He answered, still addressing himself to Sir James, his voice low, almost inaudible.

"Good family."

How original, Thea wanted to say. Instead, she said, "Absolutely. And other qualities?"

There was a beat of silence. Thea felt her disdain for this man growing. After the confidences they had shared, how could he sit beside her as if they were strangers? How could he be so bloody cold?

"I don't want a cold woman," he said, as if he'd divined her thoughts. "My mother was cold. Some say I am as well."

But he didn't used to be. A wave of sadness swept away her disdain.

"Good with children," he continued. "Our children must be her priority."

Something that hadn't been true about his mother.

Thea resisted the urge to place a comforting hand upon his arm. If Neal hadn't valued their friendship, he certainly wouldn't want her pity now.

"And she must be someone I cannot like," he said. "Admired by others . . . but *I must not like her.*"

Warm thoughts of him vanished from Thea's mind. "You don't want to 'like' the woman who will be your wife?"

At last he faced her, his features set. *"No."*

"My lord, that is a ludicrous, irresponsible position." The words had just burst out of

her, carried by her previous disappointments in him.

Apparently, few talked to Lord Lyon in such a direct manner. Sir James's mouth dropped open.

His lordship sat up even taller. "I find it very responsible."

"Then you are deceiving yourself," Thea said. She'd gone this far, she might as well go further. "Not all marriages can be built on love, but those are the best. At the very least there should be the compatibility of admiration and respect. Of *liking* the person you take a vow before God to cherish and honor."

"That is your opinion. It is not mine."

Thea looked into his eyes and saw a stranger. "Whatever happened to that boy I once knew who believed in friendship?" she said. "That lad whose confidences I valued and whose opinion I trusted?"

"Let us take a moment to consider our words," Sir James advised, as if wishing to avert a disaster.

"I can't help you arrange such a marriage as this," Thea went on, ignoring the lawyer. "Knowing what I do of you, it would not be right."

"You know nothing of me," Lord Lyon countered.

"I beg to differ, my lord. I may know more of you than you know of yourself."

"And what would that be?" he challenged.

Thea sat back, realizing she was now on very sensitive ground. How well *did* she know him? How much *had* he changed?

Certainly she wasn't the same person she'd been during those long-ago summer days.

But one thing was still clear in her mind — she believed in love.

The acknowledgement startled her. After all that Boyd, her father, her family had put her through, she still believed.

It isn't often one is struck with self-knowledge, and every time it is surprising. Suddenly, she realized why she'd set herself up as a matchmaker. She wanted to right wrongs, to guide others away from the disastrous decisions she'd made in her own life.

She softened her voice. "My lord, marriage is a difficult endeavor. I'm not saying you must love your wife, but you must like her. Otherwise you will be saddling yourself to a cold, uncompromising life." The sort of life his parents had had all those years ago.

The sort of life she remembered him vowing never to live.

Her change in tone worked. The fury in

36

his eyes died, replaced by hopelessness. "You don't understand."

"Then explain to me," she said.

"I'm cursed."

Thea blinked. Uncertain if he was being dramatic or factual. "Cursed?"

"Yes," he said with complete seriousness. "And my only hope of survival is to marry someone I don't like, that I will *never* be able to abide. It will call for a very special woman. I don't want someone I would detest. There is a difference between not liking and detesting."

Thea glanced at Sir James to see if he thought his lordship was spouting nonsense. He nodded his head as if agreeing with Lord Lyon.

"You believe him cursed as well?" Thea challenged the solicitor.

Sir James shrugged. "There is evidence to suggest it."

For a second, Thea wondered if she had wandered into a world of nonsense — and then her mind seized upon another possibility. A sinister one.

"Is my brother behind this?" she demanded.

Both Lord Lyon and Sir James acted perplexed at her accusation, but she was on to the game now. This was the only explanation that made sense. She stood. "Oh, this was very clever of him. I know Horace is not happy that I remain independent and even dare to go so far as to work for my living. But this?" She shook her head. "You should be ashamed of yourself, Sir James. And you, Lord Lyon. What a faithless friend you are. Apparently your title has destroyed whatever was good inside of you."

"I beg your pardon?" Lord Lyon said. He'd risen when she had and now pretended to be clueless in the face of her accusation.

She moved toward the door. Her excitement over a healthy commission had turned to disappointment.

Sir James came around the desk toward her. "Mrs. Martin, please, I don't know what we said to upset you —"

She cut him off by whirling around, her outstretched hand a warning that she did not want him to come closer. "*Enough.* I can't believe I wasted a half shilling on the two of you. Here you are giving in to my brother's schemes, and for what? A payment, Sir James? Some sort of cloakroom political deal in the House of Lords, Lord Lyon? Oh, yes, I know how the duke works. He's always hatching new alliances for his own benefit. But I once thought you the closest of friends, and to my great dismay, you have grown into a man much like your parents — cold, distant, everything you said you wouldn't be. *Curses,*" she said, biting out the word as if it had been an epithet. "Did you really believe I would be so gullible. Well, return to my brother and tell him no one believes in curses in this day and age. Not even his sister, the one he refuses to acknowledge." With that pronouncement, she opened the door and sailed out of the room.

"Thea, *come back here,*" Neal ordered.

Her response was to keep walking.

CHAPTER TWO

Righteous anger propelled Thea down the street and halfway home. She didn't have blood in her veins right now, she had *gunpowder.*

To think she had taken them seriously at first. She'd asked Lord Lyon what sort of qualities he was looking for in a wife? They had been very good at not snickering in her face.

And what of Lyon? Her relationship with her father had always been troubled. The duke and Thea had locked horns continually while she'd been growing up. She'd rebelled at his numerous rules, his favoritism toward her brothers and the injustice of refusing to let her study anything except deportment, painting and religion. He'd wanted docile, obedient daughters with more hair than wit, and Thea wasn't cut of that cloth.

Neal had known all that. She'd confided

in him the struggles and arguments between she and her father. With the solace of Neal's friendship, Thea had been able to face a summer of her father being unusually harsh with his strictures and criticisms, until Neal had thrown the friendship aside without a fare-thee-well. He'd just left her wondering, worrying if she had done something to set him off her, worrying if he'd been ill or, worse, dead.

Of course, he'd been fine. She'd heard through the servants that he'd been up and around the parish.

He just hadn't cared enough to explain why he hadn't wanted to see or talk to her any longer.

And that was unforgivable.

Fury consumed her. Right there, in the middle of the busy city, she walked in a small, tight circle like a madwoman with too much energy to spare. Of course, she bumped into someone . . . an orange girl who was not expecting Thea's sudden change of direction.

"Sorry, miss, sorry," the girl mumbled, adjusting the basket on her arm and hurrying on her way.

Thea looked around. She was in Picadilly. Only a few more blocks to home. She took a deep breath and released it. Enough of this nonsense. She needed to collect herself so that when she walked through the door of her apartments she had a smile on her face for her sons.

Of course, her smile would have been broader if she had actually been looking forward to a fat commission.

Money worries always plagued her, but the school fees were a particular concern. Mirabel, Lady Palmer, had offered the money, but Thea didn't want to take advantage of her friend, who was already too generous to her and her sons by half.

No, educating her sons was something she must do on her own.

As Thea turned the corner onto her narrow street, she repeated under her breath with each step, "It will all work out. It will all work out."

Her lips might be saying the words, but her mind was very anxious, an anxiety compounded by the realization that she had not shopped for their dinner that night. In her desire to save money, she sometimes let the cupboard grow a bit too bare. Her boys would be hungry.

Thea stood at the base of the four flights of stairs leading to her apartment and decided that this night, they all needed a treat. The half shilling she owed Mrs. Gray would clean out the allowance she gave herself for the week, but just this once, she should raid the Future Box for a little extra.

Perhaps she and the boys would make a night of it. They would do a bit of shopping and then buy a meat pie for their dinner. Jonathan's appetite was starting to grow, but she and Christopher could split a half pie between them, and they would enjoy it in the small park several blocks away.

Her boys grew restless when left inside all day. She didn't dare let them roam free in this neighborhood. She knew from growing up with brothers that boys of any age could find trouble if not kept under some sort of supervision. Furthermore, she was determined to raise gentlemen, not urchins.

The trudge up the stairs was always tiring, but Thea's fatigue vanished when she saw her door slightly ajar. She always kept it bolted, and, before she'd left, she had advised Mrs. Gray to do the same.

She hesitated outside the door. "Mrs. Gray?"

"We are right here, Mother," came Jonathan's voice, his relief clear.

Thea pushed the door open. Her sons were sitting side by side on the same wooden chair. Jonathan's arm was around Christopher's shoulder. She smiled. It warmed her heart to see her boys depending on each other and relieved her momentary fears.

"Hello there, my handsome lads," she said. "Mummy's home."

To that statement, Christopher burst into tears. He jumped from the chair and ran to her, catching her at the knees and almost toppling her.

"I'm happy to see you as well," she said, laughing. She gave him a hug and smiled at Jonathan, a smile that quickly died when she saw that his eyes were red and he had been crying as well. "Jonathan? Is something the matter? Where is Mrs. Gray?"

There was no sight or sound of the woman.

"She left," Jonathan said, his voice strained, as if he had the worst sort of news to tell her. Christopher buried his head deeper into her skirts and cried harder.

Thea moved into the room, walking her youngest in with her. She set her reticule aside on a chair and called, "Mrs. Gray?"

No answer.

"She's not here, Mummy," Jonathan repeated. "I told you she left."

"Where did she go? Why would she leave?"

Christopher started gasping for breath as if he would be sick. Jonathan, instead of being horrified the way he usually was when

44

his brother threatened to be ill, jumped from the chair and raced over to hug him.

Thea fell to her knees on the floor and gathered them both in her arms. "Be easy, Christopher, easy. Mummy's home. Nothing bad will happen."

"It is bad," Jonathan said. "Very bad."

"What is bad?" Thea asked, struggling to keep her voice calm. "You can tell me. Did Mrs. Gray do something bad?"

"Yes," Christopher said. "I didn't mean to tell her about the Future Box. I told her to stop."

"To stop what?" Thea asked.

"Taking the money," Jonathan said. "She took *all* the money in the Future Box."

Thea went cold with panic. She rose to her feet, ran the few steps to the bedroom.

All looked as it should. The bed was neatly made, all tidy and right, but Thea knew her sons were not teasing. She came down to the floor, reached under the bed and pressed the board so that one end would pop up.

Her boys had followed her. They stood in the bedroom doorway, their faces pale.

Thea lifted the box out. It was much lighter.

So much saving, scrimping, planning . . . *dreaming.*

She opened the box. She had to see with

her own eyes that it was empty, and it was. All was gone. Everything. The only money she had to her name was the half shilling in her purse she had been going to use to pay Mrs. Gray.

"We told her to stop," Jonathan said. "Chris didn't mean to tell her. She had us sharing secrets."

"Sharing secrets?" Thea said, confused.

"Yes, she said we all had secrets and she told us some and then wanted to know ours. It was a game," Jonathan insisted. "A game."

"Yes, she said she was thirsty and wanted to know where we hid things," Christopher said. "I didn't mean for her to take the money."

"I know you didn't," Thea answered. She had to stay calm. She must think, reason.

"I told her it was for Jonny's school," Christopher said. "She didn't listen to me."

Anger welled up inside of Thea, and disgust with her own culpability. She hadn't known Mrs. Gray other than in passing. She should not have trusted her.

But that didn't give the woman license to steal from them either.

In a blink, Thea was on her feet, the box under one arm. She marched through the apartment and out into the hall.

"Where are we going, Mother?" Jonathan asked.

"To see Mrs. Gray."

Thea took the stairs two at a time. Her sons dashed behind her to keep up, Christopher echoing her words, "See Mrs. Gray."

They were all on a mission now.

She knocked on the door at the top of the stairs. It opened immediately. Mrs. Hadley looked at the three of them standing on her landing and gave them a tired, welcoming smile. She was a thin woman with a sharp nose and pleasant blue eyes.

"Look who has come to see me," she said in her soft Irish lilt. "My, you lads are so handsome and brawny you brighten my day. You need to stop growing. Doesn't your mother put the bricks on your head to keep you little? If you aren't careful, Mrs. Martin, they will be tall as giants."

Usually when she made her comments, they all laughed, but not today.

"Where is Mrs. Gray?" Thea asked anxiously.

"Why, I don't know," Mrs. Hadley said, her manner changing to concern. "She was not here when I returned home. I went to see my husband in the hospital."

"How is he doing?" Thea stopped her own concerns to ask.

"Not well. Why do you need my husband's sister? What has she done now?"

Thea's heart sank at the wariness in Mrs. Hadley's tone. "She stole from us."

"She took the money in the Future Box," Jonathan chimed in.

Thea placed her hand on her son's back. "I did something foolish," she whispered, fearing she had only herself to blame. "I had an appointment, a rather important one, I thought, but it was a fool's errand." Thea forced herself to think clearly. "I came up here to see if you would watch my sons for an hour or so while I was gone, but you weren't home. Mrs. Gray volunteered to help. I mean, the two of you are related, and you are so good and kind to the boys. Also, she was a vicar's wife? I should have been able to trust her, shouldn't I . . . ?"

She broke off, needing, yearning for confirmation from Mrs. Hadley.

"Oh, my dear, I am so sorry," the older woman said. Tears welled in her eyes.

"What is it?" Thea begged.

"My husband's sister is too fond of gin. Her husband had the affliction. He was a vicar but one that stole from the church plate. He was run out of three parishes, and she is just as bad as he was. He died and she being alone, she came to see me. She had nowhere else to turn. The Church didn't want her. I told her she could not be sipping the gin under my roof, and I thought she was doing good. You know, some people make you think they are doing well, but they aren't. They are liars. Thieves. There has been a time or two that I sensed she was going through my things looking for a bottle or money."

"Where is she now?" Thea asked, the words hard to push past the heaviness in her chest.

"Who knows? If she has taken your money, I shan't be seeing her anytime soon," Mrs. Hadley predicted. "And don't think I'll let her stay under my roof again after what she did. I don't know what to do for you and your lads, Mrs. Martin. I feel bad, but I don't know what to do."

Thea didn't either.

"Perhaps you should call for the Watch. Let them know she's a thief," Mrs. Hadley suggested.

And then what? Thea knew the money was gone. "I might," she said, more to placate Mrs. Hadley.

"I'm so sorry," the older woman said.

"I am as well," Thea answered. She turned to her sons. "Come, boys. Let us see what we can find for supper." They wouldn't be going out for a shopping lark.

"I have a bit of bread and cheese," Mrs. Hadley offered. "Unless Mary took that as well."

"We'll be fine," Thea said, the words sounding curter than she had intended them. She softened her tone. "Truly, we will be."

They would survive, but her dream of Jonathan going to Westminster was gone . . . and she didn't know if she could revive it. Perhaps she had been fooling herself all along that she could enroll her sons there, that she could do it all on her own.

"I'm hungry, Mother," Jonathan complained.

"Me, too," Christopher echoed.

Children were so resilient. Her mind was still spinning with what had happened, while her sons had moved on to what was practical.

"Let's see what we have to eat," Thea answered, starting down the stairs, her tread heavy, her mind numb —

She pulled up short on the last three stairs as she realized she had a visitor.

Neal Chattan, Lord Lyon, stood at her open door. He'd heard them coming down the stairs and had turned to face them.

He seemed even taller, and even handsomer, here in the dingy halls of her building than he had in Sir James's office, perhaps because the refined cut of his clothes emphasized the shabbiness of her humble home.

Their eyes met. Thea tightened her jaw in resentment. She had a good notion to heave the Future Box at him. She had no doubt she could hit him right on his arrogant nose, and it might make her feel better.

As if reading her mind, he held up his hands. "We should talk, Thea. Please, just for a moment. We apparently have outstanding business between us."

Chapter Three

Neal had been taken aback by how rickety the stairs in this building were. The smoke from coal fires burned his nostrils, while the smell of ages of cooked meals seemed to have permeated the walls.

This building was so old that it had to have been standing during the time of the Great Fire. It was a pity it hadn't been burned down. He'd not live here and was surprised anyone did, most of all Lady Thea.

In the dim light of the hallway stairs, she stood tall, her eyes burning with pride. She was still dressed for going out, still in her drab hat, her gloves and her pelisse.

And he remembered her as he last saw her years ago, the memory still fresh in his mind — her hair down around her shoulders, her feet bare because she'd been wading in the stream waiting for him, a chain of bachelor buttons and daisy wildflowers forming a crown on her head.

They'd both been so young.

He'd forgotten what it was like back then. Now, responsibilities, worries, and the weight of not only his country's future but his family's were heavy on his shoulders. He'd forgotten how free he'd felt when he'd been around her.

But that was then and this was now. Gone was the blondness of her hair, which had darkened to a honeyed brown. Maturity had sharpened the lines of her face and given her character. Her eyes were just as blue, but they were no longer innocent. Knowledge of the world, of herself, had created shadows in their depth.

"I don't need this discussion right now, my lord," she said.

"I'm not here to discuss anything," he said, suddenly concerned he'd be dismissed. He needed to talk to her. He *wanted* to.

And then tears came to her eyes. Large, luminous ones that she struggled to hold back.

Like most men, Neal didn't know what to do in the face of a female's tears. His sister, Margaret, rarely cried. She was too proud. Considering the set down Thea had given him only an hour ago, Neal had assumed that she was as proud, unless something had broken her spirit.

He didn't think it was himself . . . or at least he hoped it wasn't.

Neal took a step up the staircase toward her. "What is the matter?"

"Nothing," she said, the tension in the word so tight that something had to be wrong.

"Mrs. Gray took all our money," a voice from her side said.

Neal was startled to realize they weren't alone. He'd been so focused on Thea that he hadn't noticed the two small beings who stood on either side of her.

Both had flaxen blonde hair and eyes as blue as their mother's. The youngest had a death grip on Thea's skirts, his wary expression telling Neal he wasn't about to trust him any more than his parent did.

The other was bolder. He was the one who had spoken. He'd stepped forward to make his announcement, his body taut from the top of his head to the fists he clenched at his side.

There was no doubt these were her sons. They shared her refined features and determined chin.

Neal didn't come in contact with many children. He had few relatives, and they were all aged. His day-to-day activities rarely brought him within close proximity of children and, although he saw them on the street or in shops, he rarely talked to them — even if he wanted sons of his own . . . desperately.

His desire to father a child was more than just a need to fulfill the obligations he owed his family name and title. He yearned for children in a way he didn't understand.

He now found himself both charmed and curious by these two boys. They were more than copies of their mother. They were independent souls, souls created from the spark of a connection and little more.

"Mrs. Gray stole your money?" Neal repeated, addressing the child directly while wondering who this woman was. "Did you see her take the money?"

To his surprise the youngest answered, the words coming out of his mouth so fast they tumbled over each other in his earnestness. "Yes, we did. She took the money. We told her not to, but she didn't listen to us. Jonny told her."

"Who is this Mrs. Gray?" Neal demanded, insulted for the boys.

"This isn't your concern, my lord," Thea snapped, even as her youngest answered, "The lady. Mrs. Gray. She took all our money. We don't have any."

"Chris, quiet," Jonny ordered.

His brother's response was to bury his

face in his mother's skirts but not before he explained, "We can't catch her. She's gone."

Jonny was furious that his order had been ignored. He took a step toward his brother, but Thea's hand on his shoulder stayed him, and Neal was reminded of his own battles with his brother. He and Harry were as close as two brothers could be and as far apart.

"Who is this Mrs. Gray?" Neal asked again, ready to charge after the woman.

Thea said, "I am handling the matter, my lord. This is none of your affair. Is there some outstanding business between us you wished to convey? Although I don't understand why there should be." She'd started down the last of the steps, brushing him aside as she made her way through the open apartment door, shooing her boys in ahead of her. They obeyed, the oldest taking the youngest's hand. Seeing they were safe, she turned, blocking Neal from entering the flat by leaning one hand on the door. "I thought I made myself very clear this afternoon."

"You did," Neal said.

"Then we have nothing else to say to each other," she informed him crisply.

"Actually, we do. You misunderstood me in Sir James's office. I am serious in my need for a wife, and you are not in a position to toss aside opportunities," he said, pointing to the empty wooden box she held in her arms.

Her chin lifted. A flash of new insult lit her eyes.

"A moment of your time," Neal pressed. "That's all I ask."

"A moment is too much," she answered.

Her tart reply ignited Neal's own temper. "Every inch the duke's daughter, aren't you, Lady Thea? Well, think about your sons and don't be foolish. I need your help and you need mine. Let's keep the past behind us."

The lines of her mouth flattened. "Your request is impossible to honor. That talk about a curse —"

"It's true."

She rolled her eyes and reached for the door to close it.

Neal blocked the action with his arm. "I know it sounds impossible," he said, "but I'm not known for being a frivolous man. Why would I make such a thing up?"

"I haven't a notion, my lord. Now, if you will please go?"

"Once you've heard me out."

For a long moment they were at a standstill. The set of her mouth told him she would like nothing more than to push him down the stairs and out of her life.

Well, he wasn't going, and he didn't know why, but it was now very important that *she* hear his story.

She sighed her capitulation. "All right. Explain yourself, although I'm not in the mood for explanations. You would be wise to postpone this conversation." She turned and walked into the apartment.

"Why are you so angry with me, Thea?" he said.

She looked back at him with suspicion and then frowned. "You really don't know, do you?"

"Know what?" Neal asked, closing the door behind him. Her sons still stood together, the oldest watching him warily. The youngest yawned.

Thea set the box on a wooden table. There were three chairs around the table, an unfortunate-looking settee, a serviceable cupboard. Everything was clean and neat and, in spite of the scant furnishings, it felt like a home. There was a stack of books on the cupboard and a slate board with chalk. Two horses carved out of wood had been placed there as well. They had leather saddles and bridles and appeared to be cherished toys.

She removed her gloves and started untying the ribbons of her hat as she said, "You disappeared on me years ago. I went to the stream, and you didn't show — without any explanation, my lord. You stopped coming, and I didn't know if it was something I said or did. I feared you had taken ill, until the servants said they had seen you out and about."

"It was the curse," he said.

"The curse? What, you've been cursed so that you cannot act politely to your friends?"

Her barb stung. "You've developed a sharp tongue, my lady," he said.

"It's the consequence of marriage, my lord," she shot back. "I'm not as gullible as I was when we were younger."

"Then hear me out. I don't ask that your mind is open, Mrs. Martin, but I'd like to finish a thought without your 'wisdom' being tossed at me."

She didn't like a touch of sharpness tossed right back at her. She placed her hands on her hips, her hat still on her head, the ribbons hanging down. "I don't have time to dally, my lord."

"Then let me pay you for your time," he challenged. "Provided you will let me speak."

"I don't think you could afford me," she answered. "Furthermore, after all this time, I truly am no longer interested in your excuses."

"For a woman without a shilling to her name, you are very proud."

"I'm still the daughter of a duke," she replied tightly.

"I am a wealthy man," he returned. "I want what I want and will settle for no less."

"And you must have *my* help?" she said, her disbelief clear.

His gaze drifted to the boys, who listened attentively to all that was being said. Did they understand? Could children understand the arguments of adults?

Bringing his eyes back to her, he answered, "Yes."

"Unfortunately, you will be disappointed. I choose not to work with you," she said, and he could have ground his teeth in frustration.

"You are so foolish," he said almost under his breath, but of course she heard it.

For a second, Thea appeared ready to breathe fire —

"Mother, I'm hungry," the youngest boy said.

"Christopher, one moment," his mother answered.

"No," Neal countermanded her, seizing upon an idea. "I'm hungry as well. Why don't we discuss this over dinner?" He'd be moving the lioness from her lair, and then she'd have to listen to him with a reasonable state of mind, all past grudges set aside. "Let me take all of you to dinner."

"That isn't necessary —," she started, ready to refuse his invitation.

"Have you lads been to the Clarendon Hotel?" he interrupted her, brazenly taking the argument straight to her children.

"The what?" Christopher asked. His older brother looked to their mother, not answering Neal without her approval.

Neal lowered himself to their level. "They have a French chef at the Clarendon who truly is a marvel. And there is nothing more fun than a small outing."

Jonny had placed his arm around his younger brother as if holding him back. Neal pressed his case. "Jacques makes a *poulet en croute* that is food of the gods." His mouth was watering just thinking of it.

Thea laughed, the sound bitter. "They don't know what you are talking about, my lord. They've been raised on my meager cooking. Talk to them of a rarebit and they'll understand."

"You cook?" Neal repeated in surprise and then realized it was a ridiculous question. All of this — the boys, the squalor, the married name Mrs. Martin — was a surprise.

The girl he'd known had been raised in luxury.

It was Christopher who saved him. "Do you have a horse?"

"Chris, stop talking," Jonny said, giving his younger brother's shoulder a jerk.

Neal put out his hand to steady the boy and said, "I have many."

Now he had Jonny's attention as well.

"How many horses do you have?" Christopher asked.

"More than I can ride by myself," Neal assured him. "And my brother is in the Horse Guard."

"Horse Guard?" Jonny repeated with the same awe that pilgrims reserved for a religious shrine.

"He's one of the barracks officers," Neal said.

"What color is his horse?" Christopher demanded.

"A bay," Neal said. "His name is Ajax."

Christopher broke free of his brother's hold and ran to the cupboard for his horse. He held it up. "This is my horse. His name is Regal. My mother had a horse named Regal."

"Yes," Neal said. "I remember Regal. He was a good pony."

"Mother says he was very fast."

"She and Regal beat me and my pony in every race," Neal confirmed.

Jonny glanced at his mother as if trying to picture her flying along the ground in a race.

Thea came over to her sons. "Please, boys, we need to let Lord Lyon leave —"

"What are the names of your other horses?" Christopher cut in as if he hadn't heard her speak, and he might not have. Neal remembered a time when he was that enthusiastic about life.

"It would take a while for me to tell you all of them," Neal said. "However, I have two waiting outside that you lads should meet. Would you like to see them?"

"Yes." The word practically burst out of Jonny. Christopher nodded his head vigorously. He started toward the door, holding his wood horse in front of him.

"Wait," Neal cautioned. "We need permission from your mother. We could even have a ride in my coach, if your mother would let us go to the Clarendon for our dinner."

Two pleading sets of eyes turned as one toward Thea, not, she knew, because of the treat of patronizing one of the finest public dining rooms in the city but because of the opportunity of a coach ride.

"Please, Mother," Jonny whispered.

"*I* want to go," Christopher said with his

delightful candor.

Thea stood in indecision. Neal had circumvented her wishes by catering to her horse-mad sons, and he was unrepentant.

"I don't know," she hedged. "I don't know that it is proper for a lady to go to the Clarendon with a man who isn't her husband."

Neal made an impatient sound. "Women dine at the Clarendon. You shouldn't feel uncomfortable. Yes, they are accompanied by friends or their husbands, but you have two of the most upstanding chaperones of all. Your sons." Her boys stood up a bit straighter at his words.

Thea's gaze met his, and he saw that she really did want to go. He wondered how long it had been since Thea had participated in society for the pleasure of it and not as a means to help her small family survive.

She breathed deep to register her annoyance, then released it before saying, "Very well. This one time. Go don your hats and coats."

She didn't have to repeat the order. Her sons charged off with cheers of excitement.

Thea retied the bonnet ribbon beneath her chin. "Unfair," she said to Neal.

"But necessary," he assured her, quite proud of himself. She needed this outing. He knew it. "We will talk, Thea." He paused and then added quietly, "You were important to me."

She looked away.

The boys joined them. They had matching coats and wide brimmed hats that were exactly the sort any child of the gentry would wear. Christopher was so excited that he was having trouble putting his coat on. Neal helped and then opened the door. The boys fairly ran down the stairs.

"Wait," their mother warned them. "You know the rules."

Her sons came to a halt and stood like two racehorses anxious to take off out of the gate.

"You must be gentlemen at all times," Thea chided and, after locking the door, went down the stairs to take their hands.

Neal followed, rather enjoying the boys' excitement.

On the street, Thea kept a firm hold on her sons. There was much activity, mostly neighbors sitting on the stoops and in the doorways of surrounding buildings. Christopher tried to gallop, and Jonny had to try it a step or two.

Harry and Neal used to play that game of horses when they were the ages of Thea's boys. Margaret had played too when the nanny would let her. They had spent hours at Morrisey Meadows, the family's country estate, setting up jumps and then trotting or galloping over them.

Funny, but it had been years since he'd thought of the good parts of his childhood.

"Which way shall we go, my lord?" Thea asked.

"My coach is at the end of the street. This one was too narrow for it to travel down," Neal said, pointing to the right. He saw his coachman waiting for him. "Let them go," he said to Thea. "Bonner is there waiting for them." Bonner was the name of his coachman, and he already had a small audience of children around him.

She ignored him, but her sons did not. They were both pulling on her now, anxious to have a look at his coach. She still held fast, until their excitement overcame them. They were pulling too hard, and when they were fifty feet from Bonner, she took Neal's advice and let them go.

They ran to the coach. Their first stop was Neal's matched grays.

The coach itself was Neal's pride and joy. His father had designed it out of burled wood. The seats were covered with tufted red velvet. The overall vehicle was smaller than most coaches and very comfortable for town riding. It was so distinctive that his father had never bothered placing a coat of arms on the door. It was unnecessary. Everyone recognized the Lyon when he traveled.

"They are horse mad," Thea admitted to Neal, who fell into step beside her, "and I don't know why, because they haven't been around many. They've always been that way."

"We all are at that age," Neal answered. "And remember, their mother was a bruising rider."

She glanced at him from the corner of her eye. "I did outride you on more than one occasion."

"Yes." He paused a moment and then said, "How was your money stolen?"

She looked to her sons. Bonner was telling the boys the horses' names: "Blen and Cully."

"Why did you name them that?" Christopher wanted to know.

"Lord Harry named them, laddies, after famous battles."

"He is the one in the Horse Guard, isn't he, sir?" Jonny asked.

"Aye, he is," Bonner answered.

"Don't worry about them," Neal told Thea. "They are in good hands. Bonner will have them feeding the horses molasses bits."

She crossed her arms. He sensed she wanted to tell him that how her money was stolen was none of his business. And then she surprised him by saying, "I *didn't* leave them alone if that is what you suspect. I would never do that. Those boys mean more to me than my own life. When I received Sir James's request for an interview, I went to see if Mrs. Hadley upstairs would watch them. She wasn't at home, but her sister-in-marriage was. I didn't know Mrs. Gray, and *now* I feel foolish. Mrs. Gray's husband had been a vicar. I assumed . . ." Her voice trailed off. She was not happy with herself. "I didn't know the vicar had been a thief and a drunkard, two traits that have obviously been carried on by his widow. When I returned home after our interview, I discovered the door was open and the boys left alone."

"And the box empty."

"She took all the money I'd saved," Thea said. "Every penny. Mrs. Hadley doesn't know where she is. Apparently Mrs. Gray has a fondness for drink. She could be anywhere right now."

"And what of your marriage?" he asked, pressing his luck. "I hadn't heard that you had married."

Thea's lips quirked into a smile. "Aren't

you being nosey, Neal?"

She'd called him by his Christian name, certainly a sign of a truce growing between them. "I am, but only because I care."

She shook her head, humming her disbelief. "No, we shall not go there."

Neal tamped down the desire to argue. He really was curious about what path her life had taken. If she'd been in trouble, she could have contacted him — but then she was right. He had abandoned her all those years ago. He *had* turned his back on her.

Regret was an uncomfortable emotion.

"Come, Thea. Let us have a good dinner and rekindle our friendship."

"You just want me to find a wife for you," she argued, but her words lacked their earlier heat.

"Aye, I do. I want what you have, Thea. I want children."

She nodded her understanding and gave her sons a pensive touch on the shoulders as they clambered into the coach.

In no time they were on their way to the Clarendon, one boy hanging out of one window and another boy hanging out the other so they could see all the sights along the way. They exclaimed over the stocky workhorses pulling drays, laughed at a juggler entertaining on a crowded street corner, and carried on about how "their" coach was far finer than any of the others on the road.

It was the most enjoyable trip Neal had ever made. The boys fascinated him. They had their own personalities and came up with their own thoughts. He'd equated children to being much like dogs who followed one around and did as bid. These lads were more imaginative, more engaged, more alive with life than he could ever have anticipated.

Thea was far from comfortable with him still. Even though they sat close enough that their legs brushed each other, she turned away from him, studying the passing scene outside her window, one hand on Christopher's coat in case he tumbled out in his excitement.

At this angle, she gave him a view of her very fine profile. She was a stubborn woman, a determined one, the sort he needed.

"I've had all sorts of matchmaking offers," he said.

She turned, looked at him. Her eyes had a grayish tint, like a stormy summer sky. "I am certain you have. Why were they not successful?"

"I was not interested."

She nodded as if he'd confirmed something she'd already known. However, the coach slowed to a stop. Bonner opened the door for them.

"Come, Master Martins," Neal said. "And your mother."

Christopher was reluctant to leave Blen and Cully, but a word from his mother and he was obedient. They entered the Clarendon. The doorman recognized Neal and greeted him with great fanfare.

"It is good to see you again, my lord."

"Thank you, Thomas." Neal often ate at the Clarendon. He preferred the food over that of his clubs.

The lobby was busy with much coming and going. Neal offered Thea his arm. She hesitated, as if debating whether to refuse or not, then shook her head. Neal didn't mind her standoffishness. She kept careful boundaries around herself. He understood, realizing he did the same.

Jonny and Christopher walked beside their mother, their heads turning as they were taking in all they could see. They all paused at the cloakroom to remove their headgear and the boys' coats. It was at that moment that a group of stylish women walked out of the dining area. They were all giggling and crowded around Neal's brother.

Harry was wearing one of his Horse

Guard uniforms, and the boys honed in on it.

"Lyon," Harry hailed Neal with lazy good humor. He steered his harem toward them. "You must try Jacques's *poulet en croute.* He has outdone himself . . ."

Harry's voice trailed off as he realized Neal wasn't alone. His gaze sharpened on Thea as if he sensed he should know who she was and couldn't quite place her.

The women around Harry were all smiling. The ones Neal recognized were married. Harry preferred married women. He said there were fewer complications.

Of course, Harry liked *all* women. He wasn't choosy. It was the difference between the two men. Neal fought the curse by being circumspect. Harry fought it by enjoying every pair of legs in skirts who crossed his path. In that way, he claimed, he would not and could not form a lasting attachment to any one of them.

"Who is this?" Harry asked, his tone taking on interest as he walked right up to Thea. Both Jonny and Christopher drew in their breath at the realization that one of their heroes was right there in front of them.

A bit annoyed, Neal said, "Mrs. Martin, this is my brother, Colonel Harry Chattan."

"Colonel," she said.

"Mrs. Martin?" one of Harry's companions said. "You seem so familiar. Have we met before? I am Lady Amberton." She was in her early forties but still had her looks. They said her husband turned a blind eye to her dalliances, and it was obvious that Harry had been plying her and her three companions with good wine. Their cheeks were rosy from it, and their manners more easy and forward.

Harry seemed fine. Of course, Harry could drink a cask of wine and still look unaffected. Many times Neal wished Harry did not have his prodigious predilection for ales, wines and spirits. Or a taste for other, more debilitating vices as well.

Of course there were other things Neal would change about his brother. Harry could be elegantly surly and brutally selfish when he had a mind to be. He was quick-witted, arrogant, and Neal thought him far more intelligent than himself. There were times they rubbed along well, and times they rubbed each other raw.

"I don't believe so," Thea answered. "It is a pleasure to make your acquaintance, my lady."

"We *have* met," Lady Amberton persisted. "Your name is so familiar."

Thea smiled and kept moving toward the

dining room while reaching down to bring her sons with her. Neal was happy to go with her. He murmured polite good-byes and lengthened his stride to catch up to Thea.

He could feel Harry staring after him.

"Are Lady Amberton and all those ladies with your brother?" Thea asked as the majordomo escorted them to Neal's customary table. "She is known to be a tigress."

"Then Harry shall enjoy her."

He didn't have to explain more because Thea's attention shifted to settling her sons and ensuring they understood having polite manners. "Jonathan, you take this seat on my right. Christopher, sit here on my left. Napkins in laps."

Neal took the liberty of ordering for all of them. "Tonight's *poulet*," he told the major-domo, who would handle the matter for him. He always did.

But Thea had not forgotten the thread of the conversation. "And what of yourself, my lord? Do you prefer tigresses?"

His gaze met hers. There was challenge in her voice, a hardness, as if she was waiting for him to disappoint her, as if she expected him to. Was this cynicism a result of her marriage? "I am more circumspect," he said. "Harry accuses me of being too rigid, but I

74

believe I'm the wiser —"

Before he could finish, a new member joined their party.

"I know *who* she is," Harry declared as if Neal had been hiding Thea's identity. He nabbed a chair from another table, mumbling a lame apology to the table's occupants and pulling it up to sit at Neal's. He crossed both his arms, stretching his long legs out as was his custom.

"She's a *matchmaker*." Harry said the last word as if it left a bad taste. "Don't do this, Neal. Let it end with us. Let us finish it."

Neal understood exactly what his brother was suggesting. And then he glanced at Jonathan, whose wide eyes relayed how overjoyed he was at his bounty of having the dashing Horse Guard right there at the table. Neal could remember being that young and involved in every moment of his life. Every day had been an adventure . . . but it wasn't any longer. Life had become rote, tasteless, unbearable.

Even with meals prepared by a French chef. And horses and houses and, and, *and* . . .

He hated all the "and's."

Neal wanted something *more* than possessions and money. He couldn't help himself. Life *had* to have more meaning.

He looked over to his brother. "I can't," he told Harry. "I won't."

CHAPTER FOUR

Thea looked at the two men seated on opposite sides of the table from each other. Colonel Chattan had placed himself right between her and Jonathan. Her poor son was ready to expire of hero worship, and her other son wished he could climb right across her lap, something she prevented by placing a warning hand on his leg.

The Chattans were both big-boned, handsome men. The family resemblance was obvious in the dark hair and the intelligent eyes — but there was a great difference between them. Even angry, the colonel appeared more carefree than his brother. There were laugh lines around his mouth and eyes.

Then again, appearances could be deceiving. She noticed the colonel sat with his right leg outstretched. He obviously favored it, even going so far as to reach down and massage a muscle on the outside of his thigh.

And there was no humor in the accusatory stare he slid in Thea's direction.

She attempted to avoid his glare by focusing on her sons.

The waiter broke the moment by appearing with plates of food. He asked Colonel Chattan if he wished to join them for dinner. The response was a curt hand motion waving him away.

Lord Lyon made a great pretense of ignoring his brother's foul mood. He tasted his chicken and pronounced it delightful. He then looked over at Jonathan's plate. "You must taste your chicken, Master Jonathan. And you, Master Christopher. Delicious."

The boys were too taken with having the colonel at the table to be interested in food.

Christopher leaned toward Neal. "Is his horse Ajax outside?" he asked in a whisper that could be heard by the whole table.

"*Of course* he's outside," Jonathan informed Christopher, as if annoyed by the naivete. "He can't bring him in here, can he?"

"What does his horse eat?" Christopher wanted to know, ignoring his brother and addressing himself once again to Neal.

"I don't know," Neal whispered back. "Let's ask him." He raised his voice. "Harry, what are you feeding old Ajax nowadays?"

Christopher was delighted to have a conspirator. "Yes, what do you feed him, sir?" he echoed, and even Jonathan turned to listen, as if the answer was very important.

Colonel Chattan found himself caught between two young hero worshippers and his argument with Lyon. The colonel was angry, but he wasn't a churlish man, and Lyon must have known that. Slowly, the colonel unbent a bit of his temper to answer Christopher's question. "The best hay money can buy."

Jonathan quickly jumped in with questions of his own about the life of a Horse Guard: Where do they sleep? Had the colonel been to war? Did Ajax go? Did he have as many horses as Lord Lyon?

Thea's mind raced with questions as well. Colonel Chattan was obviously displeased that his brother was contemplating marriage, and that didn't make sense. A man of Lord Lyon's rank and position should marry. It was an obligation . . . unless Colonel Chattan wished to be his heir?

She studied the officer from beneath her lashes. *"Don't do this, Neal. Let it end with us. Let us finish it."* Those were his words. His demands had been more of a plea. An urgent one.

"You young lads haven't been eating,"

79

Lyon observed. His good humor had never flagged. "I was hoping Harry would give us a tour of the Horse Guard stables, but we can't go until you've finished your suppers, right, Harry?"

A tour of the stables had obviously not been among the colonel's plans for the evening. He narrowed his gaze at his brother, but when he saw the eagerness on the boys' faces, some of his surliness evaporated. "Yes, I'd be happy to escort you on a tour."

That was all he had to say for them to start shoveling food in their mouths with incredible haste.

Neal's amused gaze went to Thea. He was enjoying her boys. In fact, the more time he spent with them, the lighter, and more likable, he became.

She was surprised. As she remembered, his parents hadn't particularly doted on their children. For that reason, Neal had told her he was very close to his brother and sister — or had been. That summer they had met, Harry had been shipped off to pursue the regimental life, and his sister, Margaret, had often escaped the quiet house to stay with a friend on the other side of the parish.

That had left Neal alone with a mother

who'd rarely spoken to him and a father who had escaped the house for London as quickly as possible and rarely returned. Neal had told her back then that his father thought more of his ledgers and investments than he did his children. She wondered if that had ever changed.

Neal reached across the table and topped off her glass of wine. "That rule applies to mothers as well," he chided. "You need to do less worrying, Mrs. Martin, and more eating."

Heat rushed to her cheeks. "How do you know I was worrying?"

His answer was an enigmatic smile. It said louder than words that he thought he knew her.

He was wrong. She'd changed. She wasn't that girl he remembered.

"Please, Mother," Jonathan said. "Eat your peas."

"Those are usually my words to you," she answered.

"Yes, well, it is good advice," Jonathan replied with perfect seriousness, and Colonel Chattan laughed. He'd been won over.

"I have to like horse-mad lads," he said. He stood, again favoring the right leg. "I'll go ahead and meet you there."

"Are you going to ride Ajax, sir?" Jonathan wanted to know.

"Of course I am." There was a beat of silence, and then the colonel said, "Would you two like to ride over with me? We'll meet your mother at the stables."

Nothing could have pleased the boys more. Christopher's eyes were so wide with his sudden good fortune that he couldn't speak. Jonathan did it for him. "*Please,* Mother, may we go?"

This would be a special treat that her sons would talk about forever. Thea couldn't say no. "Listen to what the colonel says. Behave yourselves."

"We'll follow any orders he gives us," Jonathan promised. Christopher had already climbed off his chair. He reached up and took the colonel's hand.

The sternness in Colonel Chattan's face softened. "You'll be good soldiers," he said and held out his other hand for Jonathan as he asked Lyon, "You will be coming directly?"

"Of course," his lordship answered.

"Don't tarry" was the colonel's last word before he led the boys out of the dining room, Christopher already barraging him with questions — and Jonathan walking so proudly that it almost hurt Thea's heart to see him.

Her oldest was growing up. He wouldn't be her little boy much longer. She didn't know if she could ever part with either of them. Whenever the world grew too dark and too lonely, they gave her the courage to keep going.

"It is very kind of the colonel to do this," she said.

Neal laughed. "How could he not? They've been staring at him as if he were Hercules and St. George combined. Their excitement is contagious."

Thea turned to Neal. "What happened to your brother's leg?"

"You noticed. Most people don't, and he works very hard to keep it that way." He pushed his fork pensively and then said, "Cannon fire. At Salamanca. He should have come home. The treatment here would have been better, but Harry's a military man through and through. He attempted to stay on and fight with his men, but he can't ride like he used to, and eventually Wellington moved him to his staff. Finally, Harry had no choice but to return home. He had always defined himself as a horseman. He could do anything on a horse, including riding upside down if he'd a mind to. Now he rides, but after a period of time, his leg gives him great pain."

There was something more he wasn't telling her. She sensed it. Their childhood friendship had been such that she could read him easily.

"Your brother is not pleased that you wish to marry," she observed, setting aside her napkin.

Neal shrugged. "It is not his life."

"Why is he so set against you marrying?"

Green eyes assessed her. "The curse," he answered, as if daring her to walk off again.

Thea looked around the room. There were other diners. Some were well-heeled travelers who enjoyed the meal with their families; some were bachelors here for their evening meals; others were out to enjoy the chef's excellent *poulet*.

She faced Neal. "I don't believe in curses. I don't believe in bad luck or fate or anything other than what we control ourselves."

"Not even such a thing as the hand of God?" he challenged.

"I've noticed the reasoning behind 'the hand of God' is often people making their own bad choices. It's all just life. We want to take credit for our successes but quickly point the finger at superstition or fate when something goes wrong."

He now looked around the room and appeared to notice how crowded the dining

84

room had become. "Let us discuss this in the coach." He rose from the table and she came up with him. He took her arm and guided her out of the room. They didn't say anything while gathering their coats and hats and waiting for Bonner to bring the horses around, but once inside the coach, Neal didn't waste time.

"I appreciate Harry taking the boys, because it gives us a moment for plain-speaking," he said.

"Are you afraid they will be frightened of the curse?" She let her doubt show.

"Thea, *you* don't have to believe, just accept what *I* know is true. There is more to this world than what we can touch and see."

Thea settled back into her corner of the coach. "I believe in more than what I can touch and see. But I don't believe in fairies and kelpies either. We set our own course, my lord. Mayhap your family believes there is a curse because of a lot of bad luck —"

"Yes, hundreds of years' worth," he answered, his tone stiff.

"Or perhaps it is just the vagaries of life." She leaned forward. "I don't mean to scoff, Neal, but what sort of curse is this that would expect you to marry someone you don't like? It is not logical."

He waved away her objection with a curt

motion. "It's not that I want to marry a woman I truly don't like," he said. "But she must be someone I will *never* love."

"Because?" Thea pressed.

"Because once I fall in love, I will die."

It took a moment for Thea to digest exactly what he'd said. And she still didn't understand. "Immediately, Neal? Or will you be allowed a few years of wedded bliss?"

"I thought you claimed not to scoff, Thea."

"I was being rude," she admitted. "Sorry," she tossed out, without any conviction.

"It does sound fantastic, and the truth is more so. My family has been cursed for generations by a Scottish witch. Apparently, my ancestor had handfasted with her daughter. Then he betrayed her by running away and marrying an Englishwoman from a wealthy family. The daughter was distraught and took her own life. So the witch cursed us."

The shadows of the evening were growing long. Thea sat in the swaying coach wondering if he actually believed this nonsense. "Well, one should be wary of a witch's spawn." His brows came together and she reminded him, "I explained I am a skeptic. So what makes you believe it is true?"

"The first Chattan," Neal said, "the one

who jilted the daughter died within months after his marriage. They said he was very pleased with his new wife. He'd fallen in love with her — and the curse took him."

"When was this?" Thea asked. "What year?"

"It was in 1632. The witch's name was Fenella. The daughter was called Rose."

"Fenella? That is a witchy-sounding name, but, Neal, people died of all sorts of things back then, and at relatively young ages."

"His wife was carrying a child, a son," Neal continued. "He grew into manhood, married, and died once he married, also for love. Death claimed him after a year of marriage."

"And was his wife carrying a son?"

"Yes."

"And that son grew into manhood and married and died?"

"Yes."

"And so on and so forth?" she asked.

"Yes," he reiterated, his tone growing testy.

"So your family has a history of dying at a young age," Thea concluded. "That does not mean there is a curse. However," she quickly added, "I have read stories about nonsense like curses that claim the strength of the curse is in how deeply one believes. Perhaps you should stop giving this curse any power over your own life."

He made an exasperated sound. "Do you not think that one in a long line of my ancestors has not considered the same? Of course we have. We've tried all manner of tricks to defeat this curse. My great-grandfather consulted witches and shamans and all sorts of mystics and religious men of every caste and creed to break the curse."

"What happened?"

"He fell in love with one of the witches and was dead in three months." Neal leaned toward her. "The only way we've found to hold the curse at bay is to marry out of obligation, something not unheard of for our class. But whatever we do, we can't allow ourselves any warm feelings toward our spouse."

"Which explains why your mother was such a cold woman," she said with interest.

"And explains even more why my father stayed away and did absolutely nothing to lighten the situation. He did not want to like her, and it worked. He is the first man in generations who has sired more than one child."

"Do your brother and sister carry this curse?"

"We don't know. I assume Margaret is free of it, but she has her doubts."

"And the colonel's obvious dislike of me — ?"

"Is because he hates my idea of marrying," Neal finished. "Harry, Margaret, and I are very close. They believe the three of us should not marry at all. They want the curse to end here, with us."

"That's what he meant," Thea said, half to herself. She frowned. "You obviously don't feel that way."

"I think the curse can be broken. After all, father lived many years and had three children." He dropped his gaze to his gloved hand resting on his leg. "And I want children, Thea. I want what you have. I hunger for it. I don't know if my overwhelming desire for a child is part of the curse or what, and it has created a rift between Harry and me."

Thea shook her head. "Did not your father pass away only a few years ago? He must have been of a ripe age."

"He was sixty-one."

"That is a respectable age to die, Lyon, and I mean no disrespect to his memory," she hastened to add lest he think her callous. "After all, your father had three children. Could it not mean that he has already defeated the demon of the curse?"

Neal lifted his head toward her, his expression bleak. "I wish it were so. Can you not imagine the hell of living a loveless life?" He paused and then asked, "Do you not wonder why I quit meeting you so abruptly that summer? Thea, our friendship is my fondest memory. I would not have ignored you the way I did if this curse was a hoax."

He leaned back into his corner of the coach. "My father learned of our meetings and came from London to talk to me. He explained the danger of the curse."

"But we were friends, Neal. Nothing more."

"Do you believe that, Thea? That it was nothing more?"

She frowned. "We were so young."

"Yes, we were." He turned his gaze away from her. Studied the passing scenery out the window.

"And you never questioned him?" she asked, uncertain if she was glad to finally know the reason for her friend's defection — or angry.

"I did not. Sometimes when one hears truth, one recognizes it. I knew immediately what he was saying was true."

Anger trumped gladness.

"You tossed aside our friendship over the silliness of this curse?" She moved to reach for the coach door. How dare he confess to

her. How dare he have treated her so callously years ago. The confines of the coach were suddenly too restrictive. She needed space. She needed to stomp around and have a fit.

Neal grabbed her hand and brought her around before she could open the door. "I had to, Thea. It was necessary."

"You didn't send a word to me that you weren't going to be there," she said. "You just didn't appear ever again. You could have said something. You could have sent a message or come to my father's house and explained —"

"I could not. Thea, don't you understand? My father feared our friendship."

"Why? Because he thought we were going to fall in love and you would die?" she said, throwing the words at him.

"*Yes*. And he was right to fear it. I could have fallen in love with you. Can't you understand that? I was in danger of doing so."

It took several moments for the import of his words to sink into her brain.

And when they did, she was shocked.

She pulled back and he let her go. "We were just friends," she whispered.

Neal retreated to his side of the coach. "Then why are you so angry?"

She remembered so much of that summer, but for her it had been friendship . . . or so she'd believed.

Thea looked over to him. He once again focused on the passing scenery, but she doubted if he saw anything.

What could she say after realizing how oblivious she had been? He'd been in danger of loving her. And all she'd been giddy about had been having a friend who'd understood her.

Neal broke the silence between them first. He spoke flat statements. "My mother died seven years ago. She was a lonely woman. There is a companionship in marriage which she never had. Father refused to grow close to her. But then at the age of sixty, he decided to enjoy himself. He first saw Cassandra Sweetling on stage. Cass Sweetling, the Coquette of Covent Garden."

"He fell in love with an opera dancer?"

"Madly. She was seventeen and happy to oblige him in every way."

"What did you and your siblings think of this?" Thea asked.

"What we thought didn't matter. She was everything to him. He showered her with attention. He was warm, kind and generous. He died within four months after their wedding."

"He was over *sixty*," Thea gently argued. "Men die of natural causes much younger."

"Does it matter?" Neal countered. "The curse lives." He curled one gloved hand into a fist. "I don't care about love, Thea. And I am not afraid of death. But I want a son, and I want to see him grow to manhood. My father had that blessing that none of the others in my line enjoyed. Find a wife for me, Thea. I dare not go looking on my own. The risk is too high."

"Because you are afraid you will fall in love inadvertently?"

"Exactly. She must be a decent woman who will understand that I have material goods and a fortune to offer her but little else — and she must never ask for more. Ever."

"You are condemning yourself to the selfish, the frivolous, the sort of woman who can't make any man happy."

"As long as she is an affectionate mother," he answered.

"That may be hard to find," she replied.

"I'm willing to pay handsomely. In fact, why don't I start with an advance payment, say two hundred pounds?"

If the heavens above had opened, Thea could not have been more elated. Here was the money for Jonathan's school, for better lodgings, for more than she would have let herself imagine. "It is too much," she demurred.

"I'm a wealthy man. Don't think on it."

"I shall find you a wife," she declared.

His gaze met hers. He smiled. "I thought you would."

"But I don't know if I believe in this curse yet," she said.

"You don't need to, Thea. You don't need to."

And on those words, the coach rolled to a halt, a sign they had reached the stables.

In the stables, Neal and Thea found Jonathan and Christopher working around Ajax, Harry's huge bay, brushing away at his legs and anywhere else they could reach. They had no desire to leave, but their mother insisted.

"I hope they haven't been too difficult for you," Thea said to Harry.

"Not a problem." He gave Christopher a tousle of his hair. But his eyes held no warmth for Thea, and he was absolutely cold to Neal, not that Neal minded. He could weather his brother's wrath.

Besides, Harry would find other diversions quickly enough and forget he was even angry.

Neal and Thea didn't linger. The boys begged to stay longer, but Thea wanted them home and in their beds. And of course, they fell asleep the moment the coach started to move.

"This has been a big adventure for them," Thea said. One arm was around Christopher, who had his head down in her lap. Her other hand rested on Jonathan's leg. He was leaning against her shoulder, his head back and his mouth open.

Thea saw the direction of Neal's gaze and smiled. "They are like puppies. They tear around full of energy and curiosity and then just drop where they are when tired."

"They are welcome to come see the horses in my stable," he offered.

"That's very kind of you. I shall hold such a trip over their heads to see that they do their studies." She made her threat with such delicious anticipation that Neal had to laugh, but then he sobered.

"What happened to their father?" he asked, knowing he might be treading on dangerous ground. One thing hadn't changed over the years about Thea — her pride.

"He passed away almost four years ago."

"I'm sorry."

She gave a small lift of her shoulders, a

dismissive gesture, and brushed a curl back from Christopher's forehead.

"I'm certain the boys miss him," Neal heard himself say. He wanted more information.

"Yes" was her noncommittal reply. There was a beat of silence between them, and then she added, "It is hard to raise boys without a father. I want Jonathan to attend Westminster School. I believe it will be good for him."

"It would. That is an excellent school."

She nodded and bent to place a light, loving kiss on her oldest's forehead. "Now that you have hired me, I shall be able to pay his fees, provided he is admitted. His interview for acceptance is next month."

"I'm certain he will do well."

"He is bright." There was a hesitation in her voice.

"What is it? What concerns you?"

She stroked Christopher's head again before saying, "I don't have any doubts about my sons. They are strong and bold, and I will never regret having them. But I sometimes wish I had been wiser. . . . for their sakes." She met Neal's gaze. "In my own impulsiveness, my own desire to live by my terms and in flouting all conventions of society, I may have harmed my babies, and

I never meant to do so."

"I'm certain this is not true," he started.

She smiled, the expression bittersweet. "You are obviously a person who has no regrets, my lord."

"Actually, I have too many."

Her gaze slid away from him. "But none that has harmed those who are innocent. I've robbed them of so much."

"Or will they be stronger because not everything has been handed to them? Westminster is not the only school in England, and just because your father disinherited you doesn't mean you aren't of good family. After all, you have been building a quiet little business based on those who have not forgotten your lineage or connections. Listening to Sir James rave about what you did for his nephew, I would say you are building a reputation on your successes more than your history."

"I want more than this for my sons."

He leaned forward. "We live in a new age, Thea. Any man with discipline and intelligence can make his own way in the world."

"I'm out in the world, my lord. Things have not changed as much as you imagine. One misstep and Sir James would forget he knew me."

Before Neal could answer, the coach

reached their destination. The vehicle leaned as Bonner jumped down.

Neal touched her arm. "None of us are perfect, Thea. You made choices, *honest* choices. Don't apologize for them," he managed to say before Bonner opened the coach door.

It was a small matter to carry two exhausted boys. Neal held one in each arm. In fact, their weight felt good.

Thea hovered anxiously. "Please let me carry Christopher, my lord."

"I'm fine," Neal said. "I may not be as dashing as my brother, but I'm good for some things. Catch the door for us."

She hurried to do as bid. The building's stairs creaked as Neal climbed them. Inside her apartment, he laid both Christopher and Jonathan on the pallet that served as their bed. "I wish my conscience was so clear I could sleep so deeply," he said.

"They always look like angels when they sleep," she murmured. She left the bedroom and he followed. She went over to stand by the still open door.

He hesitated.

"Thank you, my lord, for a wonderful evening. Neither the boys nor I will forget it for a long time."

"We'll see each other soon, won't we?" he

said, finding he didn't like the faint hint of dismissal in her tone. He had an urge to linger.

Her gaze slid away from his. "Of course. I shall contact you as soon as possible with a list of the young women I think are suitable for your particular needs. I'll also plan something special for you to be introduced to them. I do like house parties, because you will often meet the parents as well, and that is important."

"That sounds good." He moved to the door. He had no choice, not with her standing there waiting for him to go. Still, he had one more question.

"I know it isn't my place to ask," he said, "but I don't understand why you are here in this building, Thea. Why are you not under your family's roof?"

She crossed her arms, her whole body tightening. "My brother feels no need to offer support. He's within his rights." She was so defensive, so proud. Neal needed to be careful in how he phrased this next concern of his.

He moved to the door now but stopped before leaving. "I don't like this building or these rooms. I don't want you and your sons staying here."

"This is perfectly fine —"

"Thea, think of them," he interjected, quietly, firmly. "I have several properties throughout London. None of them fancy, but they are good homes and better than this. I want you to move into one of them."

Her chin lifted. "I'm sorry, my lord, but I cannot accept such charity from you."

"It's *not* charity. I'll lease the house to you."

"We are fine right here —"

"Damn it all, Thea, quit thinking with your pride and think of your sons. This is no neighborhood for them."

Her mouth closed. She pressed her lips together.

"My man will be over tomorrow to show you the houses I have," Neal said. "Be ready. I will not accept an argument. Understand?"

For a second, he expected her to countermand him, but then she said, "Thank you, my lord."

"And thank you for your common sense, Mrs. Martin," he answered.

She gave a small bow of her head and he left, feeling both victorious and more optimistic about life than he had for a long time. It felt right to have rekindled the friendship he had with Thea. He trusted her.

■ ■ ■ ■

Neal was not surprised to find Harry waiting for him at home.

"You are an ass," his brother informed him, waving the bottle of port he held in his hand. Neal did not like talking to him when he was drinking heavily. Fortunately, he did not act as if he'd been taking the laudanum — yet.

"Thank you, Harry, and on that comment, I'll turn in for the night." Neal started up the stairs.

His brother followed. "She's too nice a woman to do this to, Neal."

"To do what? Help me find a wife? She's a matchmaker. She has a talent for it." Neal frowned, shook his head, kept walking up the stairs. His brother could be a pest, even as an adult.

"You know what I mean," Harry accused, right on his heels.

At the top of the stairs, Neal continued to his room. "That I want a son? Of course."

With a skip, Harry placed himself in front of Neal, blocking his path. He cocked his head in disbelief. "Maybe you *don't* know, do you? Poor bugger."

"Stop talking in riddles. I'm tired —"

A door opened to his right, his sister's room. Margaret had been under the weather the last few days. She now gave them a sleepy, annoyed frown. "Won't the two of you please take the argument to another part of the house?"

"Neal is revisiting a fancy he once had for a woman and he doesn't even know it," Harry said.

"What?" Neal almost roared with laughter. "I assure you I have not taken a fancy to Thea Martin. Nothing against her, but I'm not looking for *her* sort for a wife."

"Sort?" Harry repeated. "What sort is that? Attractive female?"

"Harry, what are you going on about?" Margaret demanded.

"You don't remember Lady Thea?" Harry asked his sister. "Duruset's daughter. Her family had an estate close to ours. She and Neal were friends one summer until Father cut it off." He waggled his eyebrows on "friends."

"How do you know?" Neal demanded. "You weren't even in the country that summer."

"Father told me. Said he'd saved you. He told me the story when he explained the curse to me. He didn't want you near her, Neal."

"I'm not near her out of attraction," Neal responded.

"No, now she is a matchmaker. Don't be naive, brother. About her or yourself."

Now Margaret was awake. "Lady Thea is *the* Mrs. Martin?" she whispered. "I've heard of Mrs. Martin. She's put together several interesting matches when everyone had given up hope. Please, no, Neal. We discussed this. I thought we had a pact. Let it stop with us."

"Be like me, brother," Harry said, obviously happy now that he'd found an ally. "Women are fine. They are adorable, enjoyable, lovable — all the '-bles' — but don't marry. Don't carry this curse farther."

"Maybe I'm ending the curse," Neal muttered, pushing past his brother. "Father almost made it. If the curse doesn't claim one of us, then perhaps it will be broken. Certainly, I do not want to do as Father did and lose my head over some opera dancer."

"You poor, sorry soul," Harry said with his customary disdain. "You are already lost, and you didn't even realize it this evening. The two of you practically had an invisible cord around each other."

"That was the concern of old friendship," Neal shot back. "In your bullheadedness, you are fabricating what is not there."

Harry *ha*'d his disbelief and took a healthy swig of the port straight from the bottle.

"Neal, what is he saying?" Margaret asked, worry in her tone.

"Nothing that he knows anything about," Neal replied. "Nothing at all. Don't worry, Margaret, I will be careful."

"Men are never careful," she answered. "Your sex doesn't know the meaning of the word."

"I'm not like the others," Neal said. This was an old argument between them. "And contrary to what my tomcat brother thinks, I'm not the village idiot about women."

"We can't beat the curse, Neal," Margaret said sadly. "It isn't possible."

His response was to go to his room and shut the door.

For a moment, he leaned his back against the hard wood, every fiber of his being shouting that she was wrong. There was a way to beat this curse. There *had to* be.

He could hear Margaret and Harry talking in the hall. They were probably plotting against him and his desire to take a wife, but they were wrong if they thought he didn't know what he was doing.

Wrong.

And he would keep his distance from Thea . . . because his father had been right all those years ago. There was something about her that drew him, something he dared not explore.

But one thing he'd learned this evening is that they were two very different people now. He could keep the attraction at bay, he told himself.

He had to.

And yet he couldn't wait until he saw her again.

CHAPTER FIVE

"He moved *you* into one of *his* houses?" Mirabel, Lady Palmer, said and gave a small, glad squeal of happiness. "Oh, this is wonderful. This is more than I could have ever hoped for you! *Lord Lyon.* My dear, he is the prize, and you have *bagged* the prize —"

"No, wait, you don't understand," Thea protested. She'd been sharing with Mirabel the story of her adventure the other evening with Lord Lyon.

Mirabel brought her finger to her lips. "I understand perfectly and shall keep mum. Mum, mum, *mummmm. . . .*" She drew the last word out with delicious pleasure.

They sat in Mirabel's morning room, which overlooked the town house's garden. It was a small plot but done up with Mirabel's style so that it outshone almost any other garden Thea had ever seen — including her own father's. Mirabel did most of the work herself, claiming to adore puttering around in mud and dirt.

The boys were there now, galloping on imaginary horses around the flower beds, playing a game of Horse Guard. Thea had broken up one strong argument — both boys wanted to name their steeds Ajax — and now her sons had settled into happily entertaining themselves.

Mirabel was twenty years older than Thea, her hair still a pale, sunny blonde. She was tall, and thin, and very fashionable, and her deep blue eyes were always brimming with laughter.

When Thea had first returned to London, Mirabel had been the only one who had opened her door to her. Everyone else had been too intimidated by the duke of Duruset's power and his threats. But as Lord Palmer's wealthy widow, Mirabel hadn't cared.

And it had been Mirabel who had suggested Thea trade on her background as a duke's daughter and knowledge of society and marriage to offer a discreet but important service as a matchmaker.

Thea had rejected the idea at first, but as her situation had grown more desperate, she'd realized Mirabel was right. She did have a good understanding of the *ton.* She'd not made a good match herself, but she had discovered that she could be very clear-headed in what would be good for others.

Furthermore . . . she was the current duke of Duruset's scandalous sister, and that served her well. So far, the people who had contacted her for assistance had been the minor gentry — a squire with a beautiful daughter and no dowry, Sir James's challenging nephew, and a few aristocratic sons and daughters of middling fortune and unexceptional, sometimes even unfortunate, looks. Every one of them had mentioned her connection with the powerful duke of Duruset, and though most had known that she'd been disowned, that hadn't stopped them from engaging her services. They'd all been too desperate to find decent spouses for their family members.

Besides, amongst the *ton,* everyone liked connections, even Mirabel.

Indeed, Thea sometimes suspected her friend would give all she owned to be accepted into the first circles of society. She knew all of their names and ranking of importance. Thea had grown up with these people, and she could have told Mirabel there was nothing special about them. She far preferred Mirabel's happy spirit to their self-important ones.

"Lyon and I are *friends,*" she now stressed to Mirabel. "Nothing more. We knew each other in childhood." She wasn't about to share Neal's confession of having feelings for her at one time.

"Oh, I bet there could be something more," Mirabel speculated, wicked glee in her voice. She was arranging a vase of flowers on a table, and she placed a peony amongst the white roses she had purchased from a hothouse. Thea sat at the same table, drinking tea, ink, pen and a list in front of her.

"Men are not generous without a reason," Mirabel assured her. "Ever."

"Well, this one is. And it isn't generosity," Thea insisted. "I've paid for a lease." She actually hadn't. Mr. Givens, Lord Lyon's man of business, had offered her a period of grace until the beginning of the month before she needed to pay a rent, which Thea had thankfully accepted. In truth, she was quite pleased with the modest home with decent furnishings. It was a vast improvement over where she had been living, and she'd enjoyed the two days she'd taken to move her small family into it.

"Besides," Thea continued, "if your suspicions were true, I would have seen him by now. Over the last three days since he took us to the Clarendon, there hasn't been a word from him."

"No, just his servants to help you move," Mirabel countered with a sly smile.

Thea made a dismissive sound and poured a heaping spoonful of honey into her tea. "You are exaggerating. However, I have a larger problem. I must choose women for Lord Lyon to meet. I've been working on the problem in my mind. His wife can't be just anyone."

"What does he want in a wife?" Mirabel said, moving the vase of arranged flowers over to a side table.

"Someone he can't abide," Thea said.

Mirabel sat across the table from Thea. "What do you mean 'someone he can't abide'?"

Thea sat back in her chair. She studied her friend a moment, then pushed the list of names over an inch before asking, "Do you believe in superstitions?"

"Superstitions?" Mirabel shrugged. "I do not like spilling salt, and if I wager, I always chose the number seven because I usually win with it. Do you believe in superstitions?"

"No."

"That was very blunt of you."

"I feel that strongly. I believe we create

our own fate. There is no hand of God directing us or supernatural beings pushing us to do their whims. We have free will."

"Very well," Mirabel said, reaching for the teapot, "but what does that have to do with finding a wife for Lord Lyon? And why would you want to saddle him with a woman he can't abide?"

Thea hesitated a moment. She had to talk to someone about this, and she trusted Mirabel. "I asked about superstition because Lord Lyon believes he is cursed."

That grabbed Mirabel's attention. "In what way?"

Thea leaned across the table. "You mustn't breathe a word of this to a soul."

"I promise. What do you mean?" Mirabel vowed and demanded without taking a breath, her eyes wide with anticipation.

"He said there is a curse handed down upon his family from a Scottish witch. When a Chattan male falls in love, he dies — which is why Lord Lyon wants a woman he can't fall in love with." She felt silly just repeating it.

"Well," Mirabel said, sitting back and reaching for the honey pot, "no wonder you are denying there is anything between you. He'd fall in love with you."

Heat stole up Thea's neck. "He would not."

"Of course he would. Thea, I wish you would see yourself as others do. You are an attractive woman . . . and if Lord Lyon didn't fall in love with you, he would fall in love with your sons."

"There you are correct." Thea looked out the window to the garden, where the boys were now busy building something out of twigs and leaves and whatever rocks they could find. "He wants children."

"Most men do. Otherwise they would never settle down," Mirabel observed.

"You and Palmer didn't have children," Thea observed.

"I said 'most.' Palmer had me. I was child enough for both of us."

Thea smiled. "Everyone knows the two of you lived for each other in spite of being opposites —" Her voice broke off with sudden realization. "That's *it*."

"What is it?" Mirabel echoed.

"Lord Lyon needs a regal wife. One with excellent bloodlines."

"Like yourself?"

"Mirabel, if you insist on speaking this way, I shall leave," Thea said without any heat in her voice.

"No, don't go. I'll behave, at least as much

as I can," she promised. "What is your brilliant idea?"

Thea tapped the list she had been making. "I have very nice women here, but they are all boringly pleasant. He needs spirit. Vitality. Independence."

Mirabel stirred her tea pensively. "Yes, independence. One who will go her own way."

"And independence is also selfish," Thea pointed out. "And selfishness keeps a man at arm's length, no?"

"I'm selfish," Mirabel argued, twisting one of her blonde curls around a finger. "And men have always been after me."

"You are not. You are the most generous woman I know. And the very best friend. No, the person I'm thinking of is one who has been hard to marry off because she is almost masculine in her manner, and yet she is a woman —"

"Lady Lila Corkindale," Mirabel said, guessing accurately.

"Exactly. She's beautiful but a man-eater. However, I've heard rumblings that she needs to marry. She is the sort who wants only the best."

"And Lord Lyon is the best."

"Furthermore, she is so bold, I can't imagine any man loving her. She is not that sort of woman. However, no one could call her cold. I hear she has a temper."

"I think you have hit upon a match," Mirabel agreed.

"Perhaps," Thea hedged. Did she really want to see Neal saddled with Lila Corkindale for the rest of his life? A shudder went through her even as she reached for the silver inkstand, dipped the pen nib in ink and wrote Lady Lila's name to her list. "Now, who would be a tad tamer than Lila Corkindale?"

Before Mirabel could answer, her butler, Osgood, knocked on the morning room door. He held a silver salver in his hand. "My lady, Lady Montvale and Mrs. Harrison Pomfrey have come to call."

"Vanessa Montvale and Sarah Pomfrey? Here?" Mirabel repeated in disbelief with an incredulous look at Thea. The two women were the most fearsome hostesses of the *ton.* They only associated with "those who mattered."

"I do not know their given names, my lady," Osgood answered. "However, here are their cards."

Mirabel was up in a flash. She read the cards, turned them over as if expecting a hoax. She faced Thea in a panic. "What do they want here? They've always turned up their noses at me." Mirabel had married Lord Palmer, a man decades older than herself, to save her father from debtor's prison. Since Lord Palmer's first wife had been very popular and he'd married Mirabel with undue haste, she'd never been truly accepted in many social circles, even after all this time. "When my path crossed Lady Montvale's last year in Madame Regina's, she gave me the cut direct. Looked right past me as if I wasn't there. And neither accepted my invitation to the charity rout I held last year for St. Agnes's orphanage. I did my best to convince them to come. Oh, the toadying dance I had to jig for them — but they both turned me down flat."

"They probably didn't want to offer money to the cause." Having once been one of the upper echelon, Thea was more jaded about the likes of Lady Montvale and Mrs. Pomfrey. "They are shallow, Mirabel. They are only interested in their own gain."

"That may be true, but what gain can they have paying a call on me?"

"Go to the receiving room and find out," Thea suggested. "The boys and I will slip out the back gate." Thea knew both women were friends of her brother. She had no desire for a meeting.

"Stay right there," Mirabel ordered, rising

to her feet and putting her hand on Thea's arm to block her way. "You are *my* friend. No one chases my friends away." She made the pronouncement with her customary dramatic flair. "Osgood, I will receive my guests here in the morning room."

"Yes, my lady." The butler left.

"Mirabel, this is a terrible idea. I know how these women think. You don't want me here." Thea had already come to her feet and gathered up the list. She reached for her reticule.

"I absolutely do want you here," Mirabel declared, moving to stand in front of the door. "I don't have many friends, but the ones I have, I value."

Her words touched Thea's heart. "You are so special, Mirabel. There isn't anyone in London who can hold a candle to you."

Steps echoed on the black and white tiles in the hallway. Mirabel's eyes widened. "Oh. Dear."

Thea crossed to her side, turned her to face the door and took her arm. "Relax. They are calling on you. This meeting is under your roof. Everything will be fine."

"But why are they here?" Mirabel repeated before plastering a welcoming smile on her face.

Osgood appeared in the doorway. "Lady

Montvale and Mrs. Pomfrey," he announced in his most sonorous voice.

Mrs. Pomfrey sailed into the room ahead of her companion. She was a tall, thin woman with impeccable taste. Her graying brown hair was cut in the Juno style, and her dress of burgundy muslin trimmed in ivory lace had to have been a creation of Madame Avant's, the expensive couturier off Bond Street.

Lady Montvale wore a deep green day gown, trimmed in yellow velvet ribbon, also probably a creation of Madame Avant's. She was a petite woman with a giant attitude and a scowl made more fierce by her thick eyebrows.

Thea assumed she would receive a scowl. Instead, she was stunned when both women gave perfunctory greetings to Mirabel, then charged Thea like hounds after a rabbit.

"Mrs. Martin," Lady Montvale said, "what a pleasure to find you here!"

"We had not expected it," Mrs. Pomfrey chimed in, pulling off her lace gloves as if preparing to have a cozy chat. "We were hoping that dear Lady Palmer would have some knowledge of your whereabouts, but how fortuitous to find you ourselves."

"Yes, fortuitous?" Thea repeated. She cast a glance of confusion at Mirabel, who shrugged. She was as surprised as Thea.

"I was a friend of your dear mother," Mrs. Pomfrey said, "God rest her soul. I feel . . ." — she paused, stared hard at Thea and released a long breath before saying — "sad that I had lost touch with one of Violet's daughters."

Thea could not remember her mother ever mentioning Mrs. Pomfrey, but then her mother had died almost fifteen years ago, when her youngest brother had been born.

"I, too, was a friend," Lady Montvale echoed. "We were close."

"That is so good to know," Thea murmured with sincerity she didn't feel.

"Please, sit down," Mirabel said, as if suddenly remembering her manners. "We were having my dandelion tea. A fabulous elixir. So good for the nervous system. I'll have Osgood — ah, here is Mrs. Clemmons with the tray now."

Mrs. Clemmons was Osgood's wife and Mirabel's housekeeper. She was a narrow, efficient woman. She carried in a tray that also held plates of small sandwiches and slices of Mirabel's favorite cake. Osgood and Clemmons were Mirabel's only two permanent servants. She hired a cook and an upstairs maid for when she was in town. She liked her small household, although when she went to her country estate, there was a host of servants and retainers. "The locals depend upon me," she would often complain to Thea, who knew Mirabel was quite right. Her father's estates had employed whole villages.

The housekeeper set the refreshments upon the table and informed Thea, "I took the liberty of preparing a tray for Masters Jonathan and Christopher."

"Thank you," Thea murmured, still undecided if she should stay. Mrs. Pomfrey and Lady Montvale had already taken their places at the table. She noticed she'd left the list of names on the table, and she swiped it up, folded it and made it disappear into her reticule.

Mrs. Pomfrey tapped the place next to her. "Sit, Mrs. Martin. Sit."

"Yes, please sit, Mrs. Martin," Mirabel said, a smile on her face and a plea in her eyes.

Thea took pity on her friend and seated herself at the table.

Mirabel poured tea. There was a moment of silence while everyone took a sip and smiled at each other and Thea wondered why the mavens had called. Mirabel looked just as curious.

Mrs. Pomfrey did not waste time enlightening them. "I understand, Mrs. Martin, that Lord Lyon has been seeking your advice on a matter of much importance."

Thea wondered where she had heard that. Her question must have shown on her face, because Lady Montvale explained, "You were seen dining with him several days ago. Many of us know of your particular talents."

"Talents?" A bit uncertain, Thea looked at Mirabel, who realized first what the ladies were saying. She jumped into the fray.

"Yes, Lord Lyon is consulting with Mrs. Martin in his quest for a wife. He's decided the time has come."

Thea kicked Mirabel under the table. What was she doing?

"Ow," Mirabel had the ill grace to say. She frowned at Thea. "Why hide the fact? That these gentlewomen are here is proof enough that the word is all over town."

"Well, not all over," Mrs. Pomfrey said, "but we've heard. Then again, we've all been waiting. I was saying to Mr. Pomfrey just last week that if I had my pick of all the suitable gentlemen in London to marry my Susanne, it would be Lord Lyon."

Lady Montvale turned to Thea, giving her good friend her back. "My daughter Cynthia is of marriageable age and the leading debutante this year. They call her the

Nonpareil of the season."

"How nice for her," Thea said.

"I don't want to brag —," Lady Montvale said, leaning in to Thea as if to share confidences, until Mrs. Pomfrey placed her arm in front of her as to block any movement.

"You already have been bragging," Mrs. Pomfrey interjected bluntly. "A very unattractive habit it is."

Lady Montvale ignored her, continuing, "But Princess Caroline complimented Cynthia on her voice. Said she'd heard Italian singers who paled in comparison to my Cynthia. Of course, we've seen that she's had the finest teachers. Lord Montvale and I have poured everything we have into our daughter. Talent such as hers should not be ignored."

"Well," Mrs. Pomfrey said, setting down her teacup, "singing is fine, but *anyone* can sing. It's God given, after all. Open your mouth; let noise come out . . . However, *my* Susanne plays the pianoforte. That takes talent! The first time Prinny heard her play, he gave her a standing ovation. The Prince adores music. He said Susanne could play for him any day."

Lady Montvale's smile grew tighter. "Prinny acclaims my Cynthia's dancing. He says she is lighter than air."

"How interesting," Mrs. Pomfrey said, unimpressed. "He said the same of my Susanne. Furthermore, my husband's family has excellent bloodlines. He is descended from the Conqueror."

"As is *my* husband's," Lady Montvale returned, and Thea put her hands up to stop the conversation before it became too heated.

"Please, my ladies, I understand. You would like to have your daughters introduced to Lord Lyon."

"Of course we do," Lady Montvale said. "Why else would we track you down?"

Mirabel's gaze met Thea's over her teacup. Thea suspected Mirabel was hiding her laughter.

Mrs. Pomfrey began waxing on, "You must pardon our being forward, but Lord Lyon would be such an excellent husband for Susanne —"

"Or Cynthia," Lady Montvale added.

"— and he is so reclusive," Mrs. Pomfrey continued, "that we must resort to any means necessary to catch his attention. So tell me, how are you going to go about introducing him to my daughter? My husband and I would be very pleased to host a dinner —"

"No, it should be at Montvale House," her ladyship said. "In fact, I should have a house party in the country. That way there will be no distractions to keep him from acquainting himself with *my* daughter —"

"And *mine,*" Mrs. Pomfrey said.

"We shall see," her ladyship replied breezily. "I haven't decided the guest list."

"You would cut Susanne out? Your own goddaughter?" Mrs. Pomfrey demanded. She didn't wait for an answer but turned to Thea. "If it is a house party, then we should go to our family estate at Trumbull. It's closer to London and twice the size of Lady Montvale's."

"People would be lost in a house that size," Lady Montvale returned.

"It would be a pity if the person lost was *your* daughter" was Mrs. Pomfrey's tart reply.

"That was unkind —," Lady Montvale started, but her friend wagged a finger at her.

"This is competition for high stakes, my dear. Friendship can't be considered."

"Then perhaps it's best I not invite you when Lord Lyon comes to Wavertree for *my* house party."

"You needn't worry, my dear. He'll most certainly prefer being at *mine.*"

"And to think I *valued* your friendship," Lady Montvale spit out, coming to her feet.

"As if you would show off my daughter under your roof," Mrs. Pomfrey returned. "I know what you plan to do. It is what you do whenever a prettier girl is in the room with Cynthia. You scheme to shut her out."

"I do not," Lady Montvale said, very insulted, "because there isn't a prettier young woman in London than Cynthia."

"That's *not* what people say behind your back —," Mrs. Pomfrey returned. Thea had to cut in before they came to fisticuffs.

"Please," she said, reaching out to come between the two women. "This isn't necessary. Lord Lyon will make up his own mind."

"Then our daughters are to meet him?" Mrs. Pomfrey said.

"Yes," Thea said. "I believe he should." If the daughters were anything like the bickering, haughty mothers, then she couldn't imagine Lyon in danger of falling in love with either of them. Certainly they knew how to give their children every advantage, something that would be passed down to the grandchildren as well. Lyon wanted his children doted upon.

"However," Mirabel said, setting down her teacup and commanding everyone's attention, "the house party will be at *my* estate, Bennington Abbey. Neutral ground," she explained to the arguing friends.

For a second, Mrs. Pomfrey appeared ready to protest, but then seemed to change her mind. "That seems fair. Is it fair to you, Lady Montvale?"

Lady Montvale made a great show of considering the matter. Her eyes scanned the ceiling for a moment, as if she'd been searching for an answer there. Her chin came down. "Fair enough."

"Good," Thea said. "Lady Palmer, when will you be ready to receive guests?"

"We could plan for Thursday next?" Mirabel suggested.

Thea looked to the Lady Montvale and Mrs. Pomfrey for confirmation. They both nodded their assent.

"Very well," Thea said. "We shall make plans for that date."

Mirabel clapped her hands. "I adore house parties, and this one should prove to be very interesting."

"Are our daughters to be the only ones there?" Mrs. Pomfrey asked.

"Oh, now," Thea said, "that wouldn't be very sporting."

Neither lady appeared happy with her answer, but Mirabel was. She could now claim to have hostessed London's most hoity-toity society mavens, and Thea could tell by the grin on her friend's face she was going to enjoy every moment of it.

After Lady Montvale and Mrs. Pomfrey left, Thea penned a note to Lady Lila Corkindale inviting her to the house party. She did not mention the purpose behind the event. Mirabel had it sent off to be hand delivered by a servant, which was very kind of her.

But what was interesting was that even before Thea could gather up the boys to go home, the servant had returned with Lady Lila's acceptance and a hastily penned note.

I am looking forward to meeting Lord Lyon.

"See? Everyone knows," Mirabel said. "There are no secrets in London."

"Which is a bit unnerving," Thea said.

"Except when it works to your benefit," Mirabel answered. "Meanwhile, I shall be hosting a house party that will be the talk of the season because *everyone* will be anxious to discover who the Lyon chooses."

"As I will be," Thea threw out, becoming more preoccupied with collecting her things and her children than Mirabel's social success.

It was a good evening for a walk. The summer air was clear and velvety soft without heavy humidity.

Tonight, after spending a good portion of the day chasing each other around Mirabel's garden, the boys didn't need a trip to a park. They were happy to return to their new home.

"I like it here," Jonathan announced as Thea opened their front door.

"I like it here," Christopher echoed.

"I like it here, too," Thea agreed stoutly. "Now let us wash up and prepare for bed. I believe there is still water upstairs in the bowl. I'll read a story to you if you are speedy."

She didn't have to ask twice. Her sons liked a good tale, and they dashed up the stairs like rabbits, each trying to reach the top before the other, even if that meant some good-natured jostling.

Thea watched them, her heart filled with love. If she stopped too long and thought about their futures, she'd be frightened. They lived on an edge, where a misstep one way or the other could throw them into the streets . . . but so far she'd managed — and she would keep going. She loved her boys with a fierce passion.

She understood why Neal would want

children.

Thea turned to close the door and was startled to realize they had a visitor.

A statuesque, raven-haired woman stood on her step. Her features could have been chiseled from marble, they were so even and perfect. Her dress was of the very finest stuff, a muslin lawn so light and well woven it seemed to float around her, and it boasted an ivory lace inset around her neckline that was a work of art. She had to be of Thea's age, or perhaps a few years younger, given the smoothness of her skin.

She also seemed somewhat familiar to Thea.

"May I help you?" Thea said.

"Yes, you may help me, Mrs. Martin. I'm Lady Margaret Chattan. Lord Lyon is my brother. I'm here to ask you to leave him alone."

CHAPTER SIX

"I beg your pardon?" Thea said, a bit startled by the request.

Lady Margaret took advantage of the moment and walked right into the house. "You heard what I said," she replied. "If you value Lyon at all, if you care about him, *you* will walk away."

"Is this about his requesting my assistance to find a wife?" Thea demanded. "Or is it about the curse?" She was tired, and her tone cynical.

"You mock the curse. Many have," Lady Margaret said. "I don't blame you. I wondered at one time if it was real or not, and I was raised with it." She took a step toward Thea, her manner intense. "But it *is* true, and if you don't remove yourself from his life, you'll be signing his death warrant."

"His death warrant?" Thea repeated in disbelief, only to be interrupted by Jonathan's voice.

"Is everything all right, Mother?" He'd come halfway down the stairs. He'd removed his jacket and pulled his shirt from his breeches, but that was all he'd done in preparing for bed. Christopher waited on the top step. "Do you need me?" Jonathan asked the question with such seriousness that Thea could see the man he would one day become.

She crossed to the stairs. "It is fine, Jonathan. Now please help your brother prepare for bed. *Please,*" she reiterated when Jonathan didn't immediately do as bid. She didn't want her sons listening to the curse nonsense.

At last he reluctantly obeyed, but she knew he'd be hovering at the top of the stairs.

She turned to discover Lady Margaret standing right beside her. Her ladyship watched Jonathan as he disappeared from view. For his part, Jonathan kept his eye on her.

Thea moved away from the stairs, putting a hand on the door, a wordless suggestion for Lady Margaret to leave. "I don't know what you've been told," Thea said, "but your brother asked me to find a wife for him, not to *be* a wife to him."

Lady Margaret didn't move a muscle.

"You were very important to him at one time."

"Was I? I'm not so certain. If I'd been that important, then he wouldn't have just walked off from our friendship without one word."

"He *couldn't* be your friend," Lady Margaret said. "It's the curse. It has all of us." Her manner had changed. The fierce anger had vanished. In its place was something far more fragile. She turned and walked into the sitting room.

Biting back an impatient sound, Thea shut the front door and followed.

Lady Margaret stood by the upholstered settee, struggling to control herself. Her actions didn't make sense to Thea. She understood pride. She understood anger. Or being protective and territorial. Neal's sister acted as if afraid.

"Do you fear the curse as well?" Thea asked, gentling her voice.

Lady Margaret looked at her. "I do."

"But you have no need to fear it," Thea pointed out. "It has no impact on you. It touches only the males, does it not?"

"Are you certain?" Lady Margaret gave a sad smile. "You see, we Chattans don't know. Amazingly, I'm the first female in the line. And what of second sons? Does Harry need to fear? What of any sons I have? All of us in the family have a terrible history of dying. Even in Scotland, the name of Chattan is all but gone."

"Scotland?"

"Yes, we have Scottish roots. Many of our family hail from the countryside around Glenfinnan. Do you know of the battle of Cullendon? I've heard that the Chattan family lost more men on the Scottish side than any of the other clans fighting. In England, we are all but gone save my brothers and myself. Any other relatives are from my mother's side."

"Cullendon? Wasn't that a battle of insurrectionists? Lady Margaret, please, do not overdramatize this. Men die in battle. It's a hard truth. Furthermore, Colonel Chattan has been in battle and has not died."

"Mrs. Martin, don't assume that I am ninny-headed. Believe me, I wish what I was telling you was not true."

Thea didn't know what to say. She took a step away, looking out the front window to the street and the park. At last, she shrugged and confessed, "With all due respect, if you wish to believe in superstition and have searched for ways to twist the happenstances of life around to support your claim, well, I don't know what to do."

"I told you what I want you to do," Lady Margaret countered. "I want you to leave my brother alone. He mustn't have children. Harry and I agree none of us should. This curse must end with us."

Something deep inside Thea rebelled at the suggestion. "What you are suggesting isn't natural. We are meant to have children. And it is ludicrous to give a belief so much power. However, speak to your brother. He has hired me to help him find a wife, and that is what I will do. If he changes his mind, then I won't find him a wife."

Lady Margaret opened her mouth to protest, but Thea staved her off with a raised hand. "Yes, Lord Lyon and I were friends one summer years ago, but that was then. This is now. Life for both of us is different. In case you haven't noticed," she said, nodding to the furnishings in the room, "no one could mistake this for a ducal residence. You need not fear a match between your brother and myself."

"But what of the other women you would introduce to him?" Lady Margaret asked. "Please, don't let Lyon marry."

"I have no more control over what your brother decides to do than you do," Thea answered. "Indeed, he is determined to marry. The man wants children."

"It is more than that. Neal believes we can break this curse. He thought Father was going to break it, but then he fell in love with Cass Sweetling. You should have seen him. The father I knew — the resectable, sensible man — changed around her. He forgot about us, his obligations, his position in society. He gave in completely to the curse. Laughing, dancing, carrying on."

"Perhaps he did so because Cass Sweetling made him happy," Thea suggested.

"Perhaps she was part of the curse. Perhaps we can't help ourselves and must succumb to it."

"And perhaps it is all part of your imaginations," Thea said. "Like character traits. In my family, we all said we had uncontrollable tempers. What starts off as myth becomes a belief."

"You think I'm overreacting," Lady Margaret said, her shoulders straightening.

"I believe you are convinced this curse exists," Thea answered, not backing down. "I am not. Your father died of old age. He and your mother were an arranged marriage that was not happy. And after she died, he did what thousands of men have done before him and will continue to do until the end of time, he tumbled in love for a young, pretty girl. There is no curse involved."

The bristle left Lady Margaret's manner. "I know it isn't logical. If I wasn't part of this family, I probably would doubt the story of a curse as well. However, my coming here isn't to convince you. What I want is completely in *your* power. Stay away from my brother."

Back to that, were they?

Thea could almost have laughed at Lady Margaret's order if she hadn't been so tired. "You needn't fear I will entrap your brother. First, I am no Delilah. I'm a widow whose only thoughts, whose every energy, goes into the needs of my children. I don't have time for a man in my life, and even if I did, let me tell you now, after one taste of marriage, it is not for me. I prefer to raise my sons alone so that I do not have to answer to anyone."

"You were not happy in your marriage?" Lady Margaret tilted her head in curiosity. "We all heard about you. You were the tale of what a young woman should not do — defy our parents, marry beneath us, forget our obligations."

"I know," Thea said wearily. "I was the morality story, and I still am. I've had several mothers bring their daughters to me for lectures about the dangers of a *mésalliance.*"

"And what do you tell them?"

Thea reached over and lightly brushed the surface of an end table before saying, "I tell them that my life could have been easier if I had been more patient and wiser."

Lady Margaret waited for more, and when Thea didn't speak, she said, "That's it? That's all you have to say?"

"What more is there?" Thea answered. "Actually there is much more, but nothing those mothers would want me to tell their daughters."

"Such as?" Lady Margaret prompted.

Thea shook her head. "I'm not certain you need to hear my thoughts either."

"I believe I should." The note of regret in Lady Margaret's voice caught Thea's attention. Lady Margaret noticed Thea's change of expression and said, "Do you believe *you* are the only one who has loved outside her class?"

"Oh, no," Thea responded. "I know better than that. But I caution young women to not act on their feelings. I was the foolish one. I thought the way I felt for Boyd could overcome every obstacle. What I didn't realize is how large those obstacles were, and how he was not as strong a man as I'd thought he was."

"So you regret your marriage?"

Thea listened for any indication her sons were close at hand. She didn't hear a sound, but that didn't mean they weren't close enough to overhear anything she said. She'd been very careful not to criticize Boyd in front of them.

Of course, that didn't mean that a perceptive lad like Jonathan didn't reach his own conclusions. Since Boyd's death, they rarely talked about him.

"I don't regret my marriage because I have my sons. They are the light of my world. Of course, my marriage cost me the goodwill of my family —" She broke off, shrugged and confessed, "But we were never that close. I was the defiant one in the family, and I believe my father was secretly happy to have me off his hands. And in truth, I didn't want to marry well, breed an heir and stay out of the way. I truly felt that Boyd and I were the matching of two souls who were meant to be together."

"But you were not happy," Lady Margaret surmised.

Thea lowered her voice. "In the beginning I was. We started off with hopes and dreams . . . and gained disappointments. Boyd had many weaknesses. He really wanted to be married to a duke's daughter. My father's following through on his threats

137

to disinherit me was a disappointing blow to him. He believed Father had some respect for him. He didn't realize that while my father could be open and congenial with the help, that didn't mean he wanted one of them marrying his daughter. Then again, neither my husband nor I were perfect. That was a hard lesson for me to learn. A humbling one."

"And once the disappointments start, they don't stop, do they?" Lady Margaret agreed sadly.

"Why haven't you married?" Thea asked, suddenly having her own suspicions. "You are past the age. What are you? Four and twenty?"

"Five and twenty." Lady Margaret gave a rueful smile. "I was in love once. It was the most marvelous feeling in the world. Life made sense. I truly thought we could conquer everything."

"And then?"

"He did not love me with the same passion." Her gaze slid away from Thea's. She seemed to study the pattern of the wood floor a moment before saying stiffly, "I suppose it would be more polite to say we didn't suit."

There was more to the story. Thea would have wagered everything she owned on it.

Someone had broken Lady Margaret's trust. He'd slipped past her guard and taken all that she'd had.

It made Thea angry. How dare that man, or any man, Boyd included, take a woman's loving nature and betray it? Oh, there were women who deserved their comeuppance. Selfish creatures whose skins were tough and their wills unconquerable — but Lady Margaret was not of that ilk. She was like Thea, honest in her feelings, incapable of protecting them.

Thea crossed to the younger woman and put her arms around her. "You are *better* than him. He was not worthy of you."

Lady Margaret's face turned pinched and her nose red, as if she held back tears, but she stood still in Thea's arms.

"Go ahead and cry," Thea said. "Scream, yell curse even. The sin is his, not yours."

"I knew better," Lady Margaret said. "But even now, I wouldn't change everything that happened. He made me realize some hard truths. If we'd had children, they would have carried the curse. It's important to stop it now. To let it end here with my brothers and myself."

Thea took a step away. "Can you do that? Set yourself apart from the world? I have my sons to live for, but you would have nothing." And she wondered if Lady Margaret was making this sacrifice out of guilt more than conviction.

"I have my brothers."

"Is that enough?" Thea shook her head. "Pardon me, but my siblings and I are not close. I haven't spoken to them for seven years, so imagining they were all I had in my life is a bleak proposition. It's almost as if you are putting yourself aside in a nunnery."

Lady Margaret moved away from Thea. "Nothing of the sort. We are family. We are all we have."

"I remember your brother saying much the same thing during our summer of friendship." Thea risked pushing her point. "You were raised in a cold house, one that had no affection. Of course, it caused you and your brothers to be very close. You were all you had. I wonder," Thea continued, "what Neal would say to the request you are making of me. You choose to live a lonely life for this curse, but he doesn't. Can you not respect that it is his choice?"

"How much is he paying you, Mrs. Martin?" Lady Margaret countered, her manner growing frigid. "I wonder if the money is worth the personal cost, not just to my brother but to his children. They will either be doomed to live without a father or to that very same cold house to which you just referred. Can you live with yourself knowing what you do about our history?"

The curse again.

Thea was worn out speaking of it. "What I know of your history is that some of your ancestors died young or in battle. Your father died at a ripe age and after he'd found happiness with a woman neither you nor your brothers thought best for him. I don't question your belief in this curse. If you say it is true, it is. But what right have you to interfere with your brother's life? Who are you to make his decisions?"

"I am his *sister*. A blood relative —"

"But you are not *him*," Thea interrupted. "He is the *only* one who can make the choices for his life. I appreciate that you care enough for him to worry. But *he* isn't worried. You must respect that."

"And you do not know what you are playing with." The words she threw out sounded as if they'd been torn from Lady Margaret's heart. She looked wildly around the room as if searching for a way to convince Thea. Instead she turned on her heel and practically raced to the door. "Please, I beg of you, *rethink* what you are doing. I don't feel good about this. There are signs. She came

to me in a dream. She was laughing. It was a hideous sound. Evil."

"Who is she?" Thea demanded.

"The witch," Lady Margaret answered. She drew a great, shuddering breath. "She comes to me," she said, dropping her voice. "I haven't said anything to my brothers." She paused and then repeated, "She comes to me."

Thea's first thought was that a madness had gripped Neal's sister. Her passion, the abrupt change in demeanor, her anger at Thea's refusal to do as bid were disconcerting.

Then again, Thea's father had been this sort of person as well. Pleasant when he was pleased and absolutely vicious or whining when crossed.

But Lady Margaret didn't act vicious. She was frightened.

"Think on it," Lady Margaret ordered. "Your life is now involved in this as well." She opened the door and escaped out into the evening. Thea crossed to the door and watched the other woman dash across the street to where a hired chaise and her lady's maid waited for her.

"What was she talking about, Mother?" Jonathan said from the stairs.

Thea forced herself to smile, then shut

the door and turned to her sons. "She had some concerns about Lord Lyon," she said, giving them part of the truth.

"She was upset," Christopher declared.

"People often are when they don't have their way," Thea said, coming up the stairs. She gathered her boys close to her and gave them a hug. They smelled of the soap they'd used to scrub behind their ears, as well as dirt — a sign that the *only* place they'd washed was behind their ears. She welcomed the opportunity to take her mind off Lady Margaret's disturbing visit. "You boys haven't washed your faces and necks," she accused.

"We tried," Jonathan said.

Thea gave him a doubtful look. "I believe you did just a bit. I think you washed here, and here." She punctuated her words by giving each of them a wiggle of their earlobes. Both giggled and she felt her mood lighten.

"How did you know?" Jonathan asked.

"I'm your mother. I know everything about you because I love you so much." To her surprise, tears filled her eyes.

"What's the matter?" kindhearted Christopher asked, his expression worried. "Did someone hurt you?"

"No one hurt me," Thea answered. "I cry

because I'm happy." She pressed a kiss to his forehead. "I'm very happy."

"I'm happy too," Christopher assured her.

"Now let us go and give you both a proper washing," Thea said. She started up the stairs with Christopher. Jonathan held back. She turned to him. "Come along, Jonny."

Instead of obeying, he said with troubled eyes, "What did that woman mean about a witch?"

Thea wished he hadn't overheard. "Eavesdropping is very bad manners."

"Yes, ma'am," Jonathan answered dutifully. "Are you in trouble?"

"No," Thea quickly replied. She sat on the step in front of him so that they were eye level. "I'm in no trouble."

"Is Lord Lyon in trouble?"

This one was trickier. "I don't think so. He doesn't believe he is, and, as I said to his sister, what he thinks is all that is important. As to the witch, she was having bad dreams. You've had bad dreams before, so you know they can be scary. But we can't live our lives being afraid of dreams."

Jonathan digested this a moment and then nodded his head.

"Come upstairs," Thea instructed. "It's time for all of us to go to bed . . . after you have rewashed your faces."

Groans from Jonathan met her demand and she knew he had accepted her explanation.

She thought she was done with it.

But in the wee hours of the morning, Thea found herself staring at the ceiling, reliving the scene with Lady Margaret. The woman was not a fool. Her dreams frightened her.

Either there was madness in the Chattan family, or there really was something to fear.

"I don't see anything wrong with this list, do you, my lord?" Sir James asked Neal.

Neal sat in the chair in front of his desk. He'd brought the list to Sir James for his opinion. "No," he replied noncommittally.

"You aren't satisfied?" Sir James hazarded.

Neal wasn't certain what he felt. "They are all from exceptional families. I know many of their extended family members."

"Do they not meet your criteria?"

They met them too well. "Yes."

"Then what is not pleasing you?" Sir James sat back in his chair. "I have known you for many years, Lyon. I know when you are not happy. Do you wish me to convey your thoughts to Mrs. Martin? I will be happy to do so."

Neal stood, suddenly feeling confined in

the chair. "I told her the list was fine. It's a start."

"These are high-strung fillies," Sir James said, indicating the list.

"They are more or less what I asked for," Neal said, walking over to the window. He looked outside at the overcast day. He'd not been able to sleep the night before. Margaret had spent an hour expressing her strong objections to the endeavor.

She'd told him about her dreams.

Neal wasn't the superstitious sort. Neither was Margaret. Perhaps that was why he was so unsettled . . . that and Harry had gotten into the laudanum again last night. Neal worried about his brother. There were times he sensed Harry might be trying to take his own life. Harry put up a carefree front, but he seemed more affected by the curse, by the uncertainty of it, than Neal was. Perhaps he drank to fill the emptiness in his life? Neal himself had overindulged many a time as a way of coping with the hopelessness that was the legacy of the curse.

Or could Harry's weaknesses be connected to the war?

His brother was well respected, yet Neal had noticed the military sorts kept their distance from Harry. He had few, if any, duties with the Horse Guard. His life, once

146

full of purpose, had become aimless.

And, yes, Harry kept a bevy of women around him, but he had few male friends.

Sir James spoke, drawing Neal's attention back to their interview. "Duruset has let me know through different channels that he is not pleased to hear you are working with his sister. I know for a fact, he does not want her in London. You've already made enough of an enemy going against him in the Lords last year. Be careful you don't cross him again by wooing his sister."

"There is nothing other than an old friendship between Mrs. Martin and myself," Neal murmured dismissively. There couldn't be — about that Margaret was right. In spite of the years that had passed, the bonds between him and Thea were strong.

"Aye, I'm certain that is true," Sir James said, his voice belying his words. He tapped the list on his desk with one finger. "However, you've crossed Duruset more than once. Be wise. Keep your sights on the women on this list."

"You needn't worry," Neal told him.

"And that is why I worry," was the lawyer's reply.

CHAPTER SEVEN

Bennington Abbey had once truly been an old abbey destroyed by Henry VIII and converted a century later by one of Mirabel's late husband's ancestors into a home. Over the centuries, the Palmer family had built more wings until it had become a huge, rambling place with a great deal of charm and the layout of a rabbit warren.

Lady Palmer was the first to greet Neal when he arrived.

"My lord, we have been waiting for you. I am Mirabel, Lady Palmer, your hostess."

"Thank you, my lady. It is a pleasure to be here, and I appreciate your willingness to host this unusual gathering."

"I'm enjoying myself," she confided, taking him by the arm and steering him inside the house. She led him into a sitting room tastefully decorated in reds and golds. It would have been ostentatious except for the size of the room and the comfort of the furnishings. "I can't tell you how much fun it is to have one's name on everyone's lips. I've never had so many friends 'find' me again after ignoring me for years."

"Am I that exciting?"

"A man with your purse? Absolutely," she told him.

"I was hoping I'd be here before the others," he said. "I thought it might be best if I were to welcome them — depending on your plans, Lady Palmer."

"I have no plans except to enjoy my guests and this week," she said with an airy wave of her hand. "And please, call me Mirabel. Lady Palmer is my dull name and reserved for people I don't like."

"I'm pleased to be one of those you do like," he said.

"You should be. It's a short list. Ah, here is Thea now."

Thea walked in from a windowed side door, her arms full of daisies, larkspur, and other greenery and posies from the garden. Her cheeks were flushed from being outside, and several curls had escaped from her usually severe hairstyle. Her straw hat had fallen back and was held around her neck by green ribbons that matched the color of her dress. She appeared younger, more relaxed, carefree.

Her step slowed as she realized Neal had arrived. She smiled at him, and for a second, he felt a bit dazzled by her. In this moment, she was the very epitome, in his mind, of English womanhood.

"Welcome, my lord," she said in her low, melodic voice. "I hope your journey was uneventful."

Neal knew he should make a comment, but he was having trouble finding his tongue.

"It was uneventful," he managed to respond and immediately chastised himself for being so prosaic, which led to a beat of awkward silence. "How was your journey?"

If Thea experienced any of the same tongue-tiedness, she hid it well. She walked over to an upholstered divan and laid the flowers on a side table. "It was very good, my lord, thank you for asking." She began untying the ribbons of the bonnet. "Lady Palmer and I traveled together. Our journey was uneventful as well."

"That's good," Neal murmured, wondering why he couldn't kick his brain into operation and knowing it was from wanting Thea.

He had to let it go. She wasn't for him. She could steal his heart.

For the first time, he realized his father

might not have had any control once he'd met Cass Sweetling. Neal knew he must be stronger.

He smiled at Lady Palmer. Her arched look let him know she didn't miss a thing. If Thea hadn't noticed his halting behavior, she had.

Neal realized he'd best retreat now. There was something potent about being in the country with Thea that stirred all sorts of emotions and desires within him.

For her part, Thea seemed oblivious to him. She was rearranging the flowers, and he sensed he'd already been dismissed.

His intent to put distance between them went by the wayside as he asked, "Where are your sons?"

Thea looked up from the flowers. "They stayed in town at Lady Palmer's house with her housekeeper, Mrs. Clemmons. I thought it best they not be here. They will be sorry to have missed you. Oh, yes, and thank you for the books you sent over. They are a special treat and a welcome addition to our small library. I should have said something earlier."

"You wrote a note," Neal said.

She smiled.

He smiled.

"I should put these in water," Thea said.

"Mirabel, do you want me to use the vase in the butler's pantry?"

"That would be excellent, dear. Thank you."

"If you will excuse me, my lord?" Thea said.

Neal nodded and smiled again. Thea left the room, and all he could do was watch her leave in silence. He didn't know what had come over him. It had to be seeing her in the country, seeing her here, in the atmosphere where there had once been a close bond.

Mirabel said, a touch of sympathy in her tone, "Let me show you to your room, my lord."

He followed her out into the black-and-white-tiled hall and up the stairs. Mirabel maintained a light, running commentary. "This portrait was of my late husband in his youth," she said, pointing out a painting at the top of the stairs depicting a handsome young man dressed as St. George slaying a dragon. "I always found it a bit much, but Palmer liked it."

"It's very nice," Neal commented, his thoughts still on how diffident Thea had been to him. It was only then he realized he had been looking forward to seeing her. He'd actually wanted to deliver the books to her sons himself, but he had backed off.

She kept talking. He chided himself for his cowardice over the delivery of the books —

"You poor man," Mirabel said. She'd stopped at the intersection of two narrow hallways.

"Yes, nice," Neal muttered, until her words registered with him and he realized she was no longer giving him a tour. "What do you mean?" he demanded.

She looked around as if fearing they could be overheard. "Do you really believe you can continue playing this game of you not noticing her and she not noticing you?"

He didn't pretend to misunderstand her. "We are friends from long ago. Nothing more."

"And yet the air fairly crackles between you with attraction."

"It does not," he replied, uncomfortable with her accusation.

"Oh, not in the way young people would throw caution to the wind and all but attack each other," Mirabel said. "But you two are very aware of each other."

He hadn't noticed any interest from Thea at all.

"Tell me, Lyon, have you thought of adding our friend Thea's name to your list of possible wives?"

It was a dangerous question. "Is she interested?" he heard himself ask.

Mirabel gave the complacent smile of a cat with her sights on a mouse. "She didn't have to come in the house when she did. She knew you'd arrived."

"She was being polite." Thea hadn't given him the impression that she'd been overjoyed to greet him.

"Thea was working very hard not to notice you."

"She was successful."

"You know so little about women," Mirabel whispered. She started down the hall and stopped in front of the first door on the right. "This is your room."

She opened the door and led him into a room decorated in green and cream accessories. "Ah, your valet has already been here. His name is Whiteson." Neal hadn't traveled with his own man, preferring to use one of the house servants instead. He liked traveling light. The valet was not in the room but had already laid out fresh attire for Neal.

"Whiteson has probably gone off to fetch fresh water," Mirabel continued. "He'll return momentarily. There will be several male guests, so you will have to share his attention."

"When I'm in the country, I prefer a more simple life," Neal answered. "It shall not be a problem."

Mirabel tilted her head. "I like you, Lyon. I wasn't certain I would, but you are not as pretentious as I had feared."

"And what gave you the impression I would be pretentious?"

"It wasn't Thea, if that is what you are thinking. But usually men like yourself who are statesmen and men of commerce have a vaunted opinion of themselves. You seem a genuinely nice man."

"I was hoping for a more dashing opinion, my lady."

She laughed. "Oh, you are dashing. Handsome men always are, but they are sometimes arrogant."

"I can be."

"Yes, that is what Thea said."

"She believes me arrogant?" he said, needled by the thought. Then he decided, "Well, yes, I am. I do like to have things done my way."

"And you shall have plenty of opportunity to exercise your wishes this week, Lyon." She started to leave the room but paused by the door. "I wish you a merry chase in your hunt for a wife this week."

"Thank you," he said, uncertain if he meant the words.

And yet Neal found himself wondering if what Mirabel said about Thea's interest in him could be true. The comment about his arrogance aside, Thea had not impressed him as being as aware of him as he was of her.

But if she was, what was he going to do about it?

"He's very interested in you."

Surprised, Thea turned to see Mirabel leaning on the doorjamb of the butler's pantry. Thea had brought her flowers in here to arrange them in the yellow and gray pottery vase . . . but Neal had not been far from her thoughts.

She'd believed she'd seen him every way possible, but he'd caught her by surprise this afternoon. He'd appeared more relaxed than he had in a long time. His hair had been mussed; dust had covered his boots. His whole person had given off an air of vitality and masculinity. A dangerous combination.

Thea prayed her face hadn't betrayed the direction of her thoughts. She'd worked very hard to keep her manner welcoming but distant.

And now here was Mirabel, playing Cupid.

Thea focused on the rose in her hand. Thank heavens for thorns, which made one have to think when handling roses. "Nonsense, Mirabel. He's here to meet other women, not me. The time for us was long ago. Too much has happened to each of us since then."

"But he likes *you*," Mirabel said, inviting herself into the tight space. She leaned her hips against the cupboard where Thea was arranging. "Frankly, I was taken aback by how handsome he is."

"You'd never met him?"

"I'd seen him from a distance, but he doesn't go out in society often. He is a fine, fine man."

Indeed, he was.

"He has good looks," Thea agreed without enthusiasm as she poked the rose's stem into her arrangement.

"*'He has good looks,'*" Mirabel repeated, mimicking Thea's tone. "He's an Adonis. Probably one of the *most* handsome men I've ever met, and *you* wish to toss him away on scatterbrained, selfish chits who won't appreciate him?"

"He *wants* one of those scatterbrained, selfish chits," Thea said, picking up the vase

157

and escaping out the pantry door.

Mirabel followed, as Thea had expected her to do. Mirabel could be single-minded in the pursuit of an idea. "I don't believe that is true," she informed Thea. "He was asking me all sorts of questions about you. He's very interested, and, I believe, with something more than affection for an old friendship."

Thea pulled up short. Mirabel almost ran into her. Thea faced her. "Now you are doing it a bit too brown," she informed her friend. "Lord Lyon is not the curious sort. He wasn't asking questions." She set the bouquet on a sideboard in the dining room.

"He was in his mind," Mirabel insisted. "I thought he would eat you up with his eyes when you came in holding those flowers. You did look quite charming, and I could feel the interest *radiating* from him."

"I didn't notice anything out of the ordinary," Thea said, moving a daisy away from a rose in the bouquet, although heat rushed to her cheeks. "If anything, he seemed a bit tired."

Mirabel hummed her disbelief. "And he likes your sons."

"He likes *children*. That is why he wishes to marry," Thea said, making a beeline for the dining room door and away from Mirabel's tempting suspicions. She couldn't think this way. She mustn't. If Neal had been interested in her, then why had he kept his distance this past week when she'd been making arrangements for the house party?

"He gave your sons presents," Mirabel pointed out, following close behind her. To Thea's dismissive wave of her hand, Mirabel said, "A book is a very personal gift."

Thea stopped in her tracks. "Books are not personal. Anyone can receive a book."

Her words lacked conviction, and Mirabel pounced upon them. "Have you seen the price of books? *Very* personal. Of course, I would prefer rubies, but books would be the perfect gift for you."

Starting down the hall again, Thea said, "These books had stories that would appeal to young boys."

"Exactly my point. If a man wants to impress you, he should buy books for your sons, and Lyon knows it. You both might not admit it yet, but he wants to woo you —"

Her voice broke off as they rounded the corner into the main foyer and realized they had guests.

Lady Montvale, her husband, her daughter, and a good sampling of her servants had just arrived.

Any retort Thea had been about to launch at Mirabel caught in her throat at the realization they might have been overheard.

Her ladyship, still in her traveling coat and wearing a velvet cap embellished with rose ostrich plumes, began pulling off her gloves. "Who wants to woo you, Mrs. Martin?" she said.

Thea's first impulse was to blurt out that Mirabel had been speaking nonsense.

Fortunately, Mirabel had a cooler head. "Yvette," Mirabel said. "Lady Yvette. She is another option, but Mrs. Martin wouldn't invite her for the house party. She said she wanted to give your lovely daughter, Lady Susanne —"

"Cynthia," Thea broke in, realizing Mirabel's mistake. Mrs. Pomfrey's daughter was Susanne. "Lady Cynthia."

"Oh, yes, Lady Cynthia," Mirabel said, soldiering on. She smiled at the young girl who was truly pretty, save for the petulant set of her mouth and an air of laziness. "Lady Cynthia, what a pleasure to meet you. I am Mirabel, Lady Palmer."

Lady Cynthia looked Mirabel up and down as if she'd been beneath her.

Oh, yes, here was a woman Neal could not love.

Thea stepped forward, and introductions

were made. Mirabel entrusted her servants to show the Montvale servants to their quarters.

"Who is this Lady Yvette?" Lady Montvale asked Thea. "Is she a threat? And who else did you invite?"

Thea dodged her curiosity about Lady Yvette with some mumbled comment. She knew Mirabel had just made the name up. As to her other question, it was answered as Lady Lila and her father Lord Corkindale arrived. Within the space of forty minutes, the foyer was a scene of comings and goings. Mrs. Pomfrey and her family were the next to arrive. She barely spoke to her good friend Lady Montvale, a sign the competition between them to bring their daughters to the attention of Lord Lyon was going to be cutthroat.

Two other young women arrived with their parents. Lady Jane Birdinger and Lady Sophie Carpsley were from well-respected families and very much of the same spoiled, indolent ilk as the other women.

In fact, Lady Lila stood out because she came across as bolder and more athletic than her peers.

"Lady Palmer, I must have a rose petal bath prepared every morning," Lady Montvale informed her. "The petals are necessary for my skin."

"I must have chocolate in the morning," Mrs. Pomfrey announced. "And my husband only eats beef. No fish, no fowl, no pork."

"What time are we hunting on the morrow?" Lady Lila wanted to know.

"I must have a horse for the morrow," Lady Sophie informed them. "Mine has taken lame. Will someone bring horses up here for me to give a look over?"

So many questions. So many demands. Thea felt as if she was juggling a hundred expectations thrown at her all at once.

All the chatter came to a sudden halt.

Thea felt a sudden awareness tickle the back of her neck. She turned from listening to Mr. Pomfrey's complaints about the poor quality of the roads to see Neal standing on the stairs. He'd changed into dinner dress and cut quite a handsome figure in his elegant black.

Smiles replaced frowns.

Even on Thea's face. And she found herself wishing Mirabel's theory was correct, that there could be something more between them. Here was a man she could respect. Calm, confident . . . kind.

For the briefest moment, their gazes met. She looked away first. She had to, partly out of an awareness of how many eyes were watching his every move and partly because she felt vulnerable around him. Neal could slip past her guard and find his way to her heart.

But he *wanted* to marry someone else. He was *choosing* to do so.

And what if Neal was attracted to her with the same intensity she was feeling toward him? This horde would tar and feather her. They'd come here expecting Lyon to choose one of their daughters as his lady and, by George, Thea had better deliver.

Having him throw their girls over for the matchmaker would be very bad form.

Neal came down the stairs to welcome everyone and be introduced to those he didn't know. The young women Thea had thought rather difficult and selfish suddenly became the most pliant of souls. Even Lady Lila toned down her strong personality.

Of course, Neal said all the right things. What had seemed impossible moments ago, the meeting of all the demands and expectations of the recently arrived guests, disappeared effortlessly in his skilled hands.

Mirabel personally escorted the people she dearly wanted to impress, the Montvales and the Pomfreys, to their rooms, and Thea guided the others.

Lady Lila was the last one Thea directed to her room. Her room was next door to her father's. She looked inside at the blue and green furnishings and gave a dismissive sniff. Thea attempted to not be offended for Mirabel.

"Where is Lord Lyon's room?" Lady Lila asked.

"In the other hall," Thea said. "Will you be needing anything else?"

"*Where* in the other hall?" Lady Lila persisted.

Thea knew where his room was, but she didn't think it was proper for a young unmarried woman to be making such inquiries.

"Around the corner," she said, putting a firm note on her words. "We'll see you in an hour for dinner —"

"Mrs. Martin, when I ask a question, I'm accustomed to people answering it." Lady Lila dropped her voice, leaning close to Thea. "I intend to marry Lord Lyon. I've been waiting for a man like him. You would be wise to help me."

Thea leaned forward, dropping her voice to say sweetly, "I am helping you, but you would be wise not to threaten me."

She assumed the girl would back away. Instead, Lady Lila smiled, an expression that did not reach her eyes. "I do whatever I desire." She then shut the door in Thea's face.

Thea stared at the wood paneled door and decided right then and there that Neal would not choose Lady Lila.

Who was she to think everyone would jump to her bidding? Well, she'd just met her match.

It took Thea barely ten minutes to dress for dinner. She wore a simple lavender muslin with a demure lace neckline. She liked lavender. It reminded people that she was a widow and gave her an air of respectability that her relatively young age lacked.

When she went downstairs, she found Neal in the sitting room, lounging by the window reading a paper and enjoying a drink. When she entered the room he set the paper aside and rose to his feet.

If he was as interested in her as Mirabel claimed, she didn't see it. He seemed friendly and cordial, his usual self.

"Well," she said coming up to him, "what do you think of your prospects?" She took a seat in the chair next to his.

"They are all lovely young women," he replied, returning to his chair.

"Some not so young. Lady Lila is five and twenty." Thea had to point that out.

He nodded, took a sip of his drink. "The age of my sister," he said. Thea wanted to groan, because he said it as if Lady Lila's age was a credit to her chances.

"Sir James will be arriving on the morrow," he told her.

"Sir James? I didn't know he was coming," Thea said.

"I'm surprised Lady Palmer didn't tell you. He was supposed to ride with me today, but unfortunately business kept him in London."

"It will be a pleasure to see him again," Thea said.

There was a beat of long, uncomfortable silence. She realized an easiness with him was gone, banished by a budding sense of regret.

Perhaps she had been wrong in her thinking. She'd said she'd felt nothing but friendship that summer years ago, and yet his defecting without a reason had stayed with her. He'd hurt her more than if what she'd felt had been friendship alone.

The awkward silence was broken by the arrival of Mr. and Mrs. Pomfrey and their daughter, Miss Susanne. Thea had no need to talk as they monopolized Neal.

Very shortly, Lord and Lady Montvale and their daughter joined the group. Lady

Montvale was not happy to see the Pomfreys there but didn't hesitate to elbow the
Pomfreys aside.

Mirabel came up beside Thea. "Did you
notice the elbow? Interesting how quickly
friendship dies."

"Imagine how it will be if he chooses one
over the other," Thea said.

"All I know is that when I return to
London, I shall dine for a week on stories
of hosting Vanessa Montvale and Sarah
Pomfrey. My tale will be all the more delicious because of this little feud." She smiled
at Thea and then raised her voice. "Come,
everyone, dinner is served. Lord Lyon, will
you escort me to the table?"

"I would be honored, my lady."

Mirabel's chef had prepared an excellent
repast of pheasant, venison, and numerous
side dishes. There was one hastily cooked
beef dish. Wine and cider flowed freely.

After dinner they all returned to the sitting room, where each young woman had
the opportunity to show off her talents.
Lady Cynthia did indeed have a lovely
voice. Miss Susanne entertained them with
a complicated piece for the pianoforte, Neal
sitting beside her on the bench turning
pages.

But the others sang and played instruments as well. Lady Lila had even brought her own violin and walked over to Neal as she played it. She stood in front of him, the music a mournful piece, which she turned into a lively jig.

If this had been another gathering, there might have been dancing, but since each young woman was in competition with the other, the atmosphere was rather tense.

Thea kept an eye on Neal. She told herself it was important she gauge his reaction to each candidate.

She also had a personal interest. She found herself hoping he chose exactly the wrong woman. Then she could label him as shallow, which would put a dent in the noble armor he wore in her mind.

For his part, Neal complimented everyone and managed to spend a few minutes of private conversation with each girl. However, he appeared happy when Mirabel announced that, with the hunt tomorrow, it would be an early day and perhaps they should all retire.

There was a comical moment when not one girl wished to leave before Neal and the others did. They all hovered around him. He was too polite to just leave, so it was up to Thea to extract him from the group. Everyone followed them up the stairs for the night.

Before he turned the corner to go to his room, Neal managed to place himself beside Thea. "This is harder than I thought it would be."

"That was my wish," she said brittlely. Yes, the girls were lovely and had impeccable bloodlines and connections — but their characters were sorely lacking. He must see that? Mustn't he?

He glanced around. The two of them were at the crossway of the two halls. The fathers had gone immediately into their rooms. Their wives and daughters lingered by their doorways. A few of the girls even gave Neal little waves good night.

"And you have chosen well," he whispered, conscious that they were being watched. "I don't think I could fall in love with any of them. Thank you, Thea."

He didn't say those words happily, and Thea felt a great weight settle on her shoulders. He was pleased. "You are welcome, my lord."

He nodded and went to his room. Thea watched him open his door and disappear inside, a hollow feeling inside her. Always before, she'd felt good about putting two people together, but not this time. Neal was making a mistake wanting to marry one of these women. She knew it.

And she also felt strangely deflated.

So she took her heart and closed it off.

Thea went on the hunt with those who wished to go. It was exhilarating to be on a horse again. She'd practically grown up on them but, of course, had not been riding in years.

Lady Lila truly was an outstanding horse-woman and kept up with Neal the whole way. But it was Lady Sophie with whom he spent a good deal of time. The two of them rode back to Bennington Abbey together and seemed to be enjoying their conversation.

Thea didn't know who was the more jealous — Lady Lila or herself.

Neal's face was relaxed, and Lady Sophie laughed with giddy pleasure. Thea knew he'd wanted a woman he could not love, but did that mean he'd wanted a ninny-headed one?

Nor did he and Lady Sophie part company when they returned to the house, even upon discovering Sir James had arrived. Of course, the lawyer could easily take care of himself. He knew most of the other guests and fit right into their company.

"Lyon is showing a decided preference,"

Mirabel whispered in passing after dinner. "I would not have thought it. I spoke to Lady Sophie this morning over breakfast. She is not bright."

"She's kind," Thea said.

"Damp praise," Mirabel murmured.

Thea looked at her. "Do you mean 'faint' praise?"

A secret smile came to her friend's lips. "That, too." She leaned close. "Of course it shouldn't matter to you."

Did Mirabel see she was jealous? "It doesn't."

"Of course not," Mirabel agreed smoothly. "That's why you scowl every time you look in their direction."

Thea's immediate reaction was to school her features into a smile. She even lifted a hand to her forehead as if in thought, when in truth she wanted to be certain she didn't have a frown line.

Mirabel chuckled. "Don't worry. You are not the only one. We have a host of disgruntled women here." She floated away to see to her guests.

Thea crossed her arms. Mirabel was wrong. She didn't give a care whom Neal chose.

Still, it wasn't easy to watch Neal and Lady Sophie with their heads together over a game of cards after dinner. A part of Thea wanted to chide him over not paying more attention to the others. It seemed her responsibility. Then again, if she did approach him, would he think her jealous?

She stayed on her side of the room.

Lord Corkindale came up to her side. "My daughter is disappointed. She had thought there was a connection between herself and his lordship this afternoon."

"There was," Thea agreed. "She is a remarkable rider. Unfortunately, I have no control over whom Lord Lyon favors." If she had, she would have pulled him away from Lady Sophie by now.

"She came here to win him," Lord Corkindale answered. "Make no mistake of it. She will claim him."

"I wish her happy hunting," Thea replied, a comment that did not satisfy his lordship. He went off to repeat to his daughter what she'd said.

And Lord Corkindale wasn't the only concerned parent. After Thea had dismissed her maid but before she could climb into her bed, she was visited by Lady Montvale *and* Mrs. Pomfrey. They knocked on her door together. Apparently, the threat of Lady Sophie had restored their friendship. Their concerns were very much along the lines of Lord Corkindale's, and again, Thea had little help she could offer. "Lord Lyon is free to make his own decision."

"But you must have *some* influence," Mrs. Pomfrey insisted.

"When have you ever heard of the Lyon being easily influenced?" Thea said.

Annoyed with her response, the women left the room, their furious whispers of grievances following them out the door.

Thea sat on her bed with a sigh. Why had she ever agreed to this house party plan? It had been successful in the past, but this time, the stakes were too high. She'd never do it again. It was too stressful for all involved — except Neal.

She lay down with a yawn, but sleep eluded her. Sooner or later Neal should or *would* ask her opinion. And what would she say to him?

That the idea of marrying the silliest girl of the lot was ridiculous? Absolutely!

He wanted children. What kind of sons would such an airy girl give him?

Yes, that was *the* argument. She would appeal to Neal's intelligence, knowing he would want the same for his children. Certainly any of the other candidates would be better than Lady Sophie.

Of course, the whole debate she was having with herself could prove fruitless. Neal might not ask her opinion, and she would be stewing about nothing.

With an impatient sound, Thea tossed the covers back. She needed a book or something to take her mind off the subject. Throwing on a dressing gown, she left the room.

A footman sat at a chair next to a candle. "May I help you, ma'am."

"Can't sleep," she murmured. "I need a book."

"Would you like a candle?"

"Yes, thank you." She took the candle holder he offered and went down the stairs. The library was in the back of the house overlooking the garden.

Thea crossed to one of the bookshelves lining the wall, holding her candle up so she could see the titles —

A movement outside the window caught her attention. Taking a step closer, she saw a man's silhouette against the moonlit garden.

Neal's shadow.

There was no one else awake except for the two of them.

He stepped forward into the moonlight. He was wearing a shirt, opened at the neck, riding breeches and tall boots. He stood alone, a romantic, contemplative figure. She wished she knew what he was thinking.

Neal turned toward her, and Thea's immediate reaction was to blow out the candle. She stepped away from the window, moving far enough that he couldn't see her but she could watch him.

A terrible yearning rose in her. One she did not want to identify. That summer years ago, she'd lived for their meetings.

And now?

Now, she was a woman who'd been married, who understood desire and lust. She knew what she yearned for. She knew what she wanted. Her body ached for his touch, for him.

Thea shook her head and crossed her arms tight against her chest. Their lives had gone down different paths. Besides, if Neal had wanted her, he would have pursued.

He hadn't.

He *could* pursue now. He wouldn't.

And if she walked out into the night to him? If he opened his arms, would she be willing?

Thea turned and walked back to her room, her quest for a book forgotten.

Thea had been there in the library's darkness. Restless, feeling that the four walls of his

175

room had been closing in on him, Neal had escaped out into the night garden, but he had not found any relief. He felt trapped. Closed in, even in the open air.

Then he'd caught sight of Thea in the library.

And he could breathe again.

She hadn't lingered. He didn't fool himself. He knew she had run from him. It was the right thing for her to do.

He'd run too if he could. Something was at work. Something over which he had no control and didn't understand. He doubted if she understood as well.

This evening, he'd focused on Lady Sophie because she was simple and charming. She was also beautiful. The other young women were not only more competitive but also shrewder. He could feel them coveting him, his title and his money with their eyes.

But it was Thea he coveted. Thea, who effortlessly put the manners, the beauty, the personalities of these other women to shame. Thea, whose strength of character he admired.

Thea that he wanted to touch, to hold . . . to bed.

Margaret would tell him to leave now, but he couldn't. God help him, he couldn't.

There comes a time when every man must

meet his destiny, and Neal realized his time was nigh.

CHAPTER EIGHT

"Good morning, Lord Lyon, I trust you slept well," Mirabel said in greeting to Neal. She was sitting next to Sir James at the head of the dining table and had been the first to notice his presence. The room was busy with young women and their parents preparing their plates from the wide range of dishes set up on the sideboard.

The minute Mirabel issued her greeting, everyone turned to offer their own.

For a man accustomed to his privacy, it was a bit off-putting to have so much attention.

"There is a place to sit beside me," Lady Lila offered. She was looking fetching in a dark blue riding habit trimmed in gold braid *à la militaire.* Neal knew it was the latest fashion, but he found it disconcerting to think of women dressed for military action rather than a pleasant ride in the country.

The plan for the day was a ride to an old

church and picnic lunch. He thought of the work waiting for him back in London, the ledgers, the letters, the documents, and tried to smile. "Thank you," he said.

"There is a place next to me as well," Lady Cynthia said brightly.

"Thank you," he replied, putting his attention to his breakfast. *Thank you, thank you.* Words that could keep him out of trouble. Of course, he'd noticed that one person wasn't at breakfast yet — Thea. He thought to ask where she was, then stopped himself.

Such a request would not be appreciated by this audience.

Then, as if he'd conjured her, Thea appeared in the doorway. She wasn't dressed for riding, and she appeared very tired. Her honey brown hair had been styled for simplicity, and her eyes were dark with concern.

And still, she was the most attractive, interesting, remarkable woman in the room. There was a presence about her, a character that none of the others had.

Her gaze met Neal's for the briefest of moments, and then she announced, "I am so sorry, everyone, that I won't be able to ride with you to the ruins today. Lady Sophie has taken violently ill, and I feel I must be here with her and her family."

"Good heavens," Mirabel said. "What is the matter with her?"

"We don't know."

"Shall we call for a doctor?" Mirabel asked.

"That might be necessary," Thea said.

Neal carried a plate of food over to Thea. "Here," he said. "Take a moment and eat. I'm certain Mirabel will see to the doctor."

"That I will," Mirabel replied and nodded for one of her footmen to come to her immediately.

"You can sit here," Neal said, superseding a footman and pulling the chair next to Lady Lila out for her.

He sensed Thea's first impulse was to refuse. "You won't help anyone if you wear yourself out," he added.

Her resistance vanished. She almost gratefully sank down in the chair with a murmured "Thank you." He nodded for one of the footmen to pour a cup of tea for her.

Lady Lila cocked her head in reproof. "That chair was for you, my lord."

"And how kind of you to hold it for me," he answered. "However, I have put it to good use. After all, how can we enjoy a house party if one of our number is ill?"

"Perhaps something she ate didn't settle

well with her?" Mrs. Pomfrey said, buttering her toasted bread, a suggestion that made Mirabel's eyes widen in alarm.

"If that were true, we would all be ill," Mirabel said, looking to Thea for confirmation.

"Well, it's unfortunate she won't be able to ride with all of you today," Lady Montvale said, no sadness in her voice at all.

Neal took his plate over to the empty chair next to Miss Cynthia Pomfrey. She gave him a pleasant smile before shooting a triumphant look at Lady Lila, and Neal felt like a bone being argued over by two dogs. Well, actually five dogs — while the one *he* wanted pointedly ignored him.

Thea didn't linger over her meal but excused herself to see to Lady Sophie. Her glance had not come his way since he'd pulled out her chair.

Neal rose from the table, excusing himself, and caught up with her in the hall.

"Mrs. Martin," he said, aware that anyone could be listening. "Is there anything I can do for Lady Sophie?"

She shook her head. "No, there isn't, and I assure you I believe Lady Sophie will be fine, although it is quite worrisome." She paused. "You are sorry she won't be able to ride with you this morning?"

There was an edge to her voice, a sign of a sharper question being asked — and Neal realized that if he answered honestly, if he really didn't have a concern about Lady Sophie, that it was Thea who drew his notice, no good could come of it. His sister Margaret's worst fears would be realized, as would his own. "Of course," he responded, shrugging as he did so to take any import from his concern.

"Then it is Lady Sophie you have chosen?" she asked.

Neal took a step back. "I've not made a decision."

"But you singled her out quite often yesterday."

"I was talking to her. She's pleasant."

"Is she the one, my lord?"

Neal frowned, not liking the way she worded the question. "I haven't focused on any 'one.' Did you not tell me to become acquainted with the young women?"

"I did."

"Then I was becoming acquainted with her." He did not like the direction of this conversation. Thea was too eager to see him matched. Perhaps he was wrong in his assumption that deeper emotions were in play. "I have not made up my mind one way or the other."

"I gained the impression you had, my lord," she answered. "I was mistaken."

"Thea, don't go stiff on me," Neal said, annoyed at her cool facade. "This is devilish hard. I've never been watched so much as I am now. Lady Sophie was very safe to talk to. She's —" He paused for the right word. "Uncomplicated. If an impression has formed that I have made up my mind, then I'm sorry for it. It's not true."

If he'd thought his reasoning would placate her, he was wrong. If anything, the gleam in her eyes hardened and the furrows along her brow deepened. However, voices in the breakfast room warned that they were about to be interrupted.

"I appreciate knowing where you stand, my lord," she said and started to walk away.

He caught her arm, the action forcing her to look at him. "What do you want from me?" he demanded, his voice low. "One moment you befriend me and in the next you are distant and barely polite."

"And what do you expect of me, my lord?"

He frowned, uncertain of her meaning.

"You don't know, do you?" she pointed out, and on that cryptic remark she turned and he had to let her go.

Within minutes, Neal found himself surrounded by the other guests. Lady Lila pulled his arm one way, Lady Cynthia another, and in the end, he escaped to his room, much to Sir James's amusement.

An hour later, he found himself riding along on the most frivolous of ventures, a picnic — but his thoughts were not far from Thea.

The doctor said that Lady Sophie was suffering a stomach disorder of some sort.

"I wonder what good doctors truly are," Mirabel grumbled. "They always state the obvious." They, along with Lady Sophie's mother, Lady Carpsley, had left the patient upstairs sleeping off the effects of her illness.

"Yes, well, at least she isn't in danger of imminent demise," Thea said. "She had me worried last night."

"I'm sorry she missed the picnic," Lady Carpsley said. "I had my husband go with the group so we would receive a full report. I told Sophie she'd best be on her feet and in her prettiest frock by this evening."

"She may still not be feeling well," Thea suggested.

Lady Carpsley bristled at the suggestion. "She can't be abed when Lyon returns. I'll see that she is up. We came here to win him, and we shall."

"Are you so certain he is smitten?" Mirabel said, asking the question Thea hadn't dared voice. "Men have an amazing ability to appear interested when they are not."

"That's why Mrs. Martin is here, is it not?" Lady Carpsley said. She looked to Thea. "With Sophie taking sick at such an inopportune time, we may need your help. Sophie was gaining ground over the others. We could all see that." She folded her hands in front of her. "You wish for your son to attend Westminster School, do you not?"

"I do," Thea said, surprised that she knew and suddenly cautious. "He has an interview there in a few weeks."

"It's a very exclusive school. They don't allow just anyone to walk through their doors. My husband's cousin is the headmaster. Your son's interview will be with him. And, of course, recommendations from well-placed persons can be very important. The right word from my husband and your son will be admitted." She paused and then added, "The wrong word and your son will *never* grace Westminster's halls."

Thea looked over at Mirabel, whose eyes had widened in outrage, an outrage Thea shared.

"Lady Carpsley, that is blackmail," Thea

demurred.

"Yes, well, one does what one can for one's child. Lyon is the catch of any four seasons. The more we are around him, the more Lord Carpsley and I are convinced he is the perfect husband for our daughter. I shall expect your full assistance, that is if you wish your son to attend Westminster. There are so many bright lads from good, but modest, families. Westminster can't take them all, so they must be very selective." She smiled, the expression almost friendly, and left the room.

Thea sank down on the divan. Mirabel sat down beside her. "What are we going to do?" Mirabel asked.

"I'm disgusted that she would use my son as a bartering tool in this," Thea said, her temper taking hold.

"I am as well, but that doesn't change the fact that she is. How close do you think Lyon is to making up his mind?"

"I don't know. He's being very close-lipped. This morning when I talked to him, he seemed distant."

"He *has* showed marked attention to Lady Sophie."

Thea shrugged, a tightness settling in her shoulders. "He didn't appear overly concerned about her this morning."

"But isn't that what he wants?" Mirabel pointed out. "A woman that he can't possibly like? Once Lyon hears of this, I assume from what I've observed of his character, he will be disgusted." She shook her head. "Frankly, Thea, I sat at the breakfast table this morning, watching faces as you said Lady Sophie wasn't feeling well, and *no one* seemed concerned. In fact, a few acted quite pleased with the information. I found it unsettling."

"Mirabel, this can't be the first time you've realized how petty and selfish people can be."

"I don't live my life that way. Why should I notice?"

A new suspicion was brewing in Thea's mind. "It is a bit too fortunate that Lady Sophie would take ill. She appeared the picture of health yesterday."

"No," Mirabel said, drawing out the word as if to deny it. "Do you suspect someone made her sick? How could someone do that?"

"I don't know. It does sound far-fetched. Poison?"

"But these people are the cream of the *ton.* Thea, they are respectable people."

"Entitled? Yes. Respectable? Mirabel, don't be naive. Marrying Lyon would be a boon to any of these families. You can never tell where a person is in life just by the surface. They could be in debt or wanting Lyon's connections for their own use. His money will fill their coffers, his prestige will burnish their stars. You should have met some of the men my father wanted to marry me off to — codgers and his cronies — and he was galloping out the gate to do so. He had a number of schemes to draw me to the attention of the men he'd chosen. Of course, the thought of seeing any of them naked was enough to make me run into Boyd's arms."

"Lyon wouldn't hurt the eyes naked."

Mirabel's droll observation brought an image to Thea's mind that almost sizzled her brain and brought a flush to her cheeks. It had been a long time since she'd had a lustful thought. She'd been too busy trying to keep her small family fed and safe. Now, it was as if a part of her tamped down and kept dormant suddenly sprang to life. She rose from the divan and took a step away. "Stop this."

"What?" Mirabel asked, her eyes rounding in innocence.

"Attempting to put us together. It won't work." Thea didn't know if she was saying this for Mirabel's benefit or her own.

"It could. You must let yourself believe."

"There is nothing to believe," Thea protested. And yet a part deep inside her wistfully wondered whether Mirabel's claim was true.

"I think he likes you too much. He always stays an arm's distance away from you."

"And that means what?"

"That he is afraid to go closer," Mirabel explained, as if it should have been obvious. "Truly, Thea, you can't see the signs? Or are you so busy trying to stay away from him you don't notice?"

"He treats me with polite respect. Nothing more; nothing less."

"He likes you —"

"Mirabel, no more of that." Thea walked off before her friend could toss in a final "He likes you," something she might have heard whispered as she climbed the stairs. She went to check on Lady Sophie. She was not anxious to keep company with the Carpsleys, not after Lady Carpsley's threat, but her curiosity had been piqued.

What if someone *had* given Lady Sophie something to make her ill?

The suggestion was worth a question or two.

Lord Carpsley was taking an afternoon snooze in a comfortable chair in a corner of the room. Lady Carpsley was reading to her daughter. Lady Sophie looked like a beautiful, pale waif resting in the middle of the feather pillows and downy comforters.

"Are you feeling any better?" Thea asked.

Lady Sophie turned mournful eyes to her. "They will all be crowding around him now. He was interested in me, and I lost him." Her fingers twisted the sheets in her agitation.

"Your health is more important than this nonsense," Thea said soothingly.

"Besides, Mrs. Martin is going to see that Lord Lyon doesn't forget his interest in you, aren't you?" Lady Carpsley finished, turning to Thea with a look that her ladyship expected to be obeyed.

"He won't forget Lady Sophie," Thea allowed without committing herself. "Have you had anything to eat? Would you like a bowl of broth?"

Lady Sophie pressed her lips together and shook her head. "No, I can't eat anything."

"When did you last eat?" Thea wondered, laying a hand on the girl's brow. It was cool. She would recover. She was probably just weak from being ill.

"Dinner," Lady Sophie said.

"And nothing else?"

"No."

"Did you sleep well last night?" Thea asked.

"I did until I became ill." Lady Sophie sighed heavily. "I wasn't feeling terribly the thing earlier in the day yesterday. Just a little queasy."

"Her monthly," Lady Carpsley said, leaning toward Thea as she divulged this information, as if she didn't want the sleeping Lord Carpsley to overhear.

"Mother gave me a troche to settle me. I told her I was so nervous with excitement I didn't think I could sleep."

"And she must sleep!" Lady Carpsley declared. "We need her looking fresh."

"A troche?" Thea questioned.

"Yes," Lady Carpsley answered. "Lord Corkindale gave it to me. Said it always settles his daughter's nerves. He is such a kind man. The others are biddies, spiteful and competitive. Lord Corkindale is very much a gentleman and understands fair play. He told me he can see Lord Lyon has developed a fondness for Sophie. He was regretful his lordship didn't favor his daughter, but it is what it is."

"Lord Corkindale said this?" Thea repeated in disbelief.

"He was very supportive. Told me to have my daughter let the troche dissolve slowly

191

in her mouth. And it did settle you down, didn't it, Sophie? Of course, what we didn't know is that she was taking frightfully ill. Maybe I should have asked him for another to give her."

And maybe Lord Corkindale had dispensed with his daughter's competition along with that troche.

Thea forced a smile. "Please let us know if there is anything you need, Lady Sophie."

"Thank you, Mrs. Martin," the girl said, but then added, "have they returned from the picnic yet?"

"They have not yet returned, Lady Sophie. However, don't be anxious. Lord Lyon's character is not a shallow one," Thea said.

"But he *is* male," Lady Carpsley said. "They can't help themselves. Even that one," she finished, rolling her eyes in her sleeping husband's direction. She sighed. "No, I prefer to put my faith in you."

Thea did not appreciate the subtle reminder of what was at stake if Lyon failed to offer for Lady Sophie. She left the room. As she was coming downstairs, the picnickers were just returning.

Lady Lila had her hands, both of them, around Neal's arm, and her father appeared very happy.

The Montvales stormed up the stairs past

Thea without so much as a passing glance.

Plastering a smile to her face, Thea greeted those in the hallway. "I take it you enjoyed yourselves?" Thea asked.

"I believe we did," Neal answered. "How is Lady Sophie?"

Thea's smile grew tighter. "She might be joining us for dinner."

"That's wonderful," Lady Lila said with a sweetness that had to have been false. There was nothing "sweet" about her at all. In fact, Thea had chosen her for her callousness.

Lord Corkindale came up to their group. "That was an excellent adventure. I'm ready for my supper now."

Mrs. Pomfrey came up beside Thea. "The ruins were nothing special," she said dismissively and then turned to Lady Lila. "I hope that chafing on your cheeks improves. The sun can be so harsh on a lady's skin."

"My cheeks aren't chafed," Lady Lila countered.

"If you were *my* daughter," Mrs. Pomfrey said, putting a motherly tone behind her words, "I would advise you to run upstairs quickly and have your maid rub cream in them without delay."

"Nonsense," Lord Corkindale answered, growing blustery. "My daughter is the picture of health. Ruddy cheeks is good on a girl."

"Ruddy?" Lady Lila repeated.

"I mean you have some good color to your face," her father tried to explain, but the damage had been done, and Mrs. Pomfrey didn't hesitate to capitalize on it.

"Well, if you were my daughter . . ." She let her voice drift with the obvious implication.

Lady Lila pretended to shrug off the suggestion, but a beat later said, "I really should go upstairs and dress for dinner." She turned to Lord Lyon, gave him a dreamy smile. "Thank you for your help this afternoon, my lord. I am in your debt." Honey dripped from every syllable.

"It was nothing, my lady," Neal said. She smiled at him again and went upstairs, the sway of her hips a beckoning call — and Thea had an irrational urge to charge right up behind her, grab her arm and give her a shake.

"Harumph," Mrs. Pomfrey said as if echoing Thea's sentiments.

With the exit of his daughter, Lord Corkindale's attention turned to a more important matter. "I say," he said, addressing Osgood, "where might I find a healthy draft of something to wet my palate?"

"Where is Miss Susanne?" Thea asked, just realizing Mrs. Pomfrey was without the rest of her family.

Mrs. Pomfrey's lips pursed in disapproval. "She and my husband are coming." She forced a smile. "You will wait for her, won't you, my lord?"

Before Lyon could answer, the door opened and Mr. Pomfrey entered, followed by his daughter and Sir James, who were both chatting in an animated way. In fact, Sir James was looking years younger, and Miss Susanne's face glowed with the most becoming flush.

Mr. Pomfrey's eyes met his wife's with a resigned look. He'd obviously failed at an assigned task, which, Thea assumed, had been to nip a budding romance. Her assumption was affirmed when Mrs. Pomfrey took charge. "Susanne, you need to dress for dinner."

Miss Susanne didn't take her eyes off Sir James when she said, "Actually, I'm not ready to dress yet, Mother. It is such a lovely day, and Sir James and I thought we'd take a turn around Lady Palmer's garden."

"I *suggest* you dress for dinner" was her mother's reply.

"I will," Miss Susanne said, already starting down the hall with Sir James.

The lawyer threw over his shoulder, "I shall see that she returns with plenty of time to dress for dinner."

"Well." Mrs. Pomfrey's exclamation seemed to hover in the air, but only Thea and Lyon heard it. Mr. Pomfrey had caught wind of Lord Corkindale's interest in a good dram or bottle of wine. The two were already walking toward the sitting room, where Osgood promised to bring them two glasses and a sampling from the late Lord Palmer's highly respectable liquor cabinet.

Mrs. Pomfrey stood puzzled a moment and then retreated. "I believe I'll dress for dinner," she announced. "If you will excuse me?" She didn't wait for permission from Thea or Lyon but went up the stairs as fast as she could.

Thea turned to Neal. "It appears Mrs. Pomfrey *has* found a match for her daughter."

"And she can't ask for anyone better than James. He's one of the finest men I know and is besotted. I've never seen him this way around a woman. It was a marvel to watch romance bloom. The rest of us could have just as well not been there for all the attention they paid us."

"And *you* have been close with Lady Lila."

Thea had not meant to say anything.

Certainly she hadn't meant to sound slightly caustic.

He frowned, looking tired. "This morning you informed me I was paying too much attention to Lady Sophie and needed to spread my attention around. You can see James has captured Miss Pomfrey's attention. What should I do? Ignore Lady Lila?"

"You appeared very obliging to her," Thea had to say in the face of his reasonable explanation.

He took a step back, as if he needed a hard look at her. His voice dropped. "What do you want, Thea?"

She crossed her arms, suddenly needing a barrier between them. "I don't want anything."

"Then why do you care which woman I favor?"

"Because," she said dragging the word out while thinking of a reason. "I never thought of you as a womanizer."

"A womanizer?" he repeated as if not believing his hearing.

It did sound preposterous, yet Thea felt she had good cause to call him such. "Lady Sophie feels she has captured your affections. She believes you are very interested."

"You know how aggressive Lady Lila is. Yesterday, I used Lady Sophie to keep her at bay. This morning, you didn't like that. So, today, I let Lady Lila have her lead and, yes, she plastered herself to my side. But what can I do without being rude? She is a very forceful young woman."

"So you *are* leading both of them on?" Here was a fault to support her accusation, although, yes, she knew she was being slightly unreasonable.

"I'm not leading anyone anywhere, Thea. You know what I'm looking for. I don't understand why you are being so crotchety."

"Crotchety?" She couldn't believe he'd accused her of such a thing.

"Difficult," he amended.

"Oh, no, you said crotchety." She wasn't letting him off on this one, and it felt good to have something firm and *reasonable* to explain her feelings.

"I meant difficult," he reiterated, punctuating the word with one finger aimed at her. "As in, not knowing your own mind, as in fussy, as in hot and cold. I haven't known what to expect from you since we arrived here."

Thea took a step forward. "I've been very clear in what I've been trying to do. Marrying someone you do not like is the ridiculous notion. It's not natural."

"Do I have to explain myself again —"

"No, I don't think I could stand to hear it again." And that was true, but she wasn't certain why. It was his life. He could do what he would. Still . . . "It's not natural, my lord. It's not sane."

"It's what it is," he replied bleakly, the anger leaving him. "It's what it is."

They stood in the foyer, the door still open, the evening sun filling the room with light — and Thea wanted to grab him and shake him for all he was worth. He was too good a man to marry someone like Lady Lila or into the Carpsley family. He deserved better. Much better.

He was a man of substance, a man who had values and was respected. A *noble* man.

And yet he was so obstinate, so convinced he was right in his actions, that he'd throw himself into marriage with some ninny-headed, selfish chit —

"I don't want to see you trapped in marriage," she whispered. "I know what it is like, Neal. I was trapped. And marriage is more than having children. It has to be."

"I don't expect you to approve of my decisions, Thea."

"It's not a matter of approving or disapproving," she said. She raised a hand as if to take hold of his arm, to urge him to heed her warning, but then drew it back. "I just don't want —"

She broke off, suddenly uncertain of what she didn't want. She didn't want him in a loveless marriage . . . but did that mean she didn't want him in a marriage at all? With *any* woman?

For the past five minutes they had been circling each other. Either could have walked away at any moment, and yet they hadn't. Worse, she'd been going on like a jealous fishwife —

This could not be.

They were friends, nothing more. *Nothing* more.

He frowned, concerned. "Thea, is something the matter?"

She was so aware of him, from the cowlick that gave his hair a little lift above his brow, to the shape of his earlobes, from the weave of the material of his jacket to the dust on his boots — and yet he was here to marry another. He didn't hear the jealousy in her words.

And he'd already walked away from her before.

Neal wasn't like her. He didn't *have* to care.

"Everything is as it should be," she said, choosing her words carefully. She took a step away from him, and then another. "You are right. You are handling this whole situation well —"

"Thea —"

She held up her hand to block any more words between them. "I shall see you at supper." She took off up the stairs, running from him as fast as she could.

At the top of the stairs, she looked back. He was on the first step, as if he'd started to follow and then had thought differently of it.

For a long moment, their gazes held. She understood. *They* could not be. He would not change his path.

And then he turned away, walking toward the sitting room, where the other men were enjoying a drink.

Thea waited until he was out of sight, and she felt defeated. This was not right, but it wasn't her place to tell him. She *had* overstepped her carefully erected boundaries.

She started toward her room and almost walked into Mirabel, who had come up behind Thea without her knowledge.

Mirabel reached out and caught Thea before she ran into her. "I'm so sorry," Thea said. "I didn't see you."

"I am hard to notice," Mirabel answered. "Are you feeling quite the thing? You look pale."

"I'm fine," Thea said, moving past her friend. "Everything is fine." She kept moving and didn't stop until she reached the inner sanctum of her room, and there she collapsed.

Sitting at her dressing table, Thea studied her reflection in the mirror. "You are a fool," she told herself. "*Twice* over."

Of course, her reflection didn't argue.

But there was no time to waste feeling sorry for herself. Thea had to think of her sons. That traitorous yearning for someone special in her life, that desire for love and all it promised, were not for her. She'd had her chance, and she'd bungled it.

And perhaps her words with Lyon hadn't been such a bad thing. It brought him down to earth from her youthful dreams of "what might have been" to "what is." Since everyone had their own self-interest at heart, including Lyon, with his talk of sons and curses, and Mirabel, with her social climbing, well, perhaps Thea should be mercenary as well. If the Carpsley connection could place Jonathan in Westminster, why shouldn't she take advantage of it?

In truth, the possibility of dirty play and troches from Lord Corkindale made Thea determined to keep the willful Lady Lila from becoming the next Lady Lyon.

There, she now had a purpose.

So determined, Thea dressed for dinner.

Lady Sophie joined them at the table, and Lyon paid great attention to her. Thea decided over the creamed peas and her third glass of wine that they would make beautiful children — Sophie with her blonde beauty and Lyon with his dark handsomeness. Oh, yes, adorable children. She smiled as the footman refilled her glass.

Thea didn't usually drink more than one glass, but today had been a challenging day.

And it continued to be a challenging evening. Lady Lila did her best to reclaim Lyon. He kept his distance. He, Mirabel, Sir James, and Lady Sophie were involved in a spirited game of cards that had all the others gathered around them. Thea's presence was not needed, and it made her feel a bit alone.

He also didn't look at Thea. Not once.

She knew because she kept her eye on him.

Mirabel excused herself from the table, giving her card hand over to Miss Pomfrey. She wandered over to where Thea sat in a corner. "What is the matter with you?" she whispered.

"I don't know what you mean," Thea answered.

"You are glaring at people."

"I am not."

"Yes, you are," Mirabel insisted. "You are giving a cold, hard stare."

"You are being ridiculous."

In answer to that charge, Mirabel went away in a huff.

But the exchange did make it clear to Thea that she was not fit company. She and Mirabel never argued. She excused herself and retired to her room, aware as she climbed the stairs that, yes, she was a bit tipsy — and she missed her sons. They kept her grounded.

Of course, wine made one maudlin. As she wandered toward her room, she wondered if alone was how she would always be. She didn't regret it. She was happier alone than in her marriage, but still . . . didn't life have more to offer?

"Apparently not," Thea murmured to no one in particular. She didn't wait for a maid but undressed herself, not bothering to braid her hair as was her custom, and climbed into bed.

She was half asleep when there was a knock at the door.

Thea rolled over on her back, annoyed.

"Yes?" she said, half expecting to hear Mirabel's voice, probably on some mission to chastise her more.

"It's Nessa, Mrs. Martin. I need to speak to you."

Assuming the maid wanted to help her undress for the night, Thea said, "I am already in bed, Nessa. That's fine."

"I need to speak to you."

The hushed urgency in the maid's voice penetrated Thea's wine drowsiness. She came up on her elbows. "Come in."

The door opened, letting in light from the hallway's lamps. Nessa hurried to Thea's bedside and knelt. "I'm sorry to disturb you," she said, her voice low, as if she was afraid of being overheard, "but there is something afoot that you should know."

"What is it?"

"Lady Lila's maid has become fast friends with one of the footmen. He told me she was bragging not five minutes ago that Lady Lila is determined to marry Lord Lyon."

This was not news. "And?" Thea asked.

"She's going to his bedroom this night and place herself in his bed. When Lord Lyon comes up to bed, her father will enter the room and accuse him of taking advantage of his daughter. Lord Lyon will have no choice but to marry her."

"What of his valet?" Thea asked.

"He didn't bring one. He's been using one of the house servants. The maid said they've bribed him to make himself scarce while this all takes place."

"Not on my watch she won't," Thea said, anger bringing her wide awake. She jumped out of bed, tossing her hair over her shoulder and grabbing her dressing gown.

"What are you going to do?" Nessa asked.

"I'm going to toss that little hussy out of his room," Thea answered. "And then I am throwing both her *and* her conniving father out of Lady Palmer's house. You might wish to distance yourself from this," she advised Nessa as she went marching out the door. "It *will* become ugly."

CHAPTER NINE

Thea nodded at the footman already at his station at the top of the stairs as she turned down the connecting hallway. But before she'd gone too far down the hall, a precaution struck her. She reapproached the servant.

"Is everyone still downstairs?" she asked, knowing that he would answer because of her close friendship with Mirabel.

"All but yourself, ma'am, and one of the young ladies."

"Which young lady?" Thea tried to smile and take the edge off her question.

"I don't know her title, ma'am, but she had dark hair."

Only Lila had dark hair. The game was on.

"Thank you," Thea said, almost relishing the challenge. She knew which room was Lyon's. Mirabel would place him in her best suite.

She knocked on his door.

There was no answer.

Boldly, she entered. A lamp burned on a side table. The sheets on the bed had been turned down. There was no one in it.

That was a relief, although Thea had been looking forward to snatching Lady Lila up by the scruff of her neck and escorting her out of the room.

Thea walked over to a chair beside the cold hearth and sat, her arms and ankles crossed. Lady Lila was going to be in for a surprise when she put her little plan in motion.

The clock on the mantel ticked away the minutes. Thea waited, impatient.

Ten minutes.

Fifteen —

The door opened.

Thea rose slowly to her feet as Lady Lila backed into the room. The girl was trying to be very quiet and had her attention on not being seen by someone in the hallway, so she didn't realize she wasn't alone *inside* the room until Thea said, "Hello, my lady."

Lady Lila jumped straight into the air. Her dark, curling hair was down around her shoulders, and Thea doubted that she had anything on beneath the dressing gown she wore. "What are you doing here?"

"Waiting for you," Thea informed her smartly. "And now I'm going to escort you back to your bed."

"I'm not going," Lady Lila announced. "The Lyon asked me here. We've been meeting *every* night."

"And *I* know that you haven't," Thea responded. "I have servants who will corroborate my story if you should be so unwise as to persist with your lies."

Anger flared in Lady Lila's eyes at the mention of the servants.

"Now," Thea said, advancing on the girl, "if you are wise, you will return to your room and say nothing of this to anyone, because if you do, I shall put the word out about your schemes and you will be *ruined*. Do you understand — ?"

She wasn't able to finish her sentence because Lady Lila doubled a fist and smacked her against the side of the head. Thea's world spun. She couldn't think, could barely see. She went to her knees and reached for the floor for balance.

"No one tells me what to do. Especially if she is some ratty nobody who threw away her pride. No one cares about you. *No one*."

From the corner of her eye, Thea caught the movement of Lady Lila raising her hand to strike her again. Thea lifted an arm to protect herself.

But the second blow never came.

Thea turned to see Neal holding onto the hand Lady Lila would have struck her with. "What do you think you are doing?" he demanded in a low voice.

Lady Lila started to shout, a sound that turned into a whimper when she saw who had her. She shook her hand free from him, backed up and charged out of the room as fast as her bare feet could take her.

Thea wanted to tell Neal to stop her. The others should know how uncontrollable the girl could be, but her world was still spinning from the blow.

Neal closed the door and knelt beside her. "Thea, are you all right?"

She wanted to tell him that was the silliest question she'd ever heard. *Of course* she wasn't all right. But she was so shaken that she couldn't make her mouth work.

He put his arms around her and she gratefully leaned against him for support. "Easy, easy," he whispered. "Take deep breaths and relax."

Thea did as he said. She leaned her head against the strength of his shoulder and felt her whole body collapse against him. Her breathing became more normal, but she had a new terror to contend with — she'd started to cry, and she couldn't stop it. All she had the energy to do was bury her face in the folds of his evening jacket and release all the pent-up doubts, fears and frustrations in huge, ugly-sounding sobs.

And it felt good.

How long had she been holding all this in? She was so tired of struggling to make her life meaningful, to provide for her sons, to overcome the disadvantages she'd weighed down upon them.

Neal, God bless him, didn't say a word. He was like a stone wall, strong, dependable, present. Thea couldn't remember the last time she'd turned to a man for support. She couldn't remember when she'd trusted one enough to be vulnerable.

But this was Neal. She'd thought his friendship gone from her life forever, but now he'd returned. Good, solid, kind . . . handsome . . .

Thea didn't know really how it happened. One moment she was leaning against him, crying her heart out, and in the next, his lips were right there, inches from hers.

She didn't know who moved first. She might have. Maybe he did.

But at the first contact of his lips against hers, she was glad one of them did.

Their kiss was tentative for all of four

seconds, and then it became fuller. Deeper. More demanding.

Thea had always enjoyed the intimacy of a kiss, and yet she'd sensed there had always been something missing.

Here, in Neal's arms, she found it.

It hadn't been just any man she'd wanted to kiss. She'd wanted this one.

With stunning clarity, she realized what had been missing in her marriage. Yes, Boyd's excesses had played a role in her disappointment. Their love had been shallow, a necessity, and, from her part, a bid for freedom.

But she'd been searching in Boyd's arms for what she experienced right now. She parted her lips, wanting to breathe Neal in.

Their tongues met, touched, stroked. She tightened her hold around his neck. If she could have, she would have climbed right into his skin.

And he felt the same. He was eager, hungry. His hand slid down her shoulder, rested on her waist a moment before slipping inside her dressing gown and cupping her breast. The touch vanquished all common sense, all taboos, all fears and doubts.

This was Neal without the trappings or title, rank or responsibilities. This was the Neal she'd known all those years ago. She'd yearned for this man. She desired him. She wanted him inside her —

"I say, what are you doing with my daughter?" Lord Corkindale's voice shouted as the bedroom door was forcefully shoved open. The door hit Neal's back, which was blocking it from opening fully, and threw him against Thea. She lost her balance and the two of them tumbled to the floor, Neal turning at the last moment so that he didn't fall on her.

The way no longer blocked, the door flew open and Lord Corkindale practically stumbled into the room in his enthusiasm, almost tripping over Neal and Thea.

Nor was he alone. Mirabel was with him. "If you've compromised her —," Lord Corkindale started to threaten as he regained his balance, but then he froze as he realized it wasn't his daughter Neal was holding. He took a step back. "Mrs. Martin?" He looked around. "Where's Lila?"

"She isn't here," Neal said, coming to his feet and bringing Thea with him. Her dressing gown was hanging open, her nightdress had been up around her knees, her lips were bruised from his kisses, and her cheeks flamed with embarrassment. Everything had happened so quickly that she still hadn't registered the turn of events. She did have the presence of mind to retie the sash of her dressing gown.

"Lila has to be here," Lord Corkindale said, confused.

"I'm so sorry we disturbed you, my lord," Mirabel said, giving Thea a sly, approving look. "Good night."

She reached for Lord Corkindale as if to guide him out before anyone was the wiser, but he shook off her arm. "What *is* going on here?" Confusion was giving way to anger. "Mrs. Martin, what were you doing on the floor with Lord Lyon? And why are you wearing hardly a stitch of clothes on you?"

Thea thought her nightdress and gown was more than enough coverage, far more than Lady Lila had been wearing.

Yes, it was unseemly for her to be in a gentleman's room in night attire, but she had a good reason for being there. "I'm here because your daughter —," she started to explain, only to be interrupted by Lady Lila herself.

"Father, why are you shouting?" Lady Lila asked in a small, sweet voice as she pressed open the door. She then gave a huge gasp of horror before exclaiming in a loud voice, "*Mrs. Martin,* what have you and Lord Lyon been doing?"

Almost immediately, as if they had been summoned, the Montvales, the Carpsleys and Lady Sophie joined the gathering around the doorway.

Neal was a bit confused about what was happening.

Of course part of that was because his brain still sizzled from Thea's kiss. He hadn't intended to kiss her, but when he'd walked into the room and there she'd been —

Who knew a kiss could turn a man inside out? He'd never felt such a strong, over-whelming connection with anyone in his life. Her kiss had touched his very soul. Who cared what these people had to say? He wanted to kiss Thea again.

"Can you believe this?" Lady Lila said to the others. "Here we are thinking Mrs. Martin is a person of integrity, and she's been caught throwing herself at Lord Lyon. How incredible. How *disappointing.*"

"Now wait a minute," Thea said, ready to explain herself, but Lady Carpsley stepped forward, her eyebrows so high on her fore-head they seemed to reach her hairline.

"This is scandalous. *Shocking.* We now know why you kept steering Lord Lyon away from our daughter."

"That is not true —," Thea attempted to say.

"I can't believe my father brought me here," Lady Lila cut in with a woebegone voice.

"I shouldn't have," Lord Corkindale agreed. "This is disgraceful. And I thought you were a woman of moral character," he said to Thea.

Neal stepped forward, his fist doubling, but Thea herself pulled him back. "Don't you talk to me about character," Thea said to Lord Corkindale.

"And don't you lecture me," he returned.

"*I* have seen enough," Lady Montvale said, her voice carrying over the others. "Mrs. Martin, you have much to answer for."

"And I will," Thea said. The color had drained from her face at her ladyship's censure. "If you will all just hear me out —"

"*I* don't think any of us should listen to you," Lady Lila stated. "This is not the first time you've shown poor form, is it now? You have a history of it. I heard someone suggest you weren't really a widow. That there was never a Mr. Martin —"

Neal could contain himself no longer. *"That is enough."*

His words served to quiet Lady Lila. She

blinked as if just realizing he was present and she retreated back a step, but the society matrons were not so easily cowed.

Lady Montvale spoke. "My lord, I have the highest regard for you. You are a man, after all, and given a man's appetites, there will be, how do we say it? Ah, *peccadilloes.* But Mrs. Martin has surprised us all. Against our better judgment we involved ourselves with her. And we are now dismayed by her behavior. However, this doesn't mean we hold disapproval of *you.* We still think of *you* as an excellent suitor for our daughter's hand —"

"As *I* do," Lord Corkindale interjected, "for Lila. Quite a pair you are. Handsome couple."

"You have lovely daughters, but, unfortunately, I have been taken off the market," Neal heard himself say. He reached for Thea and gathered her protectively against his body. "Mrs. Martin has just honored me by accepting my proposal of marriage."

If the roof of the house had fallen in, the gathering in front of him could not have looked more shocked. Including Thea. She rocked back. Her head swung up to stare at him as if he'd gone mad.

Maybe he had . . . and he wasn't sorry for it.

But for the first time in his memory, he was acting according to *his* wishes, *his* wants, *his* desires.

Freedom was a heady thing.

Neal took advantage of the silence. "I hope, Lord and Lady Montvale, that you will treat my soon-to-be wife with the respect and courtesy she deserves. Lord Corkindale, Lady Lila, I register your disappointment." He noticed that Sir James and the Pomfreys had also joined the group. They had been walking toward their rooms when they had noticed the crowd in his hall. "James, wish me well. Mrs. Martin has agreed to be my wife."

The more Neal said it, the more the idea took hold with him. Perhaps it was the aftereffect of the kiss. Or perhaps it was because now Thea wouldn't have to worry about money, or where her son would be going to school. He would take care of them. He would be their protector . . . and her lover —

"I am not marrying him," Thea said. "Don't listen to his rubbish." She shoved Neal away from her with all she was worth and walked through the dumbfounded crowd and out the door.

In all his imaginings, Neal had never considered that someone would turn down his offer of marriage. Not once.

And Thea needed him. *Her sons* needed him.

"*I'll* marry you," Lady Lila announced.

Neal batted the offer away with his hand, her words as insistent and inconsequential as a black fly. "Excuse me," he murmured, and went after Thea.

CHAPTER TEN

Thea knew Neal followed. She could feel his heavier steps behind her. She began running for her room, her bare feet pounding the floor. She almost mowed down a maid as she raced around the corner. She didn't stop to apologize. She ran to the haven of her room and slammed the door, throwing her back against it, her heart pounding in her chest.

Nessa had lit the bedside table lamp. The room, with its rumpled bed, looked so peaceful. She should never have left it. Who would have predicted such a strange chain of events would uproot her world?

She was ruined. Destroyed . . . unless she could think of something to say that would erase this terrible evening from the minds of some of the *ton*'s leading personages. She pushed away from the door and started pacing in an anxious circle —

"Thea," Neal's voice said from the other

side of the door. "Let me in."

She stared at the door as if she could burn a hole through it and set him on fire.

"Thea? Talk to me."

She didn't want to talk. He'd already said enough.

"Very well, then," he said, "let me tell you what I'm going to do. Tomorrow, I will send a man to procure a special license from the bishop. That shouldn't take long. We could probably marry the day after. Of course, if you wish to marry in London so that your sons could attend —"

Thea was across to the door in a blink. She threw it open. Neal stood there, handsome, relaxed, completely in control of his emotions.

She wasn't.

"What do you believe you are doing?" she demanded.

"Marrying you," he replied.

Thea slammed the door in his face.

She turned away, raising a hand to her forehead as if her head hurt. But it wasn't her head that worried her, it was her whole life.

The door opened. "That wasn't courteous," he chastised as he walked in.

"Leave me," she ground out.

His response was to shut the door, with

him inside the room. "Thea, no one will believe we want to marry if you continue these dramatics."

His calmness threw her into hysterics. "Do you not know what you've done? You've ruined me."

Neal shook his head. "I don't agree. I think I saved you."

"And how is that?" she demanded wildly.

"No one will speak against you with me to protect you," he said, as if he was being quite noble.

"How little you know of women," Thea answered. "Protect me by marrying me? I'll be surprised if any door will be open to me. This story will fly through London. They may behave one way to *your* face, but they will let me know what they think behind your back. I'm destroyed. And what of my sons? What will happen to them?" She collapsed onto the tufted bench in front of her dressing table.

He knelt in front of her. "I don't care what those women think. They don't matter —"

"How naive you are!"

"Fine. Women control the world," he conceded without conviction. "They are all going to eat us alive —"

"They will. Lady Carpsley —"

"Is a bully. All of London knows she leads

her husband around by his boll—" He paused, catching himself before he said *bollocks,* and finished, "Nose. She leads him around by his nose. In fact most of those women handle their husbands that way. You don't think I know Lady Montvale can be a terror?" Neal shrugged. "I've managed this far in my life without her approval."

"That's because she has always approved of you, my lord. And she probably will continue the pretense of doing so, although one day you may need to speak to the Prince Regent about a matter of some urgency and find your request denied —"

"No, that won't happen. He owes me money," Neal countered, but then he frowned. "Then again, because he owes me money, he has already been avoiding me —"

"You are not listening to what I'm saying." Thea raised her hands in frustration and let them go before adding, "And you sound as if you think this is a lark."

"It is, Thea. And perhaps you are the one not listening to me. Marriage between us makes good sense. We've known each other a long time. You won't fall in love with me, and I won't fall in love with you."

"How can you say that? Didn't you toss aside our friendship because of fear we would grow too close?" And they would.

She could sense it. And *then* what would he do?

"We are older and wiser now," he replied dismissively. "Together we can beat the curse —"

Thea interrupted him with a cry of irritation. "The curse, the curse, the *curse*." She swooped off the chair and away from him, taking a good two angry steps before turning. "That's all you think about."

His brows came together in an angry V. "I don't have a choice. I must consider it."

She wanted to groan but stifled the sound. Did he know how mad he sounded? Taking a second to collect herself, she said, "Neal, have you ever wondered why I was so offended that day in Sir James's office? Why I stormed out of the place?"

"You were upset with me," he said, giving a small shrug as if it didn't matter.

"Are all men thickheaded?" Thea demanded of the room-at-large.

"Are all women so temperamental?" Neal shot back. He came to his feet. "No, Thea, I don't know why you left except that you don't believe in the curse and for some reason it made you angry that I do. All right. So be it. We have a difference. But there are many things we agree upon. In fact, we kissed rather well."

She brought her hands up as if to ward him off. "Oh, no, you didn't just say that. I thought your purpose was to marry a woman who *didn't* kiss well."

"When did I make that claim?"

"You want to marry someone you can't like," Thea pointed out.

"Yes, but I don't want to *dislike* kissing her."

Thea pounced. "Oh, so because you want to marry me, that means you don't like me."

"No, Thea, don't even jump to that conclusion."

"What conclusion am I jumping to, my lord? I'm merely restating what you said."

"But that's *not* what I said."

"Yes, it is. You said —"

Now it was Neal's turn to roar with disapproval. *"Stop twisting my words."*

It felt good to make him angry. It meant he was paying attention now.

"And you need to think about what you are saying," Thea countered. "As to that day in the office, yes, I found the talk of curse unbelievable and a bit ridiculous. But the reason I really left, Neal, is because I didn't want to help you on this quest for a wife, not with the demand you don't like her. I felt it was wrong, and I still do. Neal, I *believe* in love."

There, she'd said it, and she was a bit unnerved by her statement. But once foolish, twice damned. She couldn't stop herself from plunging on.

"I think it is important," she said, pacing the distance between the bed and the doorway as she reasoned out her words. "I know I shouldn't. If anyone should not believe in love, it is me." She had to give a small, brittle laugh at herself for having been such a fool. "I know how hard it is to find love. You think you have it, you believe you have found someone you can trust, who will stand beside you and protect you and make you feel as if you finally have a place in this world where you belong — and then you find out you are wrong. People aren't to be trusted, and no one person can give anyone everything she thinks she needs. So I *didn't* believe in love, but then here you are in Sir James's office saying you are deliberately seeking someone you can't and won't and refuse to love, and that's when something so deep inside me that I didn't know it was there rose up and said, *You are wrong . . .* because love is important, Neal. When I think of my sons, I know it is all that ever matters."

"You loved Martin?"

His question took a moment to penetrate

her mind. She was thinking about this all-encompassing emotion called love . . . and he was asking about her late husband?

What's more, he was waiting for an answer.

Thea shook her head. "Of course I did —" That wasn't completely right either. "I thought I did," she amended. "Yes, I did at one time."

"What happened?"

"What do you mean, 'what happened?' " she challenged.

Neal shifted his weight. He wasn't as overzealous as he had been a few moments ago. "You left your family and everything you knew for him. So, what happened? I gathered you were not completely happy in your marriage. What changed your affections?"

She crossed her arms, wanting to refuse an answer, then deciding it made no difference if she was candid with Neal. After all, there had been a time when he'd known all of her confidences.

"Boyd was difficult," she said. The words sounded so simple, but there was a wealth of the unspoken in each of them. She slid her gaze toward the cold hearth, remembering, and feeling disloyal. "I loved him enough to defy everyone and elope. But I don't think I knew him. No, wait," she said correcting herself, "I don't think I *trusted* him."

"You can trust me."

She had to laugh at his conviction. "My lord, I will never trust another man. Now, if you please, leave my room." She started toward the door to open it. "I am tired. Worn thin. We can discuss this night on the morrow —"

He caught her arm, swung her around and kissed her. His embrace was commanding, and she had no choice but to kiss him back.

One minute she was rational and tired, and in the next, she was suddenly vital and alive. It was that simple and the decision that quick.

Their lips did fit together well. Her body warmed to his, became warm in the places where he was hard —

He was hard.

Thea could feel the length and heat of him exactly where it should be against her, and she was undone.

There had been a time when Thea had wanted Boyd's attentions, and a time when she'd avoided all contact with him. She understood her body's signals. Hers was not a prudish nature, although she had long ago made the decision to place her needs and wants far below those of her children.

However here and now, desire burst into life with a vehemence that was all encompassing.

What was wrong with letting herself enjoy this kiss? She'd been holding herself so tight, trying to be so strong. What harm could one kiss do?

And it felt good to at last let her body enjoy being in his arms. His body heat enfolded her. His strength held her.

The kiss deepened.

He sat on the bench, pulling her down onto his lap. Thea straddled his legs.

Were her nightclothes up around her bare thighs? She didn't care.

Did his hand caress her breast? Oh, yes. Yes, yes, *yes*.

She was perfectly happy. Blissfully happy. Hungrily happy. And when he broke the kiss to brush aside her hair to nibble his way to her ear, Thea thought she was going to shoot straight from his arms into heaven . . .

Neal was intoxicated. Thea was seductive, willing, aggressive.

She cupped his head with her hands, bent over him and kissed him with an abandon he had not known existed.

Dear God, he wanted her.

In truth, he'd wanted her all those years ago when they'd met by the stream. He'd fantasized about her, yearned to see her and cherished each moment they'd been together. But *this,* having her respond to his kisses, holding her in his arms, was better than any fantasy.

The pull, the draw, the need was a hundred times stronger than it had ever been with any other woman. Neal had had dalliances over the years, but the women had meant nothing to him and he'd lost interest. Yes, he was a man with a strong drive, yet while his brother had played with every female who'd placed herself in his path, Neal had been discreet, almost celibate.

But now all caution flew to the wind.

He tasted her ear, her cheek, her nose, her eyes. Her breasts were firm and hard in his palm. He reveled in the silky skin of her thigh, his hand following the curve of her hip, the indentation of her waist.

She was moist and hot and he could not have stopped unbuttoning his breeches even if his brother had come charging into the room with the whole host of the Horse Guard behind him. He had to be inside Thea. He *must* be inside her.

She moved against his hand, as impatient as he was. He tired of feeling her breast. He found the tight hard nipple with his mouth, licking, stroking her right through the fabric of her gown.

Her breath caught in her throat as she whimpered out of pleasure, and he wanted her all the more.

And then he was free of his fumbling with buttons and material. He was hard, ready, and charged by her moist heat.

With an almost animal need, Neal lifted her hips and brought her down on top of him. Her tightness surrounded him. Her heat almost was his undoing.

She stiffened, the action allowing him to go deeper.

"Neal," she said, her voice wavering.

He kissed her ear, found her lips. "It's all right," he murmured almost desperately. She couldn't stop now. *He* couldn't. "It's *so* right. So *good.*"

She nodded even as she opened to him.

This was Thea as he'd always dreamed. Sweetly giving, yet demanding in her own right. She began moving, rolling her body against his. He copied her movements, thrust deep, eased out, came for her again. It was a dance of lust and desire. A partnership.

Her clothes became an encumbrance. Although he was still fully clothed, he ached to have her naked in his arms. He tugged at her dressing gown, freed her of it and impatiently grabbed her nightdress at the neckline, all but ripping it off her.

Naked, Thea was perfection. Their movements were growing more frenzied. He never wanted to be apart from her, not ever. He buried his head in her breasts, both arms around her waist. Her arms were around his shoulders. She moved harder, faster.

And suddenly, she cried out.

He felt her quicken, her hands gripped his shoulders, her body tightened.

Neal held her fast. She was gasping, repeating his name, whispering words he could not have made out even if he'd had sense, which he did not.

Nothing had ever felt as good as being inside Thea. No woman had ever so completely overpowered him with desire. She was quicksilver and light. She was the stars, the moon, the sun. In this moment, she owned his entire being. He could not imagine himself without her and was loathe to ever let her go.

She was his. Completely.

And he made his claim by burying himself deeper than he'd thought possible and releasing his seed with a force that robbed him of breath.

Her legs encircled his hips. She leaned against him, her body spent, her heart pounding against her chest and matching the racing rhythm of his own.

Slowly, he noticed the coolness of the room, the way the lamp sent flickering shadows around them, their reflection in the mirror. Her straight arms rested on his shoulders, her hands loose and relaxed.

Neal nudged her head where it was snuggled in the crook of his neck. She turned to him and he found her lips. This kiss was even sweeter than the others — and only then did understanding dawn.

Of course their coupling would be unlike any other. There had always been a strong connection between them. His father had realized that. It had been the reason he'd ordered the sixteen-year-old Neal to stop seeing her and sent him to London. Because of her, he'd sat Neal down and told him of the curse —

The curse. How could he have forgotten it?

Neal pulled away from the kiss and came to his feet, almost dropping her to the floor. She caught herself in time and stood.

She gave him a sleepy, seductive smile, her gaze dropping to his spent sex, which was already starting to stir at the sight of her warm, compliant, well-used body.

Dear God, he could have a go at her again. Only this time, he wanted to be naked as well. He could make love to her every hour of every day and still want her more.

Her lips were full and red from his kisses. Her skin radiated a healthy, rosy glow. Her usually properly styled hair was wildly tossed.

There was no other woman on the face of this earth more beautiful to him — and then he realized that he was in danger of falling in *love.*

Neal backed away from her, buttoning his breeches.

Dear God, what had he done?

She took a step toward him and he put up a hand. He tried to keep his mind blank, to literally freeze her out of it.

He'd refrained from chasing women not because he'd been circumspect but because he'd compared all of them to Thea. She was the ideal, the epitome . . . and he'd fallen in love with her without being conscious of it. Maybe he'd always loved her.

He stabbed his fingers through his hair. "Thea," he started but then stopped. What was he going to say? What *could* he say? He'd just rogered her lustily. She was his. She had nowhere to go, and that was his fault as well.

Her lips curved into a satisfied smile. She slid her arms around his waist. His breeches grew tight. "What may I do for you, my lord?" she murmured in a voice so sensual that he had to kiss her —

Neal dived away from her kiss. This was not right. He couldn't marry Thea.

He must. He was honor bound to do so.

He began backing toward the door. She started to follow him. He moved faster. "Tomorrow, I'll procure the special license — tomorrow," he said. "We'd best marry posthaste."

"Where are you going?" she asked, frowning as if she hadn't heard a word he'd said.

"To my bed. And you need to go to your bed."

Her mouth made a moue of disappointment, but she obeyed and backed up. He almost sighed with relief, until she lay on the edge of her bed, curling her lovely, naked body in the most beguiling way possible. She smiled, an invitation. "Are you certain you don't want to stay?"

His breeches would not be able to hold him back. The buttons would pop off in a minute. Neal clutched the door handle as if it was a lifeline.

"It's best I leave," he defended himself,

yet he wanted nothing more than to tear off his clothes and join her. Then again, what if all the other guests waited outside the door? He didn't want them to tear apart her reputation more than they already would.

"Tomorrow." The word was starting to sound weak to his own ears.

He opened the door and escaped into the hallway. Only then could he breathe again. He struggled a moment with his own weakness.

Neal had to think. He couldn't marry Thea. His father had been right. If he married Thea, he would love her more.

And it wasn't just the intimacy between them that he loved. He could talk to her and she listened to him. She was interested in what he thought and how he felt. And there was trust between them.

Now he understood the danger of the Siren. Thea had seduced him. His senses were still full of her. He faced her door, uncertain if he had the courage to leave here and return to his room. All he wanted to do was go back to her. He *needed* her.

Just as Neal started to reach for the door handle, Mirabel's voice spoke behind him.

"It's about time you came out of there," she said.

Startled, Neal turned. He'd been so lost

in his own thoughts that he'd barely registered his surroundings. Mirabel stood, a tall, regal figure in the hall's candlelight. The servant usually stationed at the head of the stairs was gone. She must have dismissed him.

"Thea and I had matters to discuss," he said, sounding to his own ears like a schoolboy who had been caught filching a sweet.

Mirabel leaned close to him. "You will marry her."

"Of course." He had no choice.

A smile tightened her face. "Good . . . because my other guests will be leaving at dawn's first light. This story will be all over London by dinner. Thea must be protected."

"My intentions are honorable."

"You *will* marry her?" she repeated.

He thought of the curse, thought of Thea having to face the biddies if he did not do what was right . . . thought of her sons. "Absolutely. I told her I would dispatch a messenger on the morrow for a special license."

Mirabel sank into a deep curtsey, taking hold of his hand. "My lord, you are a godsend. Thank you."

"I'm doing what is right."

"I don't care why you are doing it," Mirabel confessed happily. "Of course, after the noise the two of you were making, well, I believe you have good reason to marry Mrs. Martin. But most of all, she is the best person in the world. My one true friend. See you take good care of her."

"I shall."

"Good night, my lord," she said, turning and walking down the hall. "May you have sweet dreams."

Neal nodded. Alone again, he drew a deep breath and walked to his room, but it was a long time before he fell asleep. And when he did, he had the dream. It was filled with images of him making love to Thea, but in the background was a crone's wicked laughter. He could see her shadow, knew she watched them. The sound was hideous, and he woke in a sweat, fearing it was true. Had the witch been in the room with him and Thea?

Throwing his legs over the side of his bed, Neal realized he was breathing as if he'd run hard . . . or had been making love. He was covered in sweat, and the crone's wild laughter still rang in his ears.

He looked in each corner. He was alone, yet he had the uneasy suspicion there was someone there. He could almost sense her breathing, watching, waiting.

But she wasn't real. He knew that.

She'd been in his dreams before. He'd forgotten, but the evilness in the sound of her laughter had brought it all back to him. He'd dreamed of her in his youth, during that summer when he'd met Thea by the stream.

He remembered how his father had talked to him about the curse. He hadn't known his father had returned to Morrisey Meadows from London until he'd been called to the library. His father had still been in his traveling clothes.

His father had heard of Neal's clandestine meetings with Thea and had traveled with all haste to set down the rule that it had to stop . . . and then he'd told Neal about the curse.

Neal could recall every detail of that moment. The intimate glow of the candle that had created a ring of light around them in the dark, the heat of the wax, and the smell of leather and book bindings in his father's library mixed with that of horses and the dust of the road, the taste of the brandy his father had given him.

But Neal had forgotten until now that his father had asked if he'd had dreams that had included a witch's laughter. His father's reaction had been strong and decisive when

Neal had answered that, yes, he'd had strange, jumbled dreams lately that he could not remember anything of — save the maniacal laughter. It had sounded like the ravings of a mind gone mad.

His father had ordered Neal to pack. They would leave at first light for London, and his father had made him promise to never speak of Thea again.

His father, a man he'd idolized and yet had barely known.

How could Neal have forgotten their conversation about the dream?

And why did he remember it now?

CHAPTER ELEVEN

Thea woke the next morning feeling more relaxed and at peace with the world than she had been in years. She stretched, and immediately muscles she'd not used in a long time let her know they were still alive.

Alive, yes, that was what she felt.

She blushed, remembering how wanton she'd been with Neal. He'd tapped into long-suppressed desires, and she was glad he had.

Thea bound out of bed, perfectly comfortable with her nakedness. Sunlight poured through the window. She'd slept late, something she rarely did.

Her torn nightdress was still on the floor. She snatched it up and hugged it to her, reliving the memory of Neal ripping it off her body. The image sent her blood pounding through her veins. She couldn't wait to see him again.

She quickly saw to her toilette, then

crossed to the wardrobe to choose what she would wear. It wasn't a difficult decision. Her wardrobe wasn't that extensive. She chose the blue day dress she wore most often — however today was different. She was dressing for Lyon. The blue brought out the color in her eyes. Once, the butcher she'd patronized had told her that she looked fetching in it, and that was how she wanted Neal to see her — fetching. Such as perhaps he would *fetch* her back up the stairs to the bedroom.

She laughed at her own silliness. But she also wasn't as strict when styling her hair. She loosened her usually tight knot and allowed wisps to curl around her ears.

Her ears. They still tingled with the sensation of his kissing them.

But what made her happiest was that she had her friend Neal back in her life. He was her friend *and* her lover. What could be better?

And he *wanted* to marry her. After the enthusiasm with which they'd made love, she had no doubt of his desire. The man was a beast, and she practically purred her contentment.

When they had been discovered in each other's arms by the Montvales and their like, she had refused him because she'd hated the idea of his hand being forced. However, his kisses had convinced her that he, a man who could have any woman in London he desired, was indeed choosing her.

The miracle of it threatened to overwhelm her, especially since her sons would be excited over the news she had married Neal. She had no doubt how they would feel about having Neal as their stepfather. There would be no more worries about food or schooling, and they would learn to ride real horses instead of playing with wooden ones. Neal would not only restore their heritage and birthrights to them but he would also serve as a prime example of what a true gentleman was.

She met Mirabel out in the hallway. They didn't have to do anything but fall into each other's arms with sisterly hugs.

"I'm so pleased for you," Mirabel said. "I saw him last night after he left your room. He was a happy man."

Thea laughed, almost giddy with the joy she was feeling. "I am a lucky woman."

"I should say so. Every woman in London will be looking daggers of envy at you." Mirabel stepped back, smiling. "Osgood informed me his lordship sent a messenger to the bishop at first light. My dear, you could be married before this day is done."

And she would be Neal's. "I am humbled by my good fortune. I just wish my sons could be here —"

"Don't wait for them, Thea. Marry Lyon. Osgood has also told me everyone else packed up and left."

"Without waiting to say anything to you?"

"Of course," Mirabel said. "They eat my food, guzzle a good portion of Palmer's wine cellar, and then, poof, they are gone as if I didn't exist. That's the way their type is. And to think I was rather pleased they were favoring me with their presence."

Thea shook her head. "I'm so sorry, Mirabel. I would not have anything I did reflect back on you. I've destroyed your standing in society."

"Oh, no, there you are wrong," Mirabel declared, slipping her arm in Thea's. "I've been thinking about it, and let us be honest: many toady to Mrs. Pomfrey and Lady Montvale, but few admire them. We are all more intimidated by them than anything else. But this whole affair has placed me at the exact opposite of them. I will support my friend," she said, giving Thea's shoulder a squeeze, "regardless of what they say. And watch, I shall be acclaimed for it. The star of my popularity shall rise higher than it would ever have with their endorsement. People will befriend me just to hear my side of the story. I'm certain they've made a good number of enemies with their high-handed, selfish ways, and I shall richly benefit."

"I'm still sorry for all of the difficulty I've caused you," Thea said.

"I haven't had such a good time in years, my Lady Lyon."

Thea hadn't even thought that she would gain a title. Matters had advanced so rapidly that the consequences of her marriage, such as a title and a station of *her own* in society, hadn't even entered her mind yet. She'd grown up a duke's daughter but had learned how little that meant in the world when one was cut off from one's family. However, Lady Lyon would be her title alone, and a fine one it was.

All this good fortune was overwhelming.

What she was thinking must have shown on her face, because Mirabel sympathized. "Let's go downstairs and find you a strong cup of tea."

"That sounds like exactly what I need."

In the dining room they came upon Sir James finishing his breakfast. He was dressed for travel.

"Sir James, I'm glad you are still here,"

Mirabel said in greeting.

"I regret to say I shall be leaving." He cast a sheepish glance in Thea's direction. "I pray you don't think ill of me, Lady Palmer."

"Miss Pomfrey is a fortunate woman," Mirabel said.

"Yes, I hope she believes that, although her parents will need a touch more convincing to appreciate my suit for their daughter's hand. I came here expecting to help Lyon find a wife and instead found love for myself. Funny how it all works, eh? An old bachelor like me finally being brought to heel?" He cast another sheepish glance toward Thea before saying to Mirabel, "I regret I can't tarry here. Your hospitality and your late husband's wine cellar have been delightful. However, if I am to please the people whose daughter I hope to marry, I must leave. You know Mrs. Pomfrey is a bit of a Tartar."

"I understand, Sir James," Mirabel said.

He started toward the door but stopped in front of Thea. "Please take care of my friend Lyon. His is a troubled soul."

"I shall endeavor to do so," she responded, placing her hand in his.

"It won't be smooth going," he predicted and then, with a bow, left the room.

Thea frowned, not pleased to have her joy

in the day spoiled by Sir James's dire prediction.

Mirabel took her by the elbow and steered her toward the buffet. "He must be referring to the carryings-on of the Mmes. Pomfreys and Lady Montvales of the world. Pay him no mind. Lyon can handle the gossips, and so can you. Come, let us eat."

But Thea held back. "Where is Lyon?" she asked.

"He could still be abed," Mirabel answered, moving toward the sideboard. "Do you care for bacon?"

Thea didn't answer but walked out into the hall. Osgood was in the front hall, having seen Sir James on his way. She approached him. "Have you seen Lord Lyon?"

"Yes, ma'am. He went riding early this morning."

"Thank you," she murmured, turning back to the dining room. It was a beautiful day, and it would not have been out of character for Neal to want to take advantage of the weather and ride.

Still, she had hoped he would be as anxious to see her as she was him.

Thea tried to put any disquieting thoughts from her mind. Mirabel waited by the dining room door, her half-filled plate in her hand. Thea forced a smile and came to join

247

her, but she didn't have much of an appetite for food. Her stomach was unsettled by doubt.

After breakfast, Thea attempted to focus on a book and some correspondence. Time passed slowly.

In the afternoon, a rider came. It was the servant Neal had sent to arrange for the special license. He had been successful in his mission and had the license signed by the bishop . . . but there was no sign of Neal.

Mirabel kept up a running dialogue, mostly with herself, since Thea grew more introspective as the afternoon wore on, but even she was starting to worry.

"He wouldn't leave you," Mirabel burst out at one point after a half hour of silence between them. "Lyon is more of a man than that. He's not a jilt."

Thea looked up from the book she'd been staring at without comprehending any of the words. "He has before."

"When?" Mirabel demanded.

"Years ago. When we first met. We were friends for weeks and growing closer. We met at this clearing by a stream that bordered our two properties. Then one day, he stopped coming. No note, no anything. Seeing him in Sir James's office was the first time our paths crossed in years."

"Were you in love back in those days?"

Mirabel's question gave Thea pause. Had she been in love with him? Certainly she'd been deeply hurt when he'd left without a word.

"No," Thea said. "We were children, really. Very young, very protected. Our friendship was innocent. We felt free to speak our minds to each other."

"Sometimes that is how the best relationships start," Mirabel said. She set aside her needlework and leaned forward, reaching out to place a hand on Thea's arm. "When I first heard you were to find a wife for Lyon, I thought you should be that wife out of a strictly practical sense. Thea, you are well bred, intelligent, lovely — what man wouldn't want you?"

"Spoken like a true friend," Thea murmured.

"But when I saw you here together over the past few days, there is something between the two of you. His gaze would drift toward you when he didn't think anyone would notice, and he always stood so that he could keep his eye on you. Thea, he didn't have to announce he was marrying you last night —"

"He was worried for my reputation."

Mirabel dismissed the suggestion away

with her hand as she sat up. "Explanations could have been offered, and those women would have sewed their lips shut over what they'd seen if he had chosen one of their daughters. Please listen to what I'm saying. There is an attraction between you and Lyon, one that I think may be quite rare. People wax on about love and how they would spend lifetimes looking for 'the one,' but in truth most of us never do. We settle. We accept because, perhaps, we give up the dream of one special person just for us." She paused, pressing her lips together before confessing, "Palmer was that for me. He was a far better man than I deserved. He loved more than I could ever love him — until I lost him. Thea, sometimes life works in our favor. Fate may be giving the two of you a second chance."

Thea shook her head. "Fate? Some supernatural force, or being? I don't believe that things beyond our control influence our lives. It may be just happenstance that my path crossed with Lyon's. Or it might be that London is really not that big a world. Sooner or later we would meet because that is reality."

Mirabel snorted her discontent. "You are the most unromantic creature ever."

"If you are asking me to believe in fantasy,

well, yes, you may be right."

"Then what do you believe in?"

"I believe in common sense and being reasonable. We live in modern times. I ran away once over love . . . and it turned out to not be what I'd been led to believe because of unfounded romantic notions —"

The front door opened. Osgood could be heard greeting someone. It was Neal. *He'd returned.*

A hard knot formed in Thea's stomach. She wasn't certain whether she was glad he'd come back or frightfully angry that he had been gone so long without explanation.

A beat later, Neal appeared at the door. He was in riding clothes, buff breeches, a jacket of the deepest blue wool, and spurs on his boots. His neckcloth was not knotted but tied in a hasty, devil-may-care manner.

Thea didn't speak. She couldn't. Any words would give away her secret fear that he'd abandoned her again.

"Why, Lord Lyon," Mirabel said brightly, "you appear to have enjoyed an extensive ride."

He barely acknowledged her words with a nod, his gaze intent on Thea. "I need to return to London," he said.

Thea felt her heart harden. He was going to jilt her.

In her continued silence, he said, "We need to marry tomorrow morning. I have arranged for a Reverend Wells from the local parish to officiate. Osgood tells me the license has already been delivered."

Tomorrow morning? "What of my sons?" Thea heard herself say. "Should they not hear of us wedding before we do so? I should have written a note to them, but I didn't."

"Tomorrow, Thea. We must wed as soon as possible," he repeated.

She rose from her chair. "My lord, are you all right?"

"I am." His gaze shifted away from her when he spoke.

"Perhaps —," she started, thinking to argue him out of this undue haste when suddenly he walked the space of floor between then in four strides, took her by the arms and kissed her.

Thea wasn't expecting a kiss, and it wasn't a kiss that said he liked her or he was angry. No, this kiss was a plea for understanding, of needing her trust.

Doubts dissolved when he kissed her this way. She knew enough of marriage to know a kiss was often the best form of communication. She slid her arms around his neck, eager to let him know she cared, that she had worried.

He smelled of horses, fresh air, and a warm, almost spicy scent that was all his own. His body was solid and strong.

She felt his tongue brush hers, followed it with her own because it felt exactly *right*. They breathed the same air, had the same needs, were both alone and confused, and, yes, a little afraid.

Neal ended the kiss before she was ready to let go. His arms slid down to her waist. He held her, but shadows lingered in his eyes. "We will marry tomorrow. If I could, I would wed you this night."

She wanted to banish her doubts. She tried to keep her voice light as she said, "Why do I sense you are in danger of losing courage, my lord?"

"I'm here, Thea. I'm here for you." He stepped away, taking her hand and placing a kiss on her fingers.

This wasn't what Thea wanted to hear. It wasn't enough. But before she could collect the courage to speak, he turned to Mirabel. "I hope this isn't upsetting your plans for this evening, my lady?"

Mirabel had been watching them kiss, one hand up to her chest and a look of wonder on her face. "Upsetting? My lord, I am honored to have you marry my wonderful friend here under my roof."

"I must change," he said, backing away and holding his hands out to show the damage of hours of riding. Hours he'd probably spent weighing whether or not he would go through with their marriage.

Pride warred with common sense inside Thea. *He'd come back.*

Yes, she wanted him.

There was a connection between them, and she could not let it go.

But she also wanted something *more.*

He left the room, taking her silence as assent. Mirabel practically danced up to her. "I'm so excited. Aren't you excited?"

"I'm confused. He doesn't seem happy."

"He seems happy enough," Mirabel said gaily. She took Thea by the shoulders and pointed her in the direction of the door. "Come, we don't have long to make you into the prefect bride. Let us go see what is in my closet." She started forward, but Thea resisted.

"This is too quick, Mirabel."

Her friend sighed her frustration. "Is this coming from a woman who had the audacity to elope?"

"And suffered a bad marriage for it."

"Do you believe *this* will be a bad marriage?"

"No, I love him —" Thea broke off, startled by the words that had just flowed easily from her lips.

She turned, considered her words, her feelings . . .

Love was a complicated thing. And what she felt for Neal was different from what she'd felt for her husband. She'd thought she'd loved Boyd, but it had been a passionate, impulsive thing.

Her passion, her lust for Neal was real, stronger even than what her younger self had felt for her husband. But it also went beyond the physical.

She respected Neal. Admired him. Even thought him the most worthy of gentlemen in her acquaintance, and she realized that, unawares, she'd held him as a standard against whom she'd held up every male she'd known since, including Boyd. Unfortunately time and Boyd's disappointments and vices had not weathered well during their short marriage. She'd lost her respect for Boyd, and love couldn't continue or grow without it.

Thea didn't believe she could ever lose her respect for Neal.

"I love him," she repeated, sampling the statement in her own mind and discovering it was true. "I. Love. Him."

Mirabel dropped her voice to a conspiratorial whisper. "Anyone with half a brain could see you did. Especially after last night."

Heat rushed to Thea's cheeks. Mirabel laughed and tugged on her arm, but still Thea resisted.

"He doesn't love me. He won't," Thea said. "All because of this curse. He'll be like he is right now. For the duration of our marriage."

"As long as he can be as he was in your bedroom last night, you, my dear, will not have any worries."

"But what if —"

"*No, Thea,* no more questions. So he sees something you don't —"

"You don't find that mad, or at the least odd?"

Mirabel gave her a look as old as time. "Most of us have some madness in us. We believe what we believe."

"I'm not like that —," Thea started to protest.

"No, you are just expecting love to betray you. You had a bad marriage to a man who turned out not to be what you thought he was. But at some point, Thea, you must trust someone. And remember, one rarely has the opportunity to follow one's heart.

Follow your heart. Grab on to this with both hands, my friend."

"My heart betrayed me once before," Thea said.

"Did it? Or were you just not listening to what it was really saying before you made your choice? You are very headstrong, Thea. Be careful you aren't being foolishly independent." Mirabel took a step toward the door. "Furthermore, you have your sons to think of now."

Her sons. Their lives would be so much better under Lyon's protection — and Mirabel knew it.

Thea began following Mirabel to the door. "Do you believe I can defeat this curse he believes in?" she asked.

"My dear, I believe love can do anything."

CHAPTER TWELVE

Love could do anything.

Mirabel's declaration challenged Thea. It reverberated in her mind as she dressed and prepared to wed Neal.

The ceremony took place in an ancient chapel on the abbey's estate as close to noon as possible. The Reverend Mr. Wells could not arrive sooner.

Thea had spent the night in her bed alone. She had not known where Neal had been. After insisting that they marry with all haste, he'd disappeared up to his room. Of course, Mirabel had kept Thea so busy with arrangements for the ceremony that she'd not had time to worry and had fallen asleep, exhausted — but at peace with the decision.

The chapel had been rebuilt centuries before with small windows, so that it could be dark and confining, especially on an overcast morning such as this one. Mirabel had seen to it that lit candles lined the stone altar and filled the tables along the walls, so that the room glowed with warm, flickering light.

Theirs was a small gathering. Mirabel and her servants served as witnesses.

Neal looked inordinately handsome in black formal dress.

Thea wore a gown of the finest muslin in a pale shade of yellow that she had borrowed from Mirabel's closet. Her hair had been fashioned on top of her head instead of her customary knot at the base of her neck. Mirabel had wanted to loan Thea her diamond pins. Thea had politely refused and instead had fashioned a tiara of roses from the bush by the estate's gardens.

Now, as she stood before Reverend Wells, a rather portly man with tufts of hair over his ears, spectacles on his nose, and a strong sense of how important this particular marriage would be in London, Thea pledged her troth to Neal. She spoke the words of the Book of Common Prayer, repeating after Reverend Wells, but the whole time Neal did not look at her.

His stubbornness angered her. He made his vows but did so with the joy of a man facing the gallows. When Mr. Wells announced they were man and wife and could seal their vows with a kiss, Neal barely let his lips touch hers.

And then they were in the dining room, just the reverend, Mirabel, and themselves for the wedding meal.

Neal seemed to relax. He was charming, thoughtful, entertaining, but distant to Thea.

At last she could take his bewildering behavior no longer.

"Reverend Wells, does the church still perform exorcisms?" she asked.

Now she had Lyon's attention.

The good reverend apparently dearly adored having his opinion requested on ecclesiastical matters. He pushed up his spectacles in a scholarly fashion and launched into his esteemed opinion. "The church has a rite, but it is not called upon often. I have not been a party to any, and I daresay the bishop hasn't either, although the devil is amongst us."

For a second, the air in the room seemed to shift as if clouds had covered the sun, blocking its rays from the window before drifting away . . . except this day was not a sunny day.

Or was she being unusually fanciful? "How would one remove the devil?" Thea pressed on.

"Is this really a good conversation for a wedding feast?" Lyon said quietly.

"Of course it is, my lord," Thea answered. Superstition aside, she had his attention now, and she was going to keep it. "Please, Reverend, continue."

The clergyman removed his glasses and rubbed his nose before saying, "Historically church leaders have wanted us to believe the devil is a supernatural being. Something separate and apart from us. However, I hold to the more modern understanding that the devil is really the evil inside all of us. We make our own 'devil.' Take Bonaparte. He has been the mastermind behind a monstrous evil that has toppled governments and cost countless lives. Does that make him a devil? Only God knows. But in my humble opinion, I believe him to be one."

Thea was not interested in Napoleon. "What of curses, Mr. Wells. Can the church remove curses?"

His response was to burst out in laughter. "Curses? Why would we remove curses? The idea of a curse is an antiquated notion. It is the device of the uneducated mind. We now know someone can't put an evil eye out on another person with just a few words of mumbo jumbo. So there is no need of the church to provide protection. Tell me, are you afraid of curses, Lady Lyon?"

Thea shrugged. "I am merely curious."
Mirabel had a very pained expression on
her face. She was not pleased with Thea's
line of questions. Thea dared not look to
Neal, but she hoped she had made her
point.

Mirabel cleared her throat and changed
the topic. "Would you like more port, Reverend?"

"Oh, no, I must be on my way. Thank you
for your hospitality, Lady Palmer." He rose
from the table, Neal rising with him. "And
my heartiest congratulations to both you
and your lady, Lord Lyon. It has been an
honor."

"Thank you," Neal said. "Let me see you
to the door."

The second the men left the room, Mirabel waved the servants from the room before
leaning across the table. "Are you mad?"
she demanded of Thea.

"No, determined."

"This is your wedding night, and if you
want to spend it battling your husband, you
are a fool."

"I'm making a point."

"A point that will make your husband look
like a fool! Oh, that is so much better."

"Mirabel —," Thea started, ready to

explain herself, but then Neal appeared at the doorway.

He did not look pleased.

"— that was a delicious meal," Thea heard herself finish lamely. "The quail was quite succulent."

"I'm glad you enjoyed it," Mirabel responded, her jaw tight. She was truly displeased with Thea. She rose. "I believe the time has come for me to excuse myself. Many happinesses to you both." She started for the door but paused in front of Neal. "And, Lyon, please be good to my friend. She's headstrong and foolish but a wonderful woman. She'll make you a good wife once you find your way past all the armor she wears to protect her emotions."

Mirabel directed that last comment to Thea, and with those words, she left the room.

Thea didn't think she'd ever been so insulted. She sat, her gaze in front of her, waiting for Lyon to chime in with his unhappiness with her as well.

He walked into the room, his footsteps barely a sound on the carpet, but she could feel him draw close.

Lyon took the chair next to hers, turning it out so that he could sit seeing her face. He didn't speak. Not immediately.

Osgood came by the door to check on the room, saw them, and beat a hasty retreat. Neither Thea nor Lyon moved.

She was determined to let him be the first to speak. Perhaps bringing up exorcisms and curses at the table had not been wifely, but Neal needed to hear someone else's opinion besides her own.

The minutes stretched long between them, and then, finally, she could take it no longer.

"You are too intelligent to let your life be ruled by superstition," she announced.

He regarded her with a solemn face. Even angry with him, she couldn't help but marvel at how handsome he was. He had a sensual mouth, a lean, strong jaw. They were so close that she could see the line of his whiskers and smell the scent of sandalwood off his skin.

"I shouldn't have broached the topic," Thea said.

He shook his head, gave a small shrug.

"I was worried when you were gone all day."

"I had to think."

Here was the conversation she wanted, and yet she was afraid of it as well. "What did you decide? That you *must* marry me?" She heard bitterness in her voice.

He reached out and ran his fingers along the length of her arm. Where he touched, her skin tightened with expectation. "I thought that you may be right. Perhaps I shouldn't live my life afraid of a curse." He raised his gaze to meet hers.

Her heart leaped at his words. "I wasn't mocking you with my questions of Reverend Wells," she said. "I would never do that, Neal." *I love you.*

"Don't care deeply for me, Thea," he said, as if she'd spoken aloud. "Protect yourself."

"Does that mean you will walk out on me again?" she asked, a knot forming in her throat. "Or is this curse — ?"

She stopped, struck by a sudden realization. "Wait," she said before adding thoughtfully, "the curse no longer matters. Not to me." She met his eye, her mind so clear that it startled her. "All I want to do is love you."

There, she'd said it.

A second ago, such a declaration had been impossible to make, and yet here she'd spoken straight from her heart. No armor; just love.

Her words hovered in the air between them. She could picture them, bright and shining and true. A joy, a freedom she'd not known existed, filled her.

"I love you," she repeated. "I think I've

always loved you, even when I didn't realize I loved you. You caution me against feeling deeply for you, but it is too late, Neal. I believe you are the finest man of my acquaintance. While others are wrapped in their petty concerns of status and self-importance, you have tried to do what is right."

"I'm as petty as the next man."

She shook her head, almost overcome with this insight, this depth, this *honesty* of her feelings. "No, you truly are special, and if it is a curse that has caused you to think of your legacy, well, so be it. All I want to do is love you. I want a life with you and with my sons. I am all for building a fortress around us to keep away evil spirits and witches and trolls, whatever threatens us. But the one thing I don't want to avoid is love. I tried that, Neal. For the last five years of my life, I've run from love, but not any longer. I love you."

"Thea —," he started as if to defend himself *once again,* but she stopped his words by placing her fingers over his lips.

"It's too late for me to protect myself. Can't you hear the conviction in my voice? I love you, Neal, in a way I could never feel for any other. And it is all right if you wish to pretend you cannot love, but I know differently. No matter how hard you try to put distance between us, I will always be here for you, Neal. I will not turn away and I will not run. I don't believe in your curse, but I *do* believe in *you.* Whatever happens, whatever may come our way, I shall not leave your side."

"You do not know what you say, Thea."

"I know exactly what I'm saying, and I speak without fear and without doubt. You can't protect me from love, Neal, because I already love you. I started loving you all those summers ago. But now we are older. Wiser. And I still love you with that pure innocence and trust I gave you years ago. I didn't even see it back then, but this afternoon, in this moment, I realized how much you mean to me — and this time, you'd best never leave me. Do you understand, Neal? I go where you go."

"I don't deserve you, Thea. In time, you may come to hate this marriage."

"No, I won't ever. And don't fear making me a widow again, Neal. One thing I've learned is that we have only the here and now. It is all that matters. The rest is speculation and doubt and fear. But *this* day, this minute is real."

She then took his face in both hands and

kissed him with all the generosity in her spirit.

Like flame to kindling, he responded, his arms coming around her. What was between them was more than mere sex, and it had been from those days long ago.

He needed her.

She needed him.

Neal suddenly swept her up in his arms. He carried her out the door, up the stairs, and across the threshold of his bedroom.

There, in the privacy of his chambers, they began undressing each other.

The night before, they had been so eager that there had been no time for exploration. Neal made up for it now. He kissed her neck, her shoulder, her collarbone — all the while unlacing her dress and pulling it down over her shoulders.

Roses falling from her hair, Thea tilted her head back with a soft, happy sigh.

She tugged at the waist of his breeches, pulling his shirt out and then sliding her hands under his jacket. She adored the feel of his body. He was all hard planes and muscle. Her fingers danced along his rib cage before she slid his jacket off, letting it fall to the floor. She kissed his neck, nuzzling him and delighting in the texture of his skin and the scrappiness of his whiskers.

She tickled him with the tip of her tongue and he laughed, the sound startling her enough to pull back.

"What is it?" he said.

He was so handsome in the evening light. So strong and masculine. "The last time I heard you laugh was years ago."

"I want to change that, Thea. Riding yesterday, I realized I've given up too much of life."

His confession was music to her ears. "And you came back for me."

Neal nodded. "I couldn't stay away from you. Perhaps I should never have left you."

"We were both too young."

"Your feelings back then weren't as strong as mine."

His tone was light, but his claim gave her pause. His feelings had been deeper than hers. "Does the past matter, if it leads us to right here?"

His answer was to kiss her. He was already aroused.

So was she.

And they knew the answer.

In fact, Thea didn't think she'd ever wanted a man the way she wanted this one.

They didn't waste time with removing the rest of their clothing. Neal had loosened her dress enough that it fell in a heap at her feet. She stood before him in nothing more than her petticoat and stockings. She slipped out of her shoes, kicking them out of the way.

He mimicked her, kicking his off as well. She liked this new lightheartedness around him. This was the way it should be between a couple — not recriminations and nitpicking, the way things had quickly become between her and Boyd. In fact, she didn't think they'd ever laughed together. Everything had been so troubled right from the start.

She wasn't going to make that mistake with Neal.

Thea gave him a small push onto his bed's cream counterpane. He reached for her as he fell, and she landed on top of him. Neal rolled them both over so he was on top.

"Finally," he murmured. "I have you where I want you."

His shirt was of the finest lawn and felt smooth against her skin. His hair curled around her fingers. "I pray you never let me go —"

"I won't."

She searched his eyes. The shadows were gone. In their place, she saw love. He might have been afraid to use the words, but he loved her. He had always loved her, even before she had thought of loving him.

Thea kissed him, arching her body against his, then slowly relaxed, moving her hips against his. She liked the feeling of his weight upon her. She craved the texture and smell of his skin, the warmth of his body.

They wasted no time removing the last of their clothing. There were few words between them. They were not needed.

Neal raised over her. Thea ran her hands up his strong arms, over his shoulders and down his back as he slid himself deep within her.

Thea gasped at the glory of his body filling hers. She wasn't the only one caught up in this moment. Neal leaned over her. "This is good. So good."

She could have agreed — if she'd been able to speak, and then he robbed her of all conscious thought when he began moving.

There was nothing new to the mating of a man and a woman. Thea was no virgin, yet he made her feel as if this *was* the first time.

Their bodies were meant for each other. Instinctively, she knew what pleased him. He seemed aware of exactly what she wanted. She'd never made love with such intensity, such passion.

Any barriers still left between them were being destroyed through their desire.

Neal's breathing quickened. His movements took on purpose. She lifted her hips, wanting all of him.

White-hot need had driven their coupling the night before. It now gave way to something deeper, finer. A spiral of sensation began forming inside Thea, winding tighter and tighter until she didn't think she could breathe, let alone think —

The intensity of her release astonished her. It was as if she'd been moving toward a precipice and, having reached it, let herself hold for one heated beat before falling into bliss. Wave after wondrous wave of completion, of satisfaction, caught her up and wouldn't let her go.

Neal experienced the same. He cried her name. *Her* name. Then she experienced his release. She could feel it in the innermost of her being. He filled her in a way she'd not known before. Her body was his vessel, and as they were both caught up, together, in the magic of this moment, she at last realized what it meant to be "one" with another.

One. Together. For always.

Tears came to her eyes. She closed them and held him tight as slowly he let himself lay upon her. Thea hugged him with all of her strength, never wanting to let him go.

It was a long time before either of them could speak. Neal moved first, just as she started to register the cooling of her body.

He rolled over, carrying her with him. Reaching for the counterpane, he flipped it over their bodies. For a long moment, they stared into each other's eyes. This was what contentment felt like, she realized. In this moment, she wanted nothing but this man.

She pressed a kiss at the corner of his mouth. He smiled beneath her lips. "Are you happy?" she whispered.

"I am."

His eyes were closed. She decided to kiss them as well. "I am too."

She snuggled into the crook of his arm and fell asleep, only to be waked a few hours later to him making love to her. And so they spent the rest of the day into the night.

Thea even woke him up the hour before dawn. She still hadn't had enough of him. She nibbled and teased until he brought her down on top of him.

They fell asleep again, and she'd never known such peacefulness. . . .

She didn't know she was dreaming. The fire seemed real. Thea could swear she felt the heat of it. Sweat dripped from her body, and the hairs on her head and arms literally sizzled.

And there were mirrors. It was as if she was trapped in a house where every wall was a mirror; instead of one reflection of her melting in the heat, there were dozens. Instead of one fire, she was surrounded by them.

Where were her sons? Where was Lyon?

Were they trapped in this hell with her as well? She had to find them. She rushed in one direction. The flames grew higher, hotter. Her path blocked, she turned in a new direction only to find herself once again trapped.

And then she heard the laughter. Someone knew she was here. Someone had trapped her. She shouted for help. She shook her fist and challenged her captor, afraid she could not last much longer.

The laughter didn't stop. It continued even as her dress caught on fire, even as the flames climbed her body. The laughter did not stop —

Neal shook Thea awake. She'd been moaning, as if she'd been in great pain. When her eyes opened, they were glassy and full of fear. She didn't recognize him at first, and then she released a huge sigh.

"It was terrible," she said.

"What was?" he asked, already fearing her answer.

"My dream." Thea struggled out of the

covers, which her thrashing had tangled around her. She pushed her hair back from her face and frowned, as if still not certain she'd had a dream. "It seemed so real."

"What was it about?" he said, sitting back against the tufted headboard and pulling her into his arms.

She rested her head on his chest. "I don't remember." She tilted her face up to his. "Isn't that strange? I know it was vivid and frightening, but I don't remember . . . except for the laughter. Someone was laughing, and it wasn't a joyful sound. It was more triumphant." A shiver went through her, and she snuggled against him with a soft sigh. "I'm so glad you are here. I hate bad dreams."

"I hate them as well," Neal said, brushing her hair with his lips and keeping his voice calm.

"Your heart is beating fast," she murmured. She placed a palm upon his chest. "It's as if you have the fright and not myself." She pulled his arm around her and fell asleep.

But sleep didn't overtake Neal. He held her in his arms. In a very short time, she had become the most precious thing to him. He must protect her.

But she'd had the dream.
She'd had the dream.

CHAPTER THIRTEEN

Neal and Thea left for London late the afternoon the day after their marriage. Both of them were anxious to see the boys.

"Do you think the boys will be upset that we married?" Neal asked as they neared the city.

"I believe they will be very happy," Thea said. "It has been a long time since they have had a male figure in their lives."

"I don't want them to think I am going to take over their father's place."

Thea almost laughed, but she stifled it.

"What is it?" Neal asked.

"They barely knew their father," she confessed. She turned to face him. "Boyd and I spent most of our marriage apart."

"Go on," Neal said. "I admit I was curious, but I considered your marriage a private matter."

"Don't mistake me, Neal, I had strong feelings for him when I married him, or as strong as I could have for anyone at my age." She shook her head. "I was also very foolish, which many people pointed out to me after I ran away. Boyd was intelligent and handsome and seemed to genuinely care for me. He talked about how this country is divided by those who inherit their wealth and those who must work for it. I agreed with him. After all, I'd done nothing to earn my position in society, and yet I had all of these men from good families wishing to marry me. Boyd made me want to stand on my own. He challenged me to do it."

"I can't imagine your father took the match well."

"I didn't tell my father anything about it. Any time I ever expressed an opinion that wasn't his, he practically raised the roof. Besides, he wished to marry me off to a man I could not abide. He was far older than myself."

"Who was it?" Neal had to ask.

"The marquis of Tweedbury," Thea answered.

Neal frowned. He knew the marquis. He was not fond of women. However, he would have been an excellent ally for the duke of Duruset. "You are lucky you didn't marry him."

"I know. He did marry. An earl's daughter.

She is remarkably unhappy and very indiscreet about her lovers. I would not want that for my life."

"And was your marriage happy?" It was a question he'd wondered since seeing her again. She'd never criticized Boyd to him, and his interest was more than idle curiosity, although he'd not admit it.

It was a strange life he was living now. He needed to keep up barriers to Thea's charms, and yet it was harder and harder to do so. His attraction to her was strong, and it wasn't just lust. He trusted her. He always had. At no time in their acquaintance had she been anything but honest, and it was still the same now. She was a good friend . . . and an entertaining lover. Her passion matched his own.

"No, not even from the beginning, although we pretended." She reached for the edge of the door handle and rubbed it with a gloved hand before saying, "Of course, I didn't realize this at the time. I was infatuated with Boyd because he was so different from the other men I'd known and, yes, that was some love — or at least as much as I had in me for a person who knew nothing of the world beyond London's protected society. For his part, he played a gallant suitor, and I thought he did care."

"But he didn't?"

"Perhaps." She shrugged. "He was greatly offended when my father sent the letter disowning me. He was even less pleased when Father died three years later and he discovered I had been left out of the will. I knew that my father meant what he said, but Boyd felt that since *he felt* I had been the favorite daughter, my father couldn't possibly deny me. He did not know my father well."

Neal was not surprised. Thea and her father had always clashed and, yes, the duke of Duruset had been proud of his daughter and had expected her to marry very well.

Now she had. He took her hand, lacing his fingers in hers.

"I didn't know this at the time," Thea continued, "but after my father's death, Boyd went to my brother, Horace, the current duke. I believe he expected my brother to recognize me. Horace wouldn't."

"So money was the reason your marriage was unhappy?" Neal asked.

"That . . . and other reasons."

Something in her voice told him she did not wish to speak further on the topic, but Neal had one more question. "Do your sons miss him?" he asked, pulling her closer. She smelled of the lily-scented soap Lady Palmer had offered her guests.

"Christopher was still only a baby when he died," she said. "He barely remembers him, and Jonathan does not speak of him." She pulled his hand up and around her head so that his arm was around her shoulder. "And perhaps that is good."

She turned into him. Her breasts flattened against his chest as she kissed him, and any other questions Neal might have had fled his mind. For the rest of the way to London, he learned the many ways one could make love in a coach. That they had to keep quiet so that Bonner and the footman wouldn't hear only heightened the pleasure.

For that reason, Neal was in very good spirits when they rolled into London. Their first stop was Lady Palmer's house.

Mirabel had left early that morning, so she'd arrived well ahead of them. If she noticed that Neal and Thea appeared slightly mussed, she didn't make a comment, but there was a secret smile hovering around her lips.

Thea's sons were overjoyed to have her return. Neal held back as they rushed into their mother's arms. In the privacy of the room overlooking the back garden, Thea sat her boys down and explained to them that she and Lord Lyon had married.

Jonathan, bright lad that he was, immediately understood that Neal was now related to him by marriage. Both boys turned to Neal, who accepted that as an invitation to join the small family group. He sat next to Thea.

With a great deal of consideration, Jonathan said, "What are we to call you, my lord?"

Neal had not thought of this. "I shall be your stepfather. I promise I will treat you as my own. What would you like to call me?"

"I want to call you Lyon," Christopher declared. "Mrs. Clemmons was reading a story to us about a lion. He was a big cat, and he roars." He showed what he meant by giving a loud roar.

Jonathan rolled his eyes. "Ever since Mrs. Clemmons read that story, that is all he does."

His brother's response was to laugh and roar again. Neal found himself laughing as well. He couldn't help himself. Christopher looked so proud of his new talent, and Jonathan was so aggrieved by it, that Neal was reminded of himself and Harry when they were younger. Neal had forgotten about those days. That was before their father had burdened them with the curse and before the busyness of their lives had caught up with them.

"Roar once more," Neal urged Christopher.

The boy shot a triumphant look at Jonathan and roared the loudest and best roar yet.

"Call me Lyon," Neal said and held his hand out to each of the boys. They would be his sons. They would also be free of the curse. The realization was revolutionary. They had a future.

Jonathan solemnly placed his hand in Neal's. Christopher copied him, an impish grin on his face. Jonathan would always see the serious side of life, and Christopher, well, he would be Jonathan's Harry, and Neal couldn't stop from pulling them both into his arms. He had sons.

Glory of all glories, they hugged him in return, while Thea stood to the side with the dreamiest glow of pride Neal had ever seen on anyone's face. Of course, the only thing left to do was to include her in the hug.

"Shouldn't your mother be in the hug?" Neal wondered.

"Join us, Mother," Jonathan ordered, losing his earlier reserve and starting to show boyish eagerness. Neal understood. The oldest always had to be the most cautious. He'd have to make the first move with Jonathan. Christopher, of course, acted according to however he felt at the moment. So like Harry.

Thea did as commanded, and Neal found his arms full of family. A pleasure he'd not ever known before settled around him, and Neal could have stayed embraced in their hugs forever.

His wife was more practical. "We must not be a burden to Lady Palmer any longer," she said, breaking up the hug.

"Oh, poo," Mirabel said. "I adore having company. Stay for dinner."

Her offer was tempting. Neal had deliberately put off thinking of his sister and brother's reaction to his marriage. He'd sent a messenger the day before to inform them of his intentions, including whom he was marrying. He anticipated a howl of protest from Harry.

However, sooner or later he had to face them, and it might as well be sooner. Mirabel gave them each a kiss as they parted company — even Neal.

The boys were excited to ride in the coach.

"Where are we going to live?" Jonathan asked.

"In my house," Neal said.

Christopher's eyes rounded with delight,

and even Jonathan sat up straighter and looked out the window with anticipation.

Thea's hand found Neal's. She gave him a squeeze that said *thank you*. She was happy, and since making her happy made him happy, he raised her hand to his lips and placed a kiss on her fingertips.

The Chattan town home was one of the largest in London. The step boasted a huge, carved stone portico and double doors of varnished oak.

This time Jonathan did not hold back his emotions as he climbed out of the coach onto the walk. "We're living here?"

"Yes," Neal said. "Welcome home."

Both boys stood on the front step, their heads leaning back as they looked up at the portico, exclaiming over the size of the wrought-iron lamp hanging there.

Neal turned his attention to the front door. Usually a servant opened the door the moment a coach pulled up. However, it was still closed. Bonner was as surprised as Neal, although Neal didn't want to say anything in front of Thea and her sons.

The thought crossed his mind that Margaret might attempt to lock them out. She could be that stubborn and protective, but it wouldn't make sense. His sister wouldn't openly defy him. No, she'd give him a tongue lashing in private. He decided he'd best keep the boys close to him. Not even Margaret could be immune to their enthusiasm, and they might offer him a spot of protection.

Lifting Christopher up in his arms, Neal tried the handle. The front door was unlocked. He opened it. The front hall was empty. "Hello?" he called. "Dawson?"

No one answered.

He smiled at Thea. "Dawson, our butler, is usually at the front door. I don't know where he is up and about." Bonner and the coachman were making arrangements to bring in what luggage they had to the servants' entrance.

"Come into the side room," Neal said, indicating a well-furnished sitting room in tasteful blue and green. He wasn't particularly fond of the colors, but his mother had done the decorating. As Thea and the boys walked into the room, he realized how out of place they looked with so much formality.

"You have carte blanche with the house," he said. "Choose the colors you like, the furniture. It makes no difference to me. I think I would like a change."

"What of Margaret? She's been your hostess. Perhaps she would have a say?" Thea suggested.

"Yes, she might," he agreed, touched by Thea's thoughtful consideration of his sister. Margaret would not have been that generous, and that was why he loved —

Neal stopped his train of thought, backing away from the word *love.* He couldn't dwell on it. He mustn't.

He nodded. "Yes, discuss it with Margaret. As for Margaret, I wonder where she is. I wonder where anyone is. Dawson usually has someone minding the door."

Neal went out into the hallway and looked up the stairs. He checked the dining room. "Mrs. Tanner," he called, referring to the housekeeper. "Dawson?"

And then he heard a sound from upstairs and footsteps on the stair treads. He returned to the stairs. Margaret stood on the staircase landing. Her hair was loose around her shoulders. There were dark circles under her eyes and her dress was wrinkled, as if she'd slept in it. "Neal?" she said. She sounded overwhelmed.

He came up the stairs, two at a time, alarmed.

"It is Harry," she said. "He's in a bad way." She turned and dashed back up the stairs.

A bad way. It could mean only one thing,

and that was not good. Damn his brother for choosing his homecoming to be an ass.

Neal looked to Thea, who had come to the side room door, her sons beside her. "Stay in the side room. Please make yourselves comfortable. I don't know where the servants are, but I'll be right back."

He then hurried after Margaret up the stairs. She waited for him. "He came home around noon today. They carried him here."

"Who did?"

"Two big burly men, like sailors. They didn't tell me where they found him," Margaret said. "Said I most likely would not like to know. They were right."

"Wasn't Rowan with him?" Rowan was Harry's manservant. He was a short Indian with close-cropped hair and solemn, golden-brown eyes. Harry claimed that one day, while he'd been posted in India, Rowan had started following him around the market in Calcutta and had never left. He was devoted to Neal's brother and rarely spoke, but when he did, his accented English was excellent.

"No, Harry had escaped him. Rowan alerted me last night that Harry was out on the prowl. We both waited for him, hoping he would come home at a reasonable hour." She stopped in front of Harry's bedroom door and said almost defiantly, "I had him tied down, Neal. He can't go on this way, and I won't let him."

"Tied him down?"

"Yes," Margaret said. "He has to stop. He can't go on using that horrible laudanum. I told Dawson to keep the servants below stairs. You should have seen him when they brought him home. He looked dead, and then he came to his senses and started drinking again. We must stop him from destroying himself. And now he is awake and crazed and mad. We had no choice but to tie him down. You didn't look in the dining room, or you would have noticed that he turned over the buffet and has chairs against the way."

As if to punctuate her words, there came a huge crash from the bedroom. Margaret shook her head, tears forming in her eyes. She never cried. Not ever. "You and Harry are all I have," she said. "We're losing him. He's taking his own life and I can't bear it, Neal. I can't stand to watch this."

"Then go," he said. From the other side of the door, Harry yelled Margaret's name, a shout followed by a string of rude curses.

"I'll handle this," Neal said. "You need a moment to yourself."

"He's going to hate me," Margaret whispered.

"It's not him right now, Margaret. He has the devil in him. Now, go, you've done enough. Let me keep watch."

"He's never been this bad," she said before running for the haven of her room.

Neal turned the door handle, uncertain of what he'd find.

The room was chaos. A chair had been thrown against the door and a side table overturned. Rowan and a footman had their bodies on top of Harry, who was tied to the four corners of the bed with what looked to be Margaret's scarves. He was doing his best to pull free.

Usually meticulous, unless he was on the prowl for opium, Harry had a day's growth of beard, and his hair spiked every which way on his head. His face was pale, and his deep-circled eyes seemed to glow with the fire of a thousand demons. The room, its curtains pulled closed and lit by a single bedside candle, smelled of sweat and overindulged drinking.

"Neal," Harry barked out, seeing him at the door. "Come here. Rowan won't listen to me. Tell them to get off me and untie my hands."

A stone's worth of weight formed in

Neal's chest. Margaret was right. They had to do something to stop Harry from destroying himself. Perhaps if Neal had been sterner when Harry had first come home from war, things might not have gotten to this point. This was not what he wanted for his brother.

"I can't help you, Harry." Neal had to force the words out.

"You must." Bucking and rolling his body, Harry twisted against the knots holding him down. Rowan and the footman were almost thrown off the bed with the force of his surge. He was wild and seemed to have the brute strength of three men. "I have to have something, Neal. I *must* have it."

Neal took a step forward. "I can't."

"You can't? You *won't.*"

"I won't help you kill yourself," Neal said. "Please, Harry, I'll stay beside you, but I can't let you continue to do this."

"*You* fear death?" Harry answered. "Then why did you marry, Neal? Why did you give in to the curse? Why do you want me to watch *you* die?"

"Is that what this is?" Neal demanded, moving to the foot of the bed. "You are doing this because of my marriage? Then stop it. I don't want your death on my conscience."

Harry burst out into a delirious laugh. "We are all dying, brother. You, me, Margaret. We're doomed. But I need help," he went on, his voice suddenly taking that pleading note again. "I can't stand being in my own skin. I feel like I'm being eaten alive —" His voice broke off in a shuddering gasp before he tried heaving his body to and fro and pulling once again on the bonds that held him.

From behind Neal came a voice of strength. "Untie him."

Neal turned to see Thea in the doorway. She still wore her bonnet and gloves. Her gaze on Harry, she walked into the room.

Harry honed in on her with the sharpness of a hawk spotting its prey. "It's you that will kill Neal," he said, his hoarse voice sounding possessed. He tried to lunge at her, to kick out. *You will kill him.*

The words rang around the room, but Thea showed no fear. She pulled off her gloves and looked to Neal. "What is his weakness?"

He answered, almost unnerved by the force of his brother's anger. "Laudanum. An old war injury. His leg, it pains him."

She nodded, but he sensed she knew he wasn't speaking the complete truth, so he added, "And spirits. He likes the bottle.

Gin, port, wine, even Madeira if there is nothing else."

"We need more of all of it," she replied. "Will you have someone fetch bottles for me now?"

"Thea, I can't give him more. I won't. Margaret is right. This must stop," Neal said, his voice shaking with emotion.

"It can't stop until he wants it to, Neal," Thea said. "You can't make the decision for him or protect him from the world."

"Margaret and I want him to be sane enough that he realizes he must change," Neal argued. "If he doesn't, he will die."

"You are right," Thea answered. "He will die. But having all of it taken away from him before he is ready can also kill him. The man is ill. I know this is difficult to understand, Neal, but we must give him a bit of the laudanum."

"She's right," Harry said before he started coughing. A beat later, his body was heaving. Quick as a blink, Rowan was off him and picking up a bucket by the bed.

Neal watched his brother be sick. He looked to Thea. "He's a good man. A strong soldier."

"I know," Thea said. She reached out and placed her hand on Neal's arm. "This is hard. I went through this with Boyd. He liked the opium as well. But you must believe me, Neal, your brother is the only one who can stop this. If you force him, he will never change, not truly. He'll just hide it better."

Neal looked at his brother, who rolled back on the bed, his eyes closed, his breathing heavy, as if he was exhausted, his body slick with sweat.

"This is my fault," Neal said.

Thea gave his arm a squeeze, a gentle reminder that he was not alone. "He makes his own choices."

She was right. Neal had done everything in his power to stop Harry, even having servants serve as guards to keep him at home and spies to follow him when he was out. He evaded them. He always managed to have his own way.

Neal looked at his wife. "You can help him?"

"Boyd taught me a thing or two. I do not want your brother to be like this either, Neal."

Neal looked to Rowan. "Fetch some laudanum."

The valet walked over to Harry's clothes press and took out a bottle from a secret compartment.

Neal gave a bitter smile. He'd ordered all

of Harry's vices from the house too many times to count, yet here was a stash. Poor Rowan was torn between loyalty to Harry and loyalty to Neal.

Rowan brought the bottle over to Neal, but Thea intercepted it. Taking the bottle, she said, "Now I want all of you men to leave the room. Go on."

"No," Neal said, suddenly fearing for Thea. "You don't know what Harry is capable of when he is like this."

"Oh, I know all too well," Thea answered, steely eyed. "I also know that if *you* are here, he will play on every sympathy you have. Go, Neal. You don't need a hand in it."

She was right. Still, it was hard for him to walk away. He had to help his brother see reason.

Harry lifted his head and stared at the bottle in Thea's hand. "Give it to me," he begged. "Give it to me."

Neal felt his heart break for his brother. His strong, carefree, noble brother. Harry was too good a man to end this way. If Thea could help him . . .

He left the room.

CHAPTER FOURTEEN

Thea had no illusions about Harry's feelings toward her. He wanted what she held in her hand and nothing more.

His breathing was shallow as he watched her pour the drug into a glass.

"He'll need more, my lady," his manservant said.

"Here," Thea replied, offering the bottle to him. "Give him what he usually takes, less a bit."

A tear slid down the manservant's leathery cheek as he poured the liquid into a glass.

Touched by his emotion, Thea said, "What is your name?"

"Rowan, my lady."

She reached for the glass, taking Rowan's hand and holding it a moment. "This is hard. It is hard for Lord Lyon, for his sister, for yourself and everyone who cares for the colonel. But I meant what I said. The only one who can free himself of this is Colonel

Chattan."

"He's a good man," Rowan said.

"The best," she agreed. "We shall pray he has the strength to conquer this weakness. Do you know how much he's had of both spirits and opium over the last day?"

"He escaped me. I don't know," Rowan confessed. "It's my job to keep him sane. He was very angry about your marriage." He did not look at Thea as he said the latter.

Harry started pulling at his bonds again, a reminder he was there and of what he wanted.

Thea turned to the footman. "Please prepare some steaming hot water and the largest stack of towels you can gather. Oh, yes, and bring a bottle of —" She stopped, uncertain about what Harry chose to drink. Then she remembered the copious amounts of port he'd guzzled during the dinner they'd had together. "Port. Bring a bottle of port." Heavy spirits to be sure. She was certain the laudanum had been mixed with gin. Port and gin would be a potent punch.

The footman nodded and left to do her bidding.

"Rowan, please lift the colonel's head."

She poured the dosage down Harry's throat. Harry lapped at it as if he'd been a dog, his eyes closed. She eased up a bit. He literally growled, *"More."*

"Let this settle first before I give you the rest."

Harry tensed as if to argue but then sank down onto the mattress, reminding her of her sons when they were out of sorts. The colonel hadn't always been like this. She needed to keep that in mind, especially in the face of his drunken demands.

Rowan squatted on the floor next to the bed in the Indian style. He crossed his arms and began chanting in a low voice.

Harry made a sharp gesture with his fingers, indicating he wished for the rest of the contents in the glass. Thea feared giving Harry too much. The dosage had been a strong one. The colonel opened his eyes, nodded with his chin to the glass she held. He was not about to ease his demands.

This time when she administered the draft, he lifted his head on his own. He lay back down and closed his eyes with a deep sigh.

Thea retreated to a chair by the table. She crossed her arms, hugging her body close. She remembered times like this with Boyd. He'd disappear for days and then drag himself home. She'd sit and watch and pray as his body battled the ravages of his indulgences.

And then one day he'd not come home . . . and she hadn't known if she'd been sad or relieved. Months later, she'd learned of his death. They said he'd fallen off a bridge and drowned in the river Thames. It had taken time before someone had found her and delivered the news.

And sometimes she wondered if Boyd hadn't jumped off that bridge, if he hadn't taken his own life.

Harry's breathing continued at a labored rate. A shudder went through his body and he began snoring.

It was a terrible sound. Certainly nothing the dashing military man would take pride in when he was sober.

"Is everything all right now, my lady?"

"You tell me, Rowan," Thea said. "He's been like this before, hasn't he?"

Somber golden-brown eyes considered her, and then he nodded.

"Well, we shall see how he does when he wakes," she said.

At that moment, the footman returned with warm water and linen towels. "All right, gentlemen," Thea said, rising to her feet. "We have work to do. Rowan, untie and undress him." She looked to the footman. "Your name?"

"Edward, my lady."

"Well, Edward, the three of us are going to lay these cloths over his body to sweat out what we can of any poisons in him."

It wasn't the choicest of assignments. Edward did not appear pleased. He moved grudgingly toward the door. Rowan set upon the task of undressing his master.

Soon more servants were involved in bringing hot water. For three hours they worked at steaming out Harry's body. Thea had learned of this treatment from another woman whose husband had suffered from his weaknesses. She'd thought of attempting it on Boyd, but she'd never had the opportunity.

At one point, when Harry turned restless, Thea gave him a bit of port and he seemed to settle down. His breathing slowly grew more rhythmic and relaxed.

"We're done," Thea announced at last. "Rowan, your master should sleep through the night."

"Should I tie him up like Lady Margaret wishes?" Rowan asked.

Thea shook her head. "We can't keep him tied up forever. We shall have to wish for the best." She thought of her sons. Neal would have seen to them, she knew he would have, but still, she was their mother. "I must leave."

"I will keep watch, my lady," Rowan said.

"Good. Come for me if there is a problem."

Rowan answered with a deep bow.

Thea opened the bedroom door, realizing she didn't know where anything was in the house — and then stopped in her tracks at the sight of Margaret sitting in a chair across the hall from the bedroom door.

Margaret's thick, dark hair was down around her shoulders. Her face was tight and very pale. She rose from the chair. "How is he?"

"As good as can be expected," Thea said.

"He frightened me this time. He looked dead when they brought him, and then he came to life and just went wild." The woman's nerves were stretched thin. Thea knew how she felt.

"The colonel is made of stern stuff," Thea said. "He will survive this."

"But will he survive the next time he does it?"

Thea shut the door, not wanting the servants to overhear their conversation. "He needs to give it up," she said gently.

"I've told him that. He won't. He says he has nothing else in life —" Her voice broke off and she looked away, crossing her arms as if holding in all of her emotion — and Thea saw the curse's legacy.

The Chattans were not living; they were existing. They had put love, desires, dreams, wants, everything that made life worthwhile on hold because of superstition.

"He misses war, doesn't he?" Thea said.

"Perhaps. Maybe." There was a beat of silence and then Margaret said bitterly, "I believe sometimes he is disappointed he didn't die a glorious hero's death. He rode into cannon fire. He pointed his horse at where the French were the strongest, and they say he charged them like a madman. And his men followed." Her voice broke. She tightened her hold around herself. "I know Harry would have willingly died. But apparently he didn't anticipate that his men would go where he went, bravely. I believe Harry had thought to go it alone. They took out the cannons but at a great loss of life. And now Harry has their deaths on his conscience. He didn't want to leave Spain, but Wellington's staff forced him. Some think Harry is a war hero, but there are those many amongst his comrades who fault him for the deaths that day."

"What does Harry believe?" Thea asked, already knowing the answer.

"He doesn't speak of it," Margaret said. "But I believe he is unprincipled and drunk because he wishes he were dead. He doesn't care about his life, therefore he doesn't value it as much as his family does."

Thea had never considered that a man would turn to vices to escape his disappointments. Had Boyd indulged because he'd been unhappy with his life? Unhappy with her?

She had to take a step away.

Margaret raised a hand to dab at the tears that had started falling down her cheeks. "I don't like to cry. It's weak."

"It's human," Thea answered, thinking back to the way she had broken down with Neal the other night.

"Tears serve no purpose."

"They cleanse the soul," Thea said. "We all need a good soul cleansing from time to time."

Margaret shrugged her response. "Not in this family."

"Yes, in *this* family," Thea declared. "Margaret, you and I can't save Harry from the demons he faces. But you putting your life on hold is not going to help. You can't protect him. I know this. Harry must help himself. He is the only one who can. That's advice that was given to me years ago, and it is true."

"It may be too late to do anything. You saw him in there. He doesn't care if he lives or dies as long as he has laudanum and a bottle of something, anything, really. He is not choosy as long as it is spirits."

"Oh, he cares," Thea said with complete certainty. "He's a Chattan. He is made of the same stuff as you and Neal. If he wants to become better, he must learn to forgive himself and to understand that war is made up of men's sacrifices, honest lives given for a cause."

"You make it sound simple," Margaret said, anger lighting her eyes. "You talk as if you know us, and you don't. You won't, either. Because of your interference, Neal will die shortly, and I will have nothing to do with you."

On those cruel words, she walked off.

Thea sat down in the chair, shaken. She had not anticipated a joyful reception into the Chattan family, but this was too much. She needed Neal. She had to find him and her sons. Then the world would make sense again.

Of course, she had no idea where they were located in this house, and she assumed it would not be safe to ask Margaret. She glanced around at the portraits on the walls, the shining glass and bronze sconces, the thick carpet beneath her feet.

A footstep sounded on the stair. Relieved to not be alone, she turned to see a tall gentleman of advanced years coming up the stairs. He had the dignified air of a butler.

Thea stood and met him at the top of the stairs. "Dawson?" He nodded. "Please, tell me where my husband and my sons are?"

"They are in his lordship's room, my lady," Dawson said. "Please, follow me."

He took her to the end of the hall and knocked on the door. The valet answered. He recognized Thea immediately.

"Good evening, my lady. You are looking for Lord Lyon and your sons?"

"I am."

"This way, please." He opened the door, revealing a sitting room that took up almost half of the second floor. The furniture was designed with hard, masculine lines, and the colors were burgundy and brown.

It was a fitting lair for a Lyon.

"I'm Perrin, his lordship's valet. Lord Lyon and your sons are in the bedroom. They have been waiting for you. His lordship is entertaining them by reading. I took the liberty of unpacking your bags," Perrin continued. "We all know you were helping Lord Harry, so I also ordered a tray for your supper." He pointed to the silver serving dish on a table by the window.

"Thank you," Thea said. "But what of my sons and my husband?"

"Oh, they ate, and right well, I should say." He had been leading her across the room to another door, but now he stopped, one hand on the handle. "It is good to hear the sound of children's voices, my lady," he said. "All of us have commented on it. You are raising two fine young gentlemen."

"Thank you, Perrin," Thea said, pleased.

"Of course, all did not go according to plan."

"What do you mean, Perrin?" Thea's mind immediately jumped to some unforeseen disaster.

He raised a finger to his lips, signaling for her to be quiet, and opened the door.

Thea peeked inside. An oil lamp burned on the bedside table of a massive carved wood bed. On the side of the bed closest to the light were Neal and her two sons, one snuggled up on either side of him, sleeping with a peacefulness that tugged at her heart.

Both boys were in their nightclothes. Their faces appeared freshly scrubbed. Neal wore his shirt, breeches and stockings. An open book rested facedown on his chest, as if he'd been reading and they'd all drifted off to sleep. He had an arm around each boy in a loose but protective hold.

Perrin quietly closed the door behind her, leaving Thea alone with her men and a feeling of such contentment that the ugliness of the preceding hours vanished.

This was what she wanted for her sons.

This was what Neal needed.

Moving quietly so that she didn't disturb them, Thea prepared for bed. She picked the book up from his chest and read the title. *Robinson Crusoe.* Of course. She closed it. Neal's eyes opened. He gave her a satisfied, sleepy smile.

Now it was her turn to place a finger to her lips, warning him not to wake the children. She needn't worry. He wasn't going to give them up. Still smiling, he closed his eyes.

Thea picked up a coverlet at the foot of the bed and pulled it up over her men. Then she came around to her side of the bed, where her nightdress had been laid out on a chair. It looked very forlorn and dingy amid such opulence. She turned down the lamp, changed her clothes and slipped beneath the covers, turning so that she faced her little family.

They were all so tired that not one of them moved.

She closed her eyes and joined them in sleep.

The room was on fire. Thea woke, startled to see flames rising from the handsome furnishings, the upholstered chairs, the drapes, the tables. She must not have turned down the lamp —

Her first thought was of her sons and Neal. She reached for them, but they weren't there. The bed was empty save for her. She was completely alone — although she could hear a voice. A woman's laughter.

She had to leave the room. The flames would engulf her. The heat was overwhelming. She put one bare foot on the floor and snatched it back. The floor was on fire. Her foot burned where she'd placed it down.

Flames started up the carved columns of the bed. Thea looked to the bedroom door. It was aflame as well. There would be no help coming from there.

The only thing she could do was sit in the middle of the bed and watch as the fire raced up the room's walls and leaped across the ceiling.

She was sitting in an unholy inferno. And then, there was a cracking noise. The ceiling began raining fireballs down upon her —

■ ■ ■ ■

Thea woke with a gasp, sitting straight up, her heart pounding in her chest. She looked around wildly, expecting to see the room in flames —

All was fine.

The room was cool with the night air. The moonlight shone on intact chairs and tables . . . and Neal and her sons were right there beside her in the bed.

The dream had been so real. Thea had to climb out of the bed and walk around the room to convince herself that all was well.

"Thea, is something the matter?" Neal's sleep-laden voice asked.

She faced him. She could tell him about the dream, but that would be silly. "Everything's fine," she murmured. "I was just hungry."

"There is a tray for you in the other room," Neal said, yawning and closing his eyes again.

It was a long time before Thea ventured back to sleep again.

Life became better than Neal could ever have imagined possible. Thea and her sons brought a new energy, a vitality to the stately manse that had been gloomy for too long.

His first act as stepfather was to arrange for ponies for each of his boys. The first afternoon they went riding in the park, Jonathan fell off his. Brave lad that he was, he didn't cry, even though his pride was hurt. Christopher took to riding as if he'd been born to do it. Neal couldn't help but draw comparisons between Jonathan and himself, and Christopher and Harry.

Chris named his pony Victor, a bold name for such a pudgy beast. Jonathan named his horse Chattan, in honor of his new family. Neal was deeply touched.

He also discovered the true joy of married life. Thea was all he could want in a mate. She was open and inventive in bed and efficient and calm-headed during their daily life. Nothing soothed the challenges he faced more than lying beside his wife at night talking over the day's cares. She made him laugh at the absurdities of people and the frustrations of both business and government.

The days turned to weeks, with Neal discovering a renewed sense of purpose and a serenity about life he'd not known before.

Harry recovered from that terrible night and seemed determined to keep his vices in check. However, both he and Margaret kept their distance from Thea. Margaret pouted, wearing her disapproval on her sleeve.

Because Neal was not going to let anyone belittle this woman who had become so important in his life, he kept his distance from them.

Thea was exactly what the lady of the house should have been. She didn't take offense at Margaret and Harry's silence and rudeness, but she didn't hesitate to start placing her mark on the house and Neal's life.

The servants admired her. That pleased Neal. They'd been afraid of his mother. Thea managed to walk a careful line between not usurping Margaret's practices and authority and making changes to those issues that mattered to her.

As for the goodwill of society and the Montvales and the Pomfreys and their ilk, Neal could not care less about their opinions. With Thea and her sons, he had everything he'd ever wanted. Of course, Lady Palmer was a frequent and welcome guest. She helped soothe the way for Thea's reintroduction to society in her new role as his countess. The weeks flew by in a blaze of joy and contentment.

Yes, the Carpsleys attempted to keep Jonathan out of Westminster. A letter was sent to the house from the school expressing regret that they would not be able to interview Master Jonathan Martin.

Neal responded by contacting a few of his close friends, including the Prince Regent, and in short order, Jonathan was accepted. On the day they received the notice, Neal took the boy on a walk, just the two of them. He wanted to be certain Jonathan understood school life. Christopher was most annoyed to be left behind.

"It won't be easy at the school," he warned Jonathan after they had walked a good distance. "Schoolboys are harsh on each other. They play cruel pranks."

"What sort of pranks, sir?" Jonathan asked.

"They will push and shove you without cause. They may even hit you or play very mean jests that won't be funny to you. Don't complain and don't tattle. They are doing those things to see what sort of character you have."

"I believe their character is very rude if they behave that way."

Neal had to smile. At Jonathan's age, those had been his thoughts exactly. "Sometimes the older boys will do something the tutors or headmaster don't like and blame the younger boys."

"That is not fair."

"No, it isn't, but it is often the case in life. You must be brave and learn when to speak up and when to be quiet."

"I won't treat younger boys that way when I'm older."

"Very good, Jonathan. I would not want you to be so mean-spirited." They had come to a small park, and Neal let them inside. It was private here. He came down on one knee to be on Jonathan's level. "There is something I want to warn you of. The headmaster might not be kind to you."

"Why not?"

"He is not pleased with your mother and myself. However, Westminster is a very good school, and I expect him to treat you fairly. If he doesn't, you need to tell me. Not your mother — *me.*"

"But if they play pranks and blame others, how shall I know if he is being fair or not?"

"You'll know," Neal said. "And I am sorry for the trouble our marriage will cause you. But I'd wager your personality and your willingness to study hard will win the day. They will respect you, Master Jonathan."

Jonathan digested Neal's advice for a moment, and then he said, "I'm glad you and my mother married. I won't let them make me feel sorry for that."

Neal felt his heart warm and expand at the boy's words. And then Jonathan placed his hand in Neal's. So much trust in one small gesture.

The talk he'd given Jonathan had been necessary, considering how petty the Carpsleys were, but it was also a conversation he wished his father had had with him. In fact, there were many things he wanted to do differently than his father had, and he prayed he had the time left to him in life to see these matters through. Together they walked home.

Christopher was not waiting for them. Instead, they found him in the library with Harry. They were playing marbles on the floor, and Christopher was beating Harry. Their shouts and challenges could be heard all the way down the hall to the front door.

Harry looked up as they entered the library. "You shouldn't have left Christopher behind," he said. He was truly angry.

Christopher's response was to pat Harry on the shoulder. "I don't care. I like playing with you. Your turn. Your marble is on the other side of the room."

Harry groaned his ill fortune and then showed his hand at marbles by bouncing one of Christopher's to the other side of the library. Soon they had teams. Jonathan and Christopher against Harry and Neal. The competition was fierce. Neal knew he should have been going over Lord Leeds's proposal for the building of docks on the North Thames, but playing marbles was far more fun.

Harry lost the challenge for them. Jonathan and Christopher crowed like the victors they were. They even went so far as to do a jig. Harry started laughing and couldn't stop. Neal was stunned by the sound. He couldn't remember when he'd last heard his brother laugh. He had to laugh as well, just because the sound gave him so much pleasure . . . and that was when he noticed Margaret standing by the door. She appeared thunderstruck.

Seeing him notice, she started to back away, but Neal didn't want to let her escape. "Come join us, Margaret," he invited.

She hesitated. He expected her to run to her room, but then she asked, "What is going on here?"

Christopher immediately answered, "Marbles. Jonny and I beat them. We played three games and we beat them all three." He held up three fingers in case she didn't understand how victorious they were.

"Would you like to play?" Neal asked his sister.

"Girls can't play," Harry countered. Christopher nodded his head in agreement, but Neal knew what Harry was doing. Perhaps he was as worried about Margaret as Neal was.

It was Jonathan who came to Margaret's defense. "Why not?"

"Yes, why not?" Margaret echoed with a hint of her old spirit.

Neal sat up, amazed at this exchange. For too long his sister had been like a ghost around the house, a ghost of a mother hen. She clucked and worried and took care of them, never asking for anything for herself.

"They don't have the right thumbs," Harry said. "Your thumbs can't shoot marbles very far."

Both Jonathan and Christopher swerved their attention to Margaret's thumbs.

She held them up. "Oh, I don't know. I have rather strong thumbs," Margaret argued.

"No, you don't," Christopher assured her, siding with Harry.

"I think she does," Jonathan said, and Neal was charmed.

These boys had wrought a miracle in his family. They were bringing them together.

Children were safer than adults. His siblings might not have approached him, but Jonathan, Christopher and a bag of marbles provided a bridge. Neal said, "I want to make a challenge."

Jonathan's and Christopher's eyes lit with anticipation. So did Harry's. "Margaret and I against the three of you."

Oh, there was a game they couldn't pass up.

To Neal's surprise, his stylish, staid sister plopped herself down on the floor beside him with the demand "Show me how to shoot."

Neal obeyed, and within minutes they had a vigorous game going. Margaret proved to be quite adept at sending a marble after Harry's, and she and Neal almost won the challenge.

They were preparing to start another game when Thea entered the room, her manner one of concern. "Lyon, we have a visitor."

"I'm not expecting anyone," Neal said. He didn't want to interrupt the play.

"I think you should see this person," Thea said. "Certainly I can't send her away."

"Who is she?" Margaret asked. Her hair had come undone with all the rigors of crawling on the floor and she looked years younger. Her eyes sparkled in a way they hadn't in a long time.

"It's Lady Lyon, the dowager countess," Thea said.

Immediately the atmosphere in the library changed. The boys were still happy as larks, anxious to play some more, but Margaret, Harry and Neal all went tense.

"I am not receiving visitors," Neal said. How dare she call and ruin an important afternoon for his family —

"I thought you'd say that," a woman's silky voice behind Thea said, interrupting his indignation.

Thea jumped, as if surprised she'd been followed. She stepped aside, and Cass Sweetling sauntered into the library. She was a petite redhead dressed in the height of fashion in a mustard-colored dress and a wide-brimmed straw hat *à la shepherdess,* with saucy lace gloves, gold bracelets and jeweled ear bobs.

Neal rose to his feet.

Heedless of the game of marbles, Cass walked right up to him. "It's been a long time, *children,*" she said, chiding them with her position in their lives. In truth, she was the same age as Harry.

"You have lacked for nothing," Neal responded. Margaret had come to her feet, self-consciously pushing a stray strand of hair back into place. Harry didn't move from the floor, his manner defiant as he snubbed Cass.

Their stepmother did not seem to take offense. "No, I have all I need, and this isn't a social call." She looked over at the boys. Jonathan listened to the conversation with concern, while Christopher picked up marbles and put them in a bag for safekeeping. Disinterested in them, Cass swung her gaze back to Neal.

"Then what sort of call is this?" Margaret said. "You know you are not welcome here."

"I am well aware of that." Cass laughed. "And believe me when I say that I have no desire to be here. However, I promised I would deliver this to you, and so I shall. I've heard you are happy in your marriage, Lyon. Congratulations. I am pleased for you."

"Thank you," Neal responded briskly.

At his curt tone, Cass shook her head. "Always wary, never trusting. That's sad. But I'm not here for me. I've come because I am honor bound to bring this to you. You understand honor, don't you? You steep yourself in it." She reached in her reticule and pulled out a letter, still sealed and addressed *To my sons.*

"Who is it from?" Neal asked, making no move to take it from her.

"Your father," she replied.

CHAPTER FIFTEEN

Neal stared at the letter as if it had been some live thing.

Harry denied her claim, shaking his head vigorously. "That can't be from Father. Sir James had all of his papers."

"If you are so certain, why be afraid to read it?" Cass answered. She gave the envelope a little shake as if to tease them. "Can you not see the wax is sealed with the same signet design as the ring you wear on your finger, Lyon? The one your father handed to you?"

"We are not afraid," Margaret informed her. "But Father let us know directly what his wishes were. If he'd had a letter, he would have handed it to us. Now will you please leave?"

Cass glanced at Thea. "And that attitude, that certainty that they all knew their father better than I, his wife, did is the reason I haven't shared this with them sooner. I thought things had changed. I'd heard that Lyon was happy in his marriage — *as I had been in mine.* I felt the time had come for this letter. And in truth, Lyon, I'm not giving this letter to you for your benefit. I promised your father I would do it, and so I have."

Jonathan and Christopher stood silent. They had picked up the emotions of the adults in the room. Their allegiance was clearly with the Chattans.

Thea spoke. "Jonathan, Christopher, please tell Dawson we would like refreshments served in the library."

Her sons did not want to leave. For a second they hovered protectively around the Chattans. But another word from Thea sent them on their mission.

Neal was glad they were gone. The conversation could turn ugly.

Still, he made no move toward the letter.

There was a moment of silence, and Thea made an impatient sound. She took the letter from Cass's gloved hand and carried it to her husband. "Look at it. If it is false, then you may call her a liar and send her on her way. If it *is* from your father, don't you want to know what he had to say?"

Did he?

Neal could feel his siblings waiting for his

decision. They wanted to toss Cass out of the house.

But then he thought of his walk with Jonathan, of imparting advice to him. What did *his* father have to say?

Neal took the letter from Thea. The seal was still good, but the wax was brittle with age, giving credence to Cass's story.

Breaking the seal, Neal unfolded the letter. Margaret made a small sound as she recognized their father's distinctive handwriting. Cass could not have created a forgery this good. He began reading aloud.

" *'Neal, Harry, my sons —'* "

Neal had to pause. He could almost hear his father's voice.

" *'— if you are reading this, then you know we are still bound by this terrible curse. I sought to break it. However, continuing as I did with my father's cautious ways, I have denied you, my children, the only thing of importance in life — love.*

" *'I want you to understand that I have no regrets in my decision to marry Cass, and I expect her to be given all that is due her as my widow. Don't let the biddies peck her to death, and let her be who she is.'* "

Who she is. An opera dancer, a light skirt. Neal could see that Margaret struggled with this directive as much as he did, although as a family they gave Cass all she was entitled to as the dowager Countess Lyon.

" 'This curse has robbed our lives of happiness and joy. I want you to know that the six months I've spent with Cassandra have revealed to me a great truth — Love is the only true measure of a well-lived life. It is all that matters. I don't know how I existed before falling in love. No, I didn't exist. I was hollow, a martinet of a man.

" 'My sons, I thought I could escape the curse, I thought I had been prudent. I could proudly say that I had carried on the line and beaten the witch at her game. I was wrong! What I had really done was build a prison around myself. I even withheld my caring concern from you, my children. I tried to cheat Fate, but can any man escape his life?

" 'My children, forgive me for betraying you, for leading you astray. Don't follow my path. Live fully and completely. Withhold nothing from life. Find someone and love her. Life holds so much more than what I led you to believe.

" 'The curse may have claimed another victim, but I am unrepentant. I loved! What sweet words! May God have mercy on my soul. Your father, Lyon.' "

Neal looked at his brother as he finished reading. Harry still sat on the floor, an arm resting on one bent knee, his head lowered. Neal turned to Thea. She watched him closely, her expression anxious.

In truth, Neal didn't know what to think. He believed the letter did truly come from their father . . . but the thought gave him no comfort. He needed time to digest this. He needed time to understand.

He needed time to come to terms with his own turbulent thoughts.

"I've done my part," Cass said, breaking the silence. "It was a pleasure seeing you all again." On that irony, she turned to leave.

Thea immediately said, "Wait, I shall see you to the door." She left the room with Cass.

For a long moment, Neal and his siblings were quiet. Margaret spoke first. "He didn't mention me."

"What?" Neal said, caught off guard by her comment.

"Father addressed the letter to you and Harry. It is as if I don't exist."

"That isn't true," Neal said.

"It isn't?" she challenged. "Was there one word directed at me?" She didn't wait for a response but ran from the room.

Harry released his breath. "Father still had a lot to learn about love."

"He cared for Margaret," Neal said in his

father's defense.

"Yes, of course," Harry answered dully. "Just like he cared for us. Here, help me up. My game leg won't let me rise without crawling like an old man."

Neal put the letter on his desk and offered a hand to Harry, pulling him up in one smooth movement. "He *did* care," Neal had to insist one more time.

Harry's gaze met Neal's. "No, he didn't. And that is the difference between you and me, brother. You want to pretend it is all better. You are pragmatic in your business dealings and in your duties to the title, yet you ignore what is happening to you in your personal endeavors. I'm a realist. Life is hell. Death is definitely preferable." He started for the door, favoring his leg.

"Where are you going?" Neal challenged, afraid of the answer.

His brother paused and gave a mirthless laugh. "To find my own piece of heaven."

"God, Harry, the stuff will kill you."

Harry nodded to the letter Neal held in his hand. "Does it matter?" He left the room.

Neal stood, stunned by the transformation of his family. Less than an hour ago they had been laughing together. Now, they were further apart than ever before. He moved toward a leather chair, and his boot hit a marble Christopher had missed when he'd picked them up. Neal reached down and held the glass ball in his hand.

"We have the refreshments," Christopher said proudly, marching through the door. He happily stepped back for Jonathan, who carefully entered the room carrying a tray loaded with a pitcher of orangeade, cakes and sandwiches.

A maid hovered behind the boy, anxious lest he make a misstep. She held a tray of glasses. Looking to Neal, she said, "He wanted to carry it in, your lordship. I didn't think there would be a problem."

"There isn't," Neal said, watching as Jonathan placed the tray on the library's desk. "Thank you," he said to the maid, dismissing her. The girl bobbed a curtsey and left the room.

"Where is Mother?" Christopher asked. "And Harry?"

Neal sat in the chair. "I found a marble." He handed it to Chris, then placed a hand on the boy's shoulder. He looked to Jonathan. "Thank you for bringing in the tray. It is a good thing to desire to serve others."

Jonathan nodded, pleased with his accomplishment, and Neal reached out. He pulled them both close, hugging them. They

327

were honest in their emotions, without doubts or fears. "I'm proud to be your stepfather," he said fiercely. "Don't ever forget that."

"We're proud to be your sons," Jonathan answered, and Neal thought he would lose the fragile hold he had on his emotions. There was a strong chance that the Chattan name would end with his generation.

And yet here was something good. He loved these boys. He could freely love them as a father without fear of their futures.

But for how much longer?

His father's words in the letter haunted him — *"I loved! What sweet words! May God have mercy on my soul."*

Thea and Cass were quiet as they walked through the halls to the front door. Dawson opened the door, his expression grave. He, too, apparently waited for Cass Sweetling to leave.

Cass turned to Thea. "Well, it was a pleasure meeting you, albeit a short visit. I wish you good luck in your future, Lady Lyon." Cass walked out the door. Dawson started to shut it, but Thea found her voice.

"Wait," she said. She slipped out the door, catching Cass on the front step. The day was overcast, the air heavy with the threat of rain. "One moment of your time, please."

"Of course," Cass said. A sedan chair waited to carry her away. She nodded to her servants, and they set the chair down.

"Go ahead and close the door," Thea told Dawson. "I shall be fine here."

"Are you certain, my lady?"

"I am." What did he imagine the petite dancer would do to her? Thea took Cass's arm and walked her toward the corner of the house, where they were away from prying ears. Thea said, "I'm sorry for what happened in there. My husband and his family have —"

Thea stopped, needing to search for the right words while debating whether or not she should even say anything. "There is this curse they believe in —"

"*You* should believe in it as well," Cass cut in.

Startled, Thea said, "Why do you say that?"

Cass leaned close to her. "Have you had the dream?"

A coldness settled over Thea. "What dream?"

The other woman smirked, pulled back. "Pretending, are you?"

"Pretending about what?"

"You know."

Thea shook her head. "I don't *know* anything. You are talking in riddles."

"Oh, I think you understand me very well. Tell me, are you in love with Lyon?"

Thea wasn't certain she should answer. However, the truth of her love must have shown on her face, because Cass took her hand. "If you love him, then you must accept that this curse exists. People didn't think I loved my husband. He was older than myself and I was, after all, merely a dancer. Funny how love ignores all class distinctions, petty jealousies, even allegiances, and certainly the barrier of age. He was everything to me. Harold changed how I thought, what I did . . ." Her voice drifted off as her eyes became misty.

"I'm sorry his children are not kinder."

Cass shrugged away her apology. "It is what it is. You saw their expressions in there. I had the best of their father. They had a shell of the man."

"Why do you say that?"

"Harold was very proud of his children and their accomplishments. But he feared showing them any affection. He helped them, saw to their welfare and prodded them when they needed to be pushed, but he wasn't even necessarily kind about it. At least that is my observation. I don't know what impact his letter will have on them."

"I don't know either." Thea crossed her arms. "There is a strangeness here. Neal is very close to his brother and sister. They support each other, but there are walls also."

"There are always walls when one feels it dangerous to love freely and openly," Cass answered. "Harold's first wife was beautiful and wealthy, but cold and uncompromising. She was happy to keep everyone at a distance. Much like I imagine Margaret does."

Thea thought of that horrible night with Harry. "She is not so strict. She cares deeply . . . and perhaps that is what she is afraid of — caring too much."

"Harry, from all I have heard, is on his way to ruining himself. The women still like him, though. They think he is a bit of a rogue."

Thea dared not touch that statement. Over the last few weeks, her sons seemed to have brought out a better side of Harry, but that didn't mean he had changed. "And what do you think of Neal?"

"I think he's in love."

Her words filled Thea with gladness. She'd not dared let herself think as much, and yet she so wanted to believe it was true. "I love him. I've told him I love him."

Cass held up a warning hand. "Don't be

so pleased. You are in danger of losing him. Harold's death was not good. It started with a numbness, and he grew worse over time. It started in a pesky way, but he knew what would happen. His father had the numbness and his father before him. I ask again, have you had the dream?"

A gust of wind scampered along the ground, teasing their skirts, then whirling up and around them. It was a cold wind and at odds with the warmth of the day. Cass looked around as if testing the air. "She's here."

"*Who's* here?" Thea demanded.

"Fenella, the Scottish witch who put the curse on them. She knows."

Thea shook her head, backing away. "Knows what?"

"That she almost has Neal. She is going to claim another."

This was too much. Cass had obviously been a good actress as well as a dancer. Thea turned away, not liking the way Cass's eery declarations put shivers through her. There was no such thing as curses, and Thea did not believe in witches, either. . . .

Cass reached out and caught her arm. She whirled Thea to face her. "You must not be afraid."

"I'm *not* afraid."

"Then why do you deny what I'm telling you? It is of the greatest importance."

"I don't believe in curses," Thea said, but her insistence was sounding weaker.

She is here. " Cass tightened her hold on Thea's wrists. "I didn't believe either, but she came to me in my dreams. They were the most horrific ones I've ever had. She wanted to burn me alive."

Thea immediately wanted to reject the knowledge that they might have shared the same dream. "If she lived centuries ago, she is *not* alive," she said, struggling for reason.

"She reaches from beyond the grave. Her hatred is that strong. If you are having the dreams, then know she is sharpening her claws. You've heard her in the dream. I can still recall the sound of her laughter. Her evilness. She will claim Lyon." Cass released her hold on Thea. "And I'm sad, because in spite of his ill will toward me, Lyon truly is a good man."

"He has never said he loves me," Thea protested.

"But what is in his heart?"

And in that moment, Thea realized the curse was true.

The horror of what the curse meant came home to her. "He can't die," Thea whispered, almost afraid to speak aloud. "I won't let him." She loved him. Within weeks, he'd become the center of her world —

"What can I do?" she asked Cass. "How can we stop it?"

"We can't" was the bleak reply. Tears were now rolling down Cass's cheeks. "I don't know if there is a way to stop the witch. Harold tried everything. His father, his father before him. They've all tried to stop her and they've failed."

"Thea?" Neal's voice interrupted them.

With a start, Thea turned to see her husband standing on the step. He frowned, seeing her with Cass. "Is everything all right?"

"Yes, it is," Cass answered for her.

Thea was thankful she'd spoken. She was having trouble finding her voice. She loved Neal so much. She could not imagine her world without him.

Neal started walking toward them. Cass gave Thea a quick hug. "Be safe," Cass whispered. "Be strong."

"Wait," Thea said. "How much time do we have?"

"No one knows," Cass answered and started for her waiting sedan chair, as if wishing to avoid Neal. She climbed in and waved her servants onward.

"Are you all right?" Neal asked. The

concern in his voice pulled at Thea's heart.

What should she say? What *could* she say?

She drew a deep breath. Released it. "I'm fine. Your stepmother is a rather insightful person." Her voice sounded more confident than she felt.

He looked over to the sedan chair that was being carried away. "She knows how to create a scene," he answered.

"So you don't believe the letter is truly from your father?" Thea asked hopefully. If the letter was false, then other things Cass had said could have been untrue as well.

"It was from him" was her husband's blunt reply.

Thea nodded, feeling cold and hollow inside. Neal took her arm. "You don't look well. Come inside. The boys have prepared refreshments for us."

Her sons. Her poor sons. How would they take his death? He'd so quickly earned a place in their lives.

Neal led her toward the house, and she was happy to just follow.

The rest of the day was a blur to Thea. She seemed to go through the motions of living, understanding now that the happiness she had enjoyed might have been nothing more than an illusion.

She did not want Neal to die. Not on her

account. She didn't think she could live with herself if that was to happen.

Dinner was a quiet affair, with Jonathan and Christopher providing most of the chatter. Harry was not there, of course. Thea had seen Rowan pacing the upstairs hall. She knew Harry had slipped away, and the manservant feared what could happen to him. A pale, somber Margaret ate in silence and then disappeared to her room as quickly as possible. She didn't even glance once in Thea's direction. *She knew.*

And Thea felt guilty.

Only Neal seemed content to pretend all was normal, laughing with the boys and eating a robust meal.

That night, when her husband turned to her in bed, she held him tight. She never wanted to let him go. Her certainty that the curse was real had grown immeasurably, and she didn't know what to do. Holding him, being with him was her only way of fending off the danger of their world.

Neal made love to her with a gentle passion that brought tears to her eyes. He stroked, caressed, and loved every inch of her body.

And when he entered her, Thea felt the two of them meld together. She never wanted to forget this feeling of having this man she loved so deep inside her.

Together, they moved toward the inevitable, the pinnacle, the release — only this time was different.

She felt her husband's seed fill her, and she knew that it had taken. She could sense that spark of life, that spirit of a new being.

Afterward, as they lay nestled together in bed, she placed her hand upon her belly, knowing that in time it would grow . . . and the curse would live on.

Thea knew there was only one thing she could do. She had to save Neal. She had to protect him. She had to make him hate her.

Neal was scheduled to be in meetings at Whitehall all the next day. In the wee hours of the morning, while he'd been sleeping by her side, Thea had formed a plan. She knew what she had to do — she had to leave him. Desert him. Abandon him.

Then he would not love her. He might even hate her.

It was the only plan she could devise, and, yes, it was born out of fear and desperation. She did not believe she could even share her plans with Mirabel. Her friend had become a staunch supporter of Neal's and would do all in her power to talk Thea out of this decision.

She had some money. Neal was very generous in her allowance. She knew he would not begrudge her taking the funds for herself and her sons. Her sons. The thought gave her pause. Her *three* sons.

She was pregnant. She had no doubt of it, and she knew this unborn child was a male. Perhaps, if Neal lived, then this child would be safe from the curse as well. She knew she was guessing, but what other hope did she have?

While her boys were with their tutor, Thea snuck into their room and packed a few things. She did not cry as she did this but moved with steely determination. Thea would not let Fenella win.

Back in her room, she began making the same preparations. She had to leave before Neal returned, and she had to do it in a secretive manner.

Unfortunately, she was caught.

A knock sounded on the door as she was folding the last of her clothes and putting them in the bag resting on the bed. "One moment," Thea started to say, picking up the bag, thinking to hide it, but the door opened on its own.

She was surprised to see Harry standing there. He did not look well. His skin was pale and clammy, his eyes dark.

"I wanted to let you know I returned on my own this time," he said, sauntering in, his hands in his breeches pockets. "Rowan is relieved. He scolded me. Can you believe that? All these years he's put up with me, but now you are here, so I'm scolded —" He stopped, his foggy brain realizing she was holding a half-packed bag. He tilted his head. "What are you doing?"

"I'm leaving," Thea said. Why hide it? Had he not wanted her gone?

"You can't do that."

His objection surprised her. "Is that not what you wanted?"

He shook his head as if trying to clear his brain. The air around him reeked of spirits. "I can't think. Where's Margaret?"

"Harry, don't say anything to her —"

"Margaret," he hollered, going out into the hall. *"Margaret."*

With an exasperated sound, Thea set the bag back on the bed. "Harry, please," she said, going after him, but Margaret had already heard his shouts.

She came out of her room. "What is it?" she asked, taking one look at her brother and making a frustrated sound. "So you are back, are you? And looking the worse for wear!"

"Enough about me," Harry said, waving

away her chastisements. "Thea's leaving."

Margaret's whole mood changed. She came charging toward Thea's room. From the doorway, Thea turned and went inside. She wanted any arguments between them contained in this room.

"Tell her she can't go," Harry said, following his sister into the bedroom.

"Will you shut the door?" Thea ordered him in a furious whisper.

He mugged a face at her sharp tone but did as bid. Once the door was closed, he poked Margaret's arm. "Tell her she can't go."

Thea turned to her sister-in-marriage. "I must leave," she said. "The curse is real."

"Of course the curse is real," Harry responded, throwing his arms wide. "*We* know that."

"Oh, Harry, I wish you were sober," Thea said. "Then you would understand what I'm saying."

"I understand," he snipped back.

Margaret held up a hand to warn her brother back. "What is the real reason you are leaving us?" she asked.

Leaving *us*. Margaret had said that . . . Margaret, who had disliked almost everything Thea had done, even when she'd been very careful about Margaret's feelings. Margaret, who barely spoke to her.

"I don't want to," Thea replied. "But I must. I am carrying Neal's child."

The air in the room changed. Harry collapsed on the bench at the foot of the bed. Margaret raised a hand to her head. They knew what this meant.

And then Margaret said, "But how is your leaving going to do anything but tear Neal's heart out?"

So, they had noticed he loved her. "He'll be angry if I leave, and then he'll hate me," Thea said, her eyes stinging. "I don't want him to love me. He's never said the words to me. There may be time to help him. I've had the dream," she said to Margaret.

"The dream?" Margaret asked.

"You don't know about it?" Thea shook her head. "Perhaps only those who are being chosen have it. I've had dreams where I'm burning and everything is being destroyed. There is terrible laughter in the background. A woman's laughter. I can't describe it except to say it is the most evil sound I've ever heard. I started having it after I married Neal. Cass Sweetling had dreams as well, much like mine. She asked me about them. Now I know the curse is real."

Thea closed the top of the bag. "I love

him. I don't want anything to happen to him. I want Neal safe. I want our son safe. Our son will be safe. This is the only action I can think of taking."

"But you and your sons have become a part of our lives," Harry said. "We don't want you to go."

His candid admission touched Thea. "And I would not go if there was any other way out of this."

"Where is Neal now?" Margaret asked.

"He has the day at Whitehall, and then he will be dining with Lord Blayne and a few others," Thea said. "He warned me it would be a late night. That gives me time to leave London."

"And then after that?" Margaret wondered.

"I'd best leave the country," Thea answered, not willing to divulge her plans to either of them.

Margaret nodded.

"This is all rot," Harry said, jumping to his feet. He gestured wildly. "I don't want you to leave. I don't want your sons to leave. You are family now. You belong here."

"Even if it means your brother's life?" Thea asked gently.

He let his arms drop in defeat. "I can't take this," he said. "I can't stay here. I don't want to think of this." He lurched for the door.

Margaret called after him. "Going for the bottle, Harry, or more opium?"

He paused, looked back at her. "You are cruel, Margaret."

"No, your excesses are cruel, my brother. Go. Lose yourself."

"I don't want her to go," Harry said sadly. "I don't want her boys to go."

"Sometimes we must make hard decisions," Thea said.

Harry seemed to waver, then he opened the door, slamming it behind him.

"He must change," Thea said.

"Aren't you the one who said he would when *he* wanted to make the change?" Margaret reminded her.

"It's hard waiting for that moment, if it ever does come," Thea replied. She ran her hand thoughtfully over the handle of the bag. "I do love Neal. I want his happiness."

"How good you were for all of us. But you are right. We must protect Neal and the child you carry. At least he will have his brothers."

Thea nodded, feeling hollow inside.

"Do you have money?" Margaret asked.

"I have my pin money."

"Let me add mine. I never spend it." Margaret left the room and came back a few minutes later with a heavy leather purse. "Whenever you need money, contact me. Harry and I will see you are cared for, and we won't let Neal know."

"Thank you."

"How are you going to leave?"

"I will sneak this bag outside. I'll collect my sons after their lessons and we'll walk off. After that, it's best you don't know my plans or my direction."

"The boys won't want to leave."

"I know," Thea admitted. "This is going to be so hard." She broke down.

Immediately, Margaret threw her arms around her. "I won't lose track of you. We can't. You and your sons are part of us now. And, Thea, I believe you are doing the bravest thing I have ever witnessed."

Thea nodded. Margaret's support meant a great deal to her. But now was not the time to linger. "I must go."

She didn't look back.

Neal was relieved to finally return home. The dinner meeting had gone overlong, and it was now well past midnight. He had wanted to leave hours ago, but there had not been the opportunity to excuse himself gracefully.

The house was dark save for a servant waiting for him by the door. Neal took a candle and went up the stairs. He could not wait to climb into bed beside his wife. He hated spending a day like this one. He would rather have had his evening at home with his family.

The bedroom was dark. Neal cupped the candle with his hand so that the light would not disturb Thea. He thought about blowing it out, but he feared stumbling around and making noise when he crashed into things.

Placing the candle in a holder on the dresser, he set out to disrobe as quietly and quickly as he could and then join his wife —

The faint light of the candle barely reached the bed, but Neal could see it was empty.

His first thought was that one of the boys might have taken ill and she was with him. He picked up the candle, determined to go to the boys' rooms and see for himself, when a knock sounded on the door.

"Come in."

Harry pushed the door open. He was in stockinged feet, and his shirt was pulled out over his breeches. His hair was mussed, he had a growth of beard, and he had not bothered with a neck cloth. Neal's first thought was that he was foxed. His skin was pale and his eyes sunken, always signs of the worst.

"I'm cold, stone sober, if that is what you are wondering," Harry said, wandering into the room.

"That's good," Neal murmured.

"Aye, good. I don't feel *good*. I feel ill." He held out his hand. It was shaking. "But I had to be sober to talk to you."

Neal found himself impatient. He was more interested in locating his wife than talking with his errant brother. "What do you have to say?" he asked, letting his annoyance show.

"Thea is gone. She's taken her sons with her."

Now he had Neal's attention.

"I don't understand," Neal said with disbelief. "She wouldn't leave." He started toward the door, wanting to see Jonathan and Christopher.

Harry stood his ground, not letting him pass. "Sit down, brother," he said. "I want to tell you a story about love."

CHAPTER SIXTEEN

Thea took the mail coach as far as it would go. When at last she stopped, she and her sons found themselves on the Cornish coast, far removed from life in London.

Here, she let a small cottage overlooking the sea. It was a lonely place, and it fit her mood.

Her sons were furious with her.

They felt betrayed, and she didn't blame them.

When she'd taken them from their tutor, she'd told them they were going on a holiday and that Lyon would join them shortly. With that terrible lie, she'd purchased their cooperation.

For a week after they moved into the cottage, Jonathan and Christopher kept an eye out on the road for any sign of Lyon. They talked about their ponies and their schooling. They had plans, plans Thea had interrupted.

After the second week, they stopped speaking of those things. They grew distrustful of her and querulous with each other.

Finally, Jonathan confronted her. "We are going back, aren't we? Or is this like it was with Father? He just left and we didn't see him again."

Thea wasn't feeling too good. She always had difficulty with the first weeks of her pregnancy, and this time was no different. "No, Jonny, we are not going back."

"Did Lyon send us away?" her son demanded.

She shook her head. She knew that with the right words she could make them think Neal had played a hand in their leaving. Then she wouldn't be portrayed so black. However, she found she could not do that to them. They needed some of the truth.

"We had to leave," she said sadly. "I didn't want to go, and Lyon would not want us to go."

"Then let's go back," Jonathan said.

"We can't."

"Why not?"

"Someday I can tell you. Not now."

Her oldest was not pleased with the answer. He stomped off and didn't speak to her for days. Christopher acted as their intermediary, but he was not happy with his mother as well and often cried himself to sleep. He started sucking his thumb again, a habit she deplored and something he hadn't done in years.

She was also lonely. Neal was her friend as well as her lover. She missed him to the point it physically hurt to be without him.

But she hadn't had the dream.

If she had, she would have gone running back to London as quickly as she'd been able. However, the lack of the dream gave her hope that her plan would work.

Still, it was a lonely life.

Autumn came more rapidly on the coast. The wind off the sea grew colder. Thea had enough money to last them a long time. There wouldn't be extras, but they would not lack for what was important.

And all the time, the baby within her grew.

On an October morning, Jonathan gave a shout that a visitor was riding down the road toward their cottage. They didn't have visitors. Thea kept to herself and rarely ventured into the local village unless she had to do so.

She went out into the cottage garden. A rider was at the top of the hill above the house and starting his way down. She recognized him immediately.

Neal had found her.

"Boys, come into the house," Thea ordered.

Christopher hurried to her, but Jonathan charged toward the dirt path in front of the house. "I know him," Jonathan said. "I know that man." He began running up the road. "It's Lyon," he shouted. "Lyon has come."

Christopher tried to take off after him, with a happy "Lyon."

Thea grabbed his arm, wanting to hold him, but her youngest defied her, twisting his way free and chasing after his brother. Thea watched in helpless wonder as her children jumped and danced as they welcomed Neal.

She didn't know what to do. Her belly was not showing that much. Perhaps she could bluff her way into making him think she wanted nothing to do with him. But first she had to control her own wild emotions at realizing that he was here. He had come for her, and she realized she'd been waiting for him.

Thea escaped into the cottage. It had a wood floor and was decorated in a comfortable, homey style — yet she could not wait to leave it. She grabbed hold of a chair and clutched it with all she had. She had to be brave. She had to convince Neal that she had left him because she did not love him.

Even if she went back with him, *she could not let him love her.*

She heard his voice out in the yard. The tone of it reverberated through her being. Her sons were speaking over each other in their enthusiasm to share how much they'd missed him. She took a step toward the window to look outside. He was holding them both in his arms and hugging them as if he would never let them go.

How many times when she'd been married to Boyd had she longed for her sons to know this exact sort of commitment and love from a father? And here it was.

Was she willing to take this away from them?

Neal saw her watching them. He stood. He looked very handsome in an open greatcoat over his riding clothes and tall boots. His hair was longer than it had been, and his whiskers were almost as rough as Harry's.

Neal said something to her sons. They looked in the direction of the cottage and then took the reins of his horse. Neal started walking toward the door.

Thea wanted to run. She thought about charging into the back room and hiding, but there was no lock to stop him.

No, Neal had found her and the least she

could do was face him.

A step sounded on the floor behind her. She could feel his presence, feel the bond that was between them. The bond she had to deny.

She turned, not knowing what to expect. He should be angry with her. Furious.

Instead, she discovered an expression of such compassion on her husband's face that she could have wept.

"I don't deserve you," she said.

"I think differently." His voice was harsh with pent-up emotion, emotion she could feel as clearly as if it had been her own.

"We can't, Neal. We mustn't. I can't let you love me."

"It is too late," he said. "I already do."

His words were a knife to her heart. "No, no, the witch will win. I've had the dreams, Neal. *I've had the dreams.*"

Neal was in front of her in a thrice. She started to turn away, but he put strong arms around her, holding her fast. "Now, listen to me. Fenella will *never* win. Do you understand? She won't."

Thea shook her head. "You are safe only if we are apart. We must not be together."

"I can't live without you," he said. "Do you hear me? I love you, Thea. *I love you.*" He shouted the words, and his voice rang in the rafters. "I will not run from love."

"But it will mean your death." Thea reached up and placed her hands around his neck. He felt so good and solid to her. "I don't want to lose you, Neal. I am so afraid."

He hugged her tight. He smelled of the sea air and horses. "Don't be afraid, my love," he whispered. "I'm not. Of course, I've spent a good portion of my life avoiding love. But having you and the boys has made me realize that living without the family I love is worse than death." He drew back to look her in the eye. "Thea, none of us knows how much time we have on this earth. Whatever happens, I don't want to feel as if I've wasted the time I've had. I need you, Thea. You are my mate, my companion, my love, my wife."

"But can my love save you?"

"No, it does something better — it makes my life meaningful. Before you, I had nothing. Now, having you in my arms, I know I'm the richest of men."

She kissed him then. She kissed him with all the love in her being, and he kissed her back.

"Does this mean we are going back with Lyon?" Jonathan's voice said from the door.

Thea and Neal turned to see Jonathan,

Christopher and the horse's head in the doorway.

Neal looked to Thea. "Does it?" he asked with a smile that said he knew the answer.

"Yes," Thea said. "Yes, we are."

It didn't take long to pack up their few belongings. Thea left a note to the owner of the cottage and shut the door.

Neal, with Jonathan riding in front of him, had ridden into the village in search of a vehicle for them to use for their trip. They managed to locate a coach for hire from a posting inn. It was an ancient conveyance that smelled musty inside. Thea took one whiff and felt violently ill.

"What is the matter?" Neal asked as she hurried around to the back of the cottage.

"She does that from time to time," she heard Jonathan assure him.

"Every morning," she heard Christopher chime in. "She doesn't feel good in her tummy, but then she is all right."

Thea knew by the time she came from the back of the cottage that Neal had guessed her secret. He took her aside.

"When were you going to tell me?" he said.

She found it hard to meet his eye. She placed a hand on his chest, right over where his heart was. "Soon. I knew I was carrying our baby when I left London."

"Is that why you left?"

"I left to save you."

He gathered her close. The wool of his greatcoat was soft against her cheek. "Don't save me, Thea. I don't want to be saved."

"I was saving the baby as well. I'm afraid for him, Neal. What will become of him?"

"He will be like me. He will grow up to be the best man I hope he can be, and to live his life fully." He pressed a kiss against the top of her head. How she had missed his closeness. "He will manage, Thea."

A calmness settled over her. An acceptance. Neal was right. Fear was not the answer. Love was. Love, love, love.

Her being was filled with it. She hugged her husband back. He smiled, took her hand and led her to the coach.

He opened the door. "After you, my lady."

Jonathan and Christopher were by his side, and they echoed his words with small bows. Thea laughed. Her sons climbed into the coach behind her. Neal gave orders to the postboy, checked to see that his own horse was securely tethered to the coach, and off they went, the windows on both sides of the coach completely open.

That night, the boys sound asleep in an

adjoining room at the inn, Thea and Neal made love.

It felt good to be touched.

It felt good to touch.

He knew what she liked and he quickly brought her to arousal. Together they found the magic that always sealed the bond of their love.

Afterward, lying in his arms, Thea asked, "How can you forgive me so easily? I would have thought you'd be furious with me."

"Harry," he said.

"Harry what?" Thea asked, coming up on one elbow to look down at her husband. "When I last saw him, he was not well."

He reached up and stroked her hair away from her face, and then with his fingers followed the line of her shoulder and down around her breast before dropping his hand and answering, "Harry is your strongest ally now. Margaret is your second strongest. They both wanted me to bring you home."

She frowned. "Even Margaret? Harry put up a protest, but Margaret understood what I was doing."

"I explained my feelings to them, the way I did to you. They worry for me. They are not pleased at the implications, but they have no choice but to accept them."

"I pray we have long lives," Thea said.

"I do as well," he answered, pulling her closer. "But the love I have for you, Thea, will last forever. The heart is a shield, my love, and mine will keep us safe forever."

Thea hadn't ever believed life could be so easy or so good.

Their homecoming to London was everything she could have wished. Margaret hugged her, and even Harry acted happy, although Thea believed him more pleased to see her sons.

Harry was still the same. He drank heavily, womanized, and twice a month disappeared for a day or two. But Thea couldn't concern herself with his vices. She wanted to enjoy every moment she had with Neal. Daily, she prayed to God that they would escape the curse, and the prayers seemed to work. Neal was healthy.

Margaret and Thea became fast friends. They spent at least an hour each day in needlework. Mirabel often joined them, although she disdained plying a needle. She was most upset that Thea had taken off without a word to her, but one word of the baby and Mirabel freely forgave the transgression. Margaret had decided that she would embroider the baby's christening gown and it would be a garment that would be the envy of all who saw it.

Jonathan seemed to like Westminster very much, but Thea would often catch him talking earnestly to Neal. She wondered what they said, but she didn't pry. Instead, she was thankful for Neal's listening ear.

The dreams began.

Only this time was different.

Before, she and Neal had kept silent. Now they discussed those nightmares and kept a journal on them. In the sharing of their dreams, they searched for clues that might help them defeat the curse. They each had many dreams when they first reunited, but the frequency seemed to slow, and they took that as a good sign.

Perhaps they could beat the curse with prayer and bravery. Certainly her love for Neal had helped defeat her fear.

In fact, even Harry and Margaret began to lose their own anxiousness about the curse. The atmosphere in the house grew more cohesive, warm and nurturing. Every day was busy and fulfilling.

In mid-November, there was an evening drive of open vehicles through Hyde Park. The boys had been looking forward to participating, and Neal and Thea had thought it would be an enjoyable outing, since many of their friends' families would be there.

They all bundled up against the chilled air and piled into Neal's open curricle. Soon they were part of a moonlit procession, one that was almost wheel-to-wheel.

Neal drove the vehicle, but he let both Christopher and Jonathan have a turn at the reins. With a wool lap blanket wrapped around her legs and hot bricks at her feet, Thea enjoyed watching her sons learn how to drive.

In preparation for the drive, her husband had given her a blue velvet cape lined in fur, with a matching muff. It was very stylish, and she quite enjoyed showing it off. Soon she would retire from social occasions until her child was born, but tonight, she delighted in the fresh night air and the company of so many people enjoying the same.

Thea spied Mirabel in another vehicle and gaily waved at her.

Even more interesting, she caught sight of her brother Horace and his wife. Since Thea had married, her path had not crossed his until this night. Horace was staring right at her, a huge scowl on his face — and Thea discovered she had no animosity toward him. Whatever grievances she'd once had over what she'd felt her brother should or should not have done had disappeared, vanquished by the happiness in her life.

Thea blew an air kiss at him, and he looked away. Instead of being offended, Thea laughed.

"Who is that, Mother?" Jonathan asked.

"Someone I used to know," she answered. "But Lady Palmer is over there." She indicated Mirabel's direction, and he shouted for her attention, rising as he did so, that she might see him better.

However, at that moment, the horses pulling their curricle started to bolt. They bumped into the vehicle ahead of them and panicked in the way horses did sometimes.

Jonathan toppled forward and would have tumbled out of the curricle except for Thea's reaching out and grabbing his coat in time. "Neal," she said to warn him something was wrong, but her husband had his hands full with the horses. With a start, she realized that half the reins had dropped to the ground.

Neal leaned over the front of the curricle, reaching for the reins before something worse happened. Thea noticed that he only used his right hand, which was still holding the right reins. He kept his left hand tucked into his side.

He snatched up the loose reins and quickly

brought the animals back under control.

Christopher grabbed Thea's arm, his eyes wide. She still had her arms full of Jonathan, and she didn't think she'd ever let him go.

If he'd fallen to the ground, he could have been hurt in the fall or found himself kicked by the horses.

"Don't be afraid," Thea said soothingly. "Everything is all right. Lyon has the horses under control." She couldn't help but add, "In the future, Christopher, you must be careful to always hold the reins tightly." She assumed her youngest had been driving, since he'd been on Neal's lap.

"I didn't have the reins," Christopher said. "Lyon had them."

"You dropped them," Thea asserted, keeping her voice low.

"No, Mother. Lyon dropped them."

Thea frowned, then shrugged it off. The horses were under control, and that was all that mattered.

But she did notice that her husband was still favoring his left arm. He did most of his driving the rest of the night with his right hand, using his left only for a bit of balance. The driving had to have been a difficult task, considering the skill needed to maneuver their vehicle in such a crowd.

Come to think of it, the night before, she had noticed Neal massaging his left hand, circling the thumb. On an occasion or two, she'd caught him doing the same with his whole left arm.

Later that evening, after she'd put the children to bed, Thea sought out her husband. He had not yet come upstairs for bed. Indeed, for the last several weeks, he'd been working in his office late into the night. Thea found him there.

He wasn't working. He sat behind his desk, cradling his left arm against his body.

Seeing her at the door, he looked up and said, "It is starting."

"What is?" she asked, wanting to pretend that she didn't know.

"The curse, Thea."

"Why do you say that?" she demanded.

"My arm is numb. I thought I'd injured a muscle, but it is not healing. In fact, it is growing worse." He frowned. "I dropped the reins this evening. My hand froze, and I couldn't move my fingers. The horses startled and we could have caused an accident. I hate to think what could have happened to Jonny."

Thea came around the desk to him. She knelt on the floor, taking his left hand into hers. "Such beautiful hands," she whispered.

"Strong hands."

"Not much longer," he said. "This is how it starts."

"And then what happens?" she asked, and she found herself strangely unafraid. Holding his hand, a calmness settled over her. He was so alive, so vital. Nothing could harm him. She wouldn't let it.

"The paralysis spreads. Father had a month. Some have up to a year, with the numbness growing and claiming every limb. Eventually, my heart will cease to work."

The death he described was horrifying to her.

"Thea, hold me."

She obeyed instantly. She threw her arms around him and held him tight. "I won't let you go. You've done nothing to deserve this."

"My hope is to live to see my son born," Neal said.

She couldn't bear thinking of his death. She denied it by kissing him. Their kiss grew heated, and Neal's right hand drew her into his lap. His left arm came around her. The paralysis was gone — for now — and she silently vowed her love would keep it at bay.

He was hard for her. She remembered that first night, with its frenzied passion. She began unbuttoning his breeches. He needed this. She needed it.

Slowly he entered her. How she loved this man, and loved making love to him. He was the center of her world, and she told him with her body how much he meant to her.

They took their time. He kept smoothing his hand over the curve of her hip and across her slightly rounded belly.

What would she tell this son about his father? Or would it be necessary? Would not Jonathan and Christopher share their stories? Oh, yes, they would. Neither she nor her sons would let the memory of this wonderful man die.

Sweet, wondrous love. Once again, he took her to the very heights of pleasure. Every time he made love to her, he claimed more of her soul.

She could not let him go. She wouldn't.

"We will fight this," Thea vowed.

Neal's answer was a sleepy, lazy smile.

He had given up. He'd accepted.

But she wouldn't.

The heart is a shield.

Thea woke with Neal's words in her mind.

Well, if they were true, then she needed to find a sword to go with her shield.

She waited until Neal left the house on business before she knocked on Harry's door. Rowan answered. "Please have the colonel up and downstairs in half an hour."

"That will be a challenge, my lady."

"Is he not here?" she wondered.

"He is . . . but he drank port last night."

Thea felt her patience snap. She had a war to wage, and she needed all the help she could muster. "Have him up."

She made the same request of Margaret.

Within the hour, she was pleased when both Harry and Margaret joined her in the breakfast room. Harry slumped into a chair and placed his head facedown on the table. Margaret gave her brother a look of disgust.

Thea said, "Neal is dying. It has started."

Now she'd captured their attention. Harry's head came up.

"How do you know?" Margaret asked.

"His left arm occasionally has bouts of paralysis," Thea said. "He says that is how it starts. I want you to know *I am not giving up*." She jabbed the table with her finger to emphasize her words.

"He's not the one who should die. I should die," Harry muttered. "Why doesn't the curse take me instead?"

"Because you are too soused to fall in love," Margaret said without pity.

Her brother glared at her. She glared back and then said, "Be honest, Harry. You are too selfish to love, and I'm too difficult."

She turned to Thea. "What do you think we should do?"

Thea had the dream journal she and Neal had been keeping. She opened it up. "We've been writing descriptions of the dreams. There is always fire. One of us is always burning. And quite often there is laughter. It is the most hideous cackle, like a crone's laughter."

"That must be Fenella," Margaret said. "She is the one who placed the curse upon us."

"Where can we find her?" Thea asked.

"Find her?" Margaret questioned. "She's been dead for hundreds of years. She died the night she placed the curse upon our line."

"Or perhaps she has been in hiding?" Thea leaned toward Harry and Margaret. "Has anyone gone after her?"

There was a beat of silence as they considered her words. Harry lifted his head and answered, "Thea, did you not hear Margaret? Fenella died almost two hundred years ago. I would hope she is not around. She'd be a hideous-looking hag."

"Where was she from?" Thea asked. "Where did she place the curse on us?"

Again there was puzzlement. Harry glanced at his sister. Margaret spoke. "Well, the family back then was from Glenfinnan. Charles of Glenfinnan was the first to be cursed. I don't think any of us have a record of where Fenella and her clan were located. It's one of those details lost in history."

"Then we must find answers, and we don't have much time," Thea said. "Neal wants to live to see his son born. I pray he does. But I want *more*. I want to defeat this curse. Neal says that over years your family has tried exorcisms and hiring witches for reverse spells. But nothing has worked. So, we must try something else. Harry, will you go to Glenfinnan?"

Harry had his elbow propped on the table so he could hold his head up. He turned bloodshot eyes on Thea.

"Will you go, Harry?" she pressed. "At one time, you were the most fearless of warriors. Can you be fearless once again for your brother's sake — ?"

"What is going on here?" Neal's voice said from the doorway.

Thea's gaze went straight to his left arm. He appeared normal, but she knew she wouldn't be able to relax until the curse had been lifted.

"I thought you had an appointment this morning," Thea said, trying to shield the journal with her arm. She wasn't certain how her husband would feel about her sharing it.

"Gilroy had to cancel our meeting," Neal answered. "What are you hiding there, Thea?"

It was his sister who answered. "We are joining you and Thea in the fight against the curse," Margaret said stoutly. "We don't want to lose you, Neal."

"She told you about my hand," Neal said. A sad smile came to his face. "I wish you hadn't, Thea."

"They would have noticed sooner or later," Thea defended herself. "And we have a plan. Harry is going to Glenfinnan."

"Glenfinnan? What for?" Neal asked.

"Because that was the home of Charles Chattan before he married his English heiress and started our line," Margaret answered.

Thea was heartened by the enthusiasm in Margaret's voice, but Harry was quiet.

Neal entered the room, coming around to stand by Thea. He placed his hand on her shoulder. "I want you to know that I have no regrets loving my wife. She has made me the happiest of men. I have done more living with her these past months than I had all the years before my marriage. I'm at peace with whatever comes my way."

"But I'm not," Harry said, speaking at last. He pushed himself up from the table. "Thea is right. It's never good to wait upon the enemy. I *shall* go to Glenfinnan."

Neal shook his head. "Harry, you are not in good shape —"

"I'm going, brother. I'm going for you . . . and for me. I will not let you die without a fight. The only people who truly see me for what I am are in this room."

"Harry, we love you," Neal said.

"Can you?" Harry said. "I can barely abide myself. What better man than I to wrestle with a witch?"

"It will not be an easy task," Thea predicted. "Think on it. Her magic must be strong. It has lasted all of this time."

"Yes, well, she hasn't met this devil," Harry answered. He moved toward the door. He stopped and looked back at them. "And for your information, Margaret, I do love. I love you and my brother very much. You are all I have." He left the room.

"I feel rotten," Margaret confessed. "I've been horribly mean to him. Excuse me while I make an apology." She followed after her brother.

Thea and Neal were alone.

He didn't speak. Instead, he leaned over the table and flipped a page of the journal.

His fingers brushed over her writing.

"What made you think of this?" he asked, breaking the silence.

"Something you said to me. I woke with it in my mind, and I realized how right you were. You said the heart is a shield. Your forebears have tried so many ways to defeat this curse, but what if we embraced it, Neal? What if we used our hearts as a shield against her evil? What if we went to her and let her know she can steal our lives, but the love we feel for each other is stronger than her powers."

Neal pulled her up from the chair. He placed his arms around her. "Dear God, I am blessed to have you for my wife."

Thea smiled up at him. "And I am glad you recognize the fact, my lord."

His response was to tilt his head back and laugh. The sound was carefree, and Thea put her arms around his waist and hugged him as tight as she could.

"We will defeat this," she promised. "I won't let you go without fighting with everything I have."

"Then Fenella had best watch out," he whispered. "But whatever happens, Thea, you are my wife and my love. Not even death will be able to change that."

And then he kissed her.

No man's kiss had ever had such power over her. He claimed her every time his lips met hers. She loved! And his father had been right when he'd written in his letter that they were sweet words.

At that moment, they were joined by Jonathan and Christopher. The boys had obviously been out in the cold, because the tips of their noses were red. They often went to the stables down the street to help feed their ponies.

"Good morning," Christopher said in a happy voice. He was always in a good mood in the mornings. He came right over to Neal and Thea and threw himself into the hug. Jonathan did the same. The boys giggled at their audacity, their arms reaching around Thea and Neal's legs — but Thea didn't laugh. She thought it was a blessing that her sons had found a father. A blessing that she had found a man she could love for all eternity.

Neal reached for her hand with his left one. He laced his fingers with hers, showing her that his strength had returned. His grip was strong.

It might weaken again. Or it might not.

But in this moment, having it return was the confirmation they needed.

They would defeat Fenella. She knew they would.

As her sons climbed into chairs around the table for their breakfast, she leaned her head against her husband's shoulder.

The heart *was* a shield, and the love she felt in this moment was enough to protect them all.

Fenella had best beware.

HARRY

It takes hard courage for a man to defeat his demons.

His brother needed him. His family needed him.

And Harry was not ready.

In all his years in the military, he had always been ready . . . but not any longer. His hands shook, his head ached and his body yearned for more drink even after the copious amounts he'd consumed over the preceding day and night.

He'd been trying to ease his dose of laudanum. He'd never really taken it for his leg. Yes, his leg pained him but not beyond something a good soldier could accept.

A good soldier. How long had it been since he'd thought of himself that way?

But now he had another chance to be a hero.

His siblings suspected he'd been attempting to kill himself with heroics that day he'd charged the French cannon position. Perhaps they were right. He certainly was not afraid of death. However, he was not a suicide.

He'd attacked that post because doing so had been needed to win the day. He'd felt invincible at the moment of his decision. War depends upon bold acts, foolhardy acts . . . and men willing to pay the ultimate sacrifice.

Harry had seen the weakness in the French position and had believed that one armed man with daring could take it. Unfortunately, his strong, valiant men had thought otherwise.

Out of loyalty or foolishness, they had disobeyed his orders to stay in rank and had followed him into the attack.

One man could have made it through.

A large number of troops had been easy targets for French sharpshooters.

And the horrific thing was that Harry had been right. He and Ajax had succeeded in their attack. He'd quickly secured the cannon. The French had run from his sword. Wellington could then march forward. However, when he'd turned to give the signal all was well, he'd had to watch his beloved men being mowed down.

Wellington had not faulted him for what

he'd done. His actions had enabled British forces to win the day and had saved many lives. There were witnesses who had heard Harry tell Lieutenant Fleshman to stay in position.

Being right didn't make Harry feel less guilty.

These had been men with wives and families along with feckless bachelors such as himself. He'd drunk with these men, laughed with them, fought beside them. That they would march after him to their own deaths out of nothing more than misguided loyalty humbled him.

It had also become an unbearable burden to carry.

Opium had helped ease it. Drink had always offered solace, and he had embraced it with a willingness beyond what he'd shown before.

And now he was in danger of never being the man he'd once hoped to be. There had been a time, and not too long ago, when he'd thought *he* controlled his vices. But now they controlled him, and he wasn't certain when the change had come about . . . perhaps around the time of Thea's arrival?

Stumbling up to his room, he opened his door and practically fell through it.

Rowan was tidying the bed. He looked up in surprise at Harry. "Colonel, you are not well. Here, let me help you to bed."

Harry shook him off. "No, not here." He knew this would not be pleasant. He walked over to the desk by the window, pulled open a drawer and took out a purse. "There is a man, an Alexander Rimmer on Fife Lane, who says he has a cure. Tell him I am coming to his house. Have him prepare a room."

Rowan took the money, bowed and left, meeting Margaret at the door. She didn't ask permission but walked in.

Harry sat at the desk, clasping his head in his hands. Just the thought of leaving the crutches he'd used these past two years more than filled him with anxiety.

"What are you going to do?" his sister asked.

"I want to save Neal," Harry said. "He's always been here for me. Yes, sometimes he's been a pain in my backside, but what brother isn't?"

"I want to help," Margaret said.

Harry shook his head. "No."

"Yes." She walked over to stand before him. "You weren't here when Father died. He went quickly, Harry. Faster than I could imagine. You will need my help."

Visions of his men following him into

combat formed in Harry's mind, only this time it was his sister at risk.

"I go alone."

She didn't like his command. Margaret was the headstrong one in the family.

He reached over to pick up one of Christopher's marbles resting on his desk. It was the shooter. Harry had won it from the boy in a challenge. Christopher had enthusiastically vowed to win it back.

"Life has to mean more than what we have here," Harry said half to himself, rolling the marble in the palm of his hand. "It must."

"Neal seems happy," Margaret answered. "Even knowing what is happening to him, he seems at peace."

Harry looked up at her. "Are you at peace?"

His sister shrugged. "Love is not for me. I'm better alone. Happier."

She didn't sound happy, and the thought went through his mind that she was hiding something. Margaret was a beautiful woman, yet she kept herself apart from the rest of the world.

Of course, he'd chosen to be alone as well, but that was because of the curse . . . and besides, what woman with any sense would want him? He was a shambles of a man, a fool. Then again, he had a legion of senseless ladies who vied for his attention, but they weren't the sort a man loved.

Harry stood, putting the marble in his coat pocket. "I'm going to Glenfinnan, Margaret, but first, I must take a cure."

"What sort of cure?"

"I don't know. They say it is successful, but we shall see."

"Let me help you, brother. I don't want you to feel alone against this."

Harry walked to her, leaned forward and pressed a kiss upon her forehead. "You cannot come with me. I do not want you to see me the way I will be."

"I've seen you at your worst."

He shook his head. "I wish I could erase the memory of those times from your mind. But you need to be here. We don't know what will be happening to Neal. Thea will need help."

"Thea sounds as if she can take care of herself," Margaret argued.

"Does she? I don't know. Certainly she wants us to do battle in a way no one seems to have tried before. We've all been afraid of it. But I'm tired of being afraid. I'm tired of being who I am."

"Well, who you are is important to us. Please, Harry, be gentle with yourself, and be careful of the world or of searching out this witch."

He smiled, felt the weight of the marble in his pocket. "I've never lost in battle, Margaret. I shall not lose now."

With those confident words, he walked out the door, feeling less confident than he ever had before in his life. He didn't stop to say good-bye to Neal and Thea. He could hear them in the breakfast room, laughing and talking with the boys. His brother sounded as if he didn't have a care in the world.

How he envied Neal.

And Neal dreamed. Harry had noticed his brother's comments in the journal Neal and Thea had been keeping. Harry didn't dream. He had nightmares of the men who'd given their lives for him. A dream of a witch would be a welcome relief.

Harry walked out of the house, heading for Fife Lane and Rimmer's cure.

"A determined man can do anything," Mr. Rimmer said. "However, I must warn you, my cure may kill you."

"But will I be done with drink, with laudanum if I live?" Harry demanded. Up and down the hall of the tidy house, moans and shouts could be heard coming from beyond the bedroom doors. It sounded like bedlam or a brothel with unhappy clients.

"We shall see," was the cryptic answer.

For the next two weeks of his life, Harry found himself in a special kind of hell. Rimmer's cure was really little more than what Margaret had attempted when she'd ordered him tied and held down to his bed. It had been painful, nauseating, frightening then, and it was worse now.

Rowan stayed faithfully by his side.

Harry cried, swore and begged, but his servant would not release him from the bonds holding him in place. The visions tore at his soul. If he thought his dreams before had been troubled, the visions, the hallucinations he had now were more horrific, and all too real.

And then one day, the pain wasn't as bad. The anxiety, the delusions lessened.

Rimmer started the next phase of his cure. Harry was treated to scalding hot baths designed to rid his body of poisons. Thea's cure! Who knew his sister and sister-in-marriage were so wise?

Harry kept Christopher's marble shooter on the table beside the bed. During his worst moments, he clutched the marble, using it to remind him of all that was at stake.

At the end of two weeks, he was pronounced "cured." His eye was clear, his hand steady, and, for now, his demons were at bay. He had lost weight, most of it the bloat of his vices, and his hair had gone prematurely gray at his temples.

"Fetch Ajax," he ordered Rowan, "and bring me my pistols and my sword. I'm ready to hunt for a Scottish witch."

Harry plucked the marble off the bedside table and placed it in his pocket.

He was prepared to do battle.

And if she would not fight, then he would beg her to take his life instead of his brother's.